MALL

ERIC J. MCCONNELL

MALL

BY

Eric J. McConnell

❀ Created with Vellum

ZERO

Every day for the rest of my life, I'll hear the same fourteen words:

Attention MetroMall guests: please prepare for imminent nuclear detonation. This is not a drill.

I'm not the kind of guy who goes to the mall unless I have a very specific purpose in mind. Today, I've come to Metro-Mall to get my phone fixed at the Electronix store. It's so dumb. Some pocket lint got into the charging port and I needed to get it cleaned out.

Turns out I may owe my life to that pocket lint.

I had just arrived at the Electronix—first floor, next to the Candleworks—and was waiting at the bar while a technician cleaned my phone in the back. I was killing time playing on one of the tablets. I slept in that morning—my friggin' alarm didn't go off—and I was late for my nine o'clock appointment. I rolled out of bed, threw on my favorite blue-and-white-striped tank top and blue shorts, and ran out the door. It wasn't until I got in my car that I realized my socks were mismatched, pink on my left foot and green on my right.

I rushed out of the house without saying goodbye to my mom. My dad was not present as he had conveniently chosen to die two years prior.

Good move on his part.

"What on God's green earth was that?" someone asks. A woman, wearing a lime-green hat and a yellow skirt.

I hear a voice behind me. "This is a joke, right?"

I turn around. It's an Electronix employee, a different technician from the guy who had taken my phone a few minutes before. Rectangular glasses, uneven stubble, and messy blond hair. He's wearing a light-blue polo emblazoned with the company logo. He's thin, and a few inches taller than I am. His hand begins to tremble.

"Yeah, I'm sure it's a prank," a man across the store says. Sweat glistens over his brow and soaks through the pits of his lavender T-shirt. He probably just came from the gym. "Some punk probably got hold of the paging system."

My heart is racing, but I smile at the Electronix employee and glance at his nametag. *I'm Jack, how can I help you?* "Hey Jack, I'm Luke. Luke Chesterfield."

My dad always told me to greet salespeople by their names if they had tags. *That's why they're there, Luke.*

I extend my hand. Jack's hand meets mine. He's still shaking.

"H-Hi Luke, we're pleased to help you today. What brings you—"

Then the alarms start. High-pitched sirens screeching as if from the depths of hell. My eardrums tear into pieces. Green Hat Lady screams. Lavender Pit Stains Guy bolts. The silver gate at the front of Electronix comes crashing down. I look at Jack. His eyes are wide and his mouth is agape. He isn't moving. Neither is half the store. The other half runs out as the metal gate descends.

My mind races. Should we get out of here? What the hell is even going on? Could this still be some juvenile prank? Or is it the real thing?

And if it *is* the real thing, how *real* is the real thing?

I don't know why, but I can't leave Jack. Some force is tethering me to him. He's the only person in the store who seems to be close to my age. I'm twenty-three years old, home from grad school for the summer. I'm making some extra cash working at the library by my mom's house, but today—Tuesday—is my day off. I wanted to go get my phone fixed on a weekday to avoid the crowds.

Jack's maybe a few years younger than I am. He's swimming in that light-blue polo, and he looks about the same age as my little brother, Greg, who's twenty. I wouldn't leave Greg in there, so I shouldn't leave this guy. That would be wrong, right?

Right?

"Hey, it's fine." I awkwardly tap Jack on his shoulder. "The gates and alarms are probably just a formality. Some kid probably broke into security and pulled the alarm. There's no way in hell anyone is targeting a shopping mall in boring-ass Jackson City."

Jack doesn't respond. He just stares blankly, his eyes wide. The alarms continue to blare. They're getting louder. My vision starts to blur.

The Electronix gate hits the floor. Then—

The Boom.

I only hear the first half-second of The Boom. After that my ears stop working. The room shakes. Phones and tablets fall from their displays. A huge shelf full of accessories comes down on Green Hat Lady, pinning her by the legs. Jack the Technician and I both tumble to the floor.

I scurry underneath one of the display tables—I remember seeing videos from the fifties of kids huddled under desks for nuclear bomb drills. Seems like a smart move. One small thing to control while the world ends around you.

Jack joins me under the table. My hearing comes back, thanks in part to the piercing screams of Green Hat Lady. My first instinct is to help her, but I'm unable to move from under the display table. And I have no desire to have something heavy fall on me.

It doesn't matter. It's all gonna be over in a few minutes.

Oh, God. *Over*.

I'm too young to die.

Ugh. *What an unoriginal thought.* Everyone thinks they're too young to die. I can't help but roll my eyes even as adrenaline pumps through my veins.

I look over at Jack. He's silent and still shuddering. So this is the person next to whom I will spend my final moments on Earth. I always assumed I'd be surrounded my friends and family in a hospital, with some heart-shaped balloons and flowers bought from the gift shop, maybe a half-eaten container of gelatin next to my bed. I definitely imagined a lot less broken glass and screaming and alarms. And I haven't even gotten my damn phone fixed.

I'm going to die with a broken phone.

Huh. *Less unoriginal.*

1

———

Turns out I lived. Jack and I are both alive.

The alarms have ceased.

We've been under that table for a few hours, or so it seems. I have no way of telling the time without my phone. Green Hat Lady has stopped screaming.

Oh, God, she *stopped screaming.*

Other survivors inside Electronix have brazenly stolen my idea of huddling underneath the store's display tables. No one has said a word since the alarms went off.

For some reason, I miss the sounds of the alarms. At least then I knew something was going on. This silence pierces my ears in a way the alarms never could.

It's far worse.

On top of the silence—and I realize that this sounds incredibly basic for someone my age—I really want my phone. I have reflexively reached towards my right jeans pocket for it about once a minute since I got under the table. It just really isn't fair. All these freaks have *their* phones. Why did this bomb—or whatever—have to be deployed in the one ten-minute period when *I* was phoneless?

Things are calm now. I decide to get out from under the table and check things out. Will there be a second Boom? I have no idea. Screw it. I poke my head out.

Jack grabs my arm. "*No*," he whispers. "You can't leave!"

"Why not? Whatever happened is over."

"You don't know that. That might have just been the first one."

"The first what?"

"I don't *know*. The first of whatever just happened. All I know is it can't be safe."

"Can't argue with you there." I can't help but grin. I've always had a penchant for dark humor, and it's kicking in. My definitely-not-toxic defense mechanism in the face of trauma. "But one of your technicians has my phone, and I'd like to google whatever the hell that big-ass Boom was."

I tug my arm out of Jack's grasp and gingerly stagger to my feet. My legs tremble a bit, like the baby giraffes on the nature channel. All the blood has to flow back into my legs. Every eye in the store burns into me as I stand up. I can't help but feel a little proud of myself. Kind of like being the first kid in your class to hand their test in.

I look around Electronix. Phones and tablets litter the ground, their screens all cracked beyond repair. All the shelves in the store fell in The Boom. Green Hat Lady wasn't their only victim, just their loudest. I count three bodies, each one surrounded by a pool of half-dried blood. The reddish-brown puddles really hit the eye in contrast to the immaculate white tile flooring.

All this carnage, and I feel nothing. This isn't real. This is some grotesque dream from which I'll wake up in just a few moments. I remember feeling the same way the night my dad died. The gore I behold doesn't disturb me in the slightest. This is just the way things are in this moment in time.

I cross behind the cashier's desk into the back room. The guy who took my phone also wore a blue polo. Dark, long greasy hair, and an average build. Oh, and he was wearing a white skinny tie. Truly unsettling in tandem with the polo. Very middle school dance. The tie, along with the man around whose neck it was wrapped, had just disappeared behind the door when the first announcement blared.

Now he's nowhere to be found. The whole back room is a mess. Unlike the store itself, which was practically bare—since anything other than minimalism is *passé* at this point in human history—this room is bursting with cardboard boxes, filing cabinets, and way too much paper strewn about. A broken coffeepot and a toppled refrigerator add to the eclectic atmosphere.

Oh, *there* he is! Under the fridge.

Yikes.

A string cheese wrapper lies on the floor. My technician was apparently helping himself to an early lunch as he fixed my phone. I don't love the fact that he was going to be eating while he cleaned out my charging port, but then again he also appears to have been crushed by the refrigerator, so I doubt the irony of the whole situation was lost on him in his final moments.

The location of my phone, however, is unclear. Fridge Guy doesn't have it in his hands, and it isn't nearby. It must be on the floor. Of course, so is every sheet of paper ever printed in the store's history. I get on my knees and dig, but I can't find it.

Dammit. It must be in Fridge Guy's pocket, and I don't

have the strength to pick the fridge up off of him. I also have no desire to see what a grown man's body looks like after having been crushed by a refrigerator. I accept defeat and exit the back room.

Electronix is just as I left it. No one has moved. I walk back to the table where Jack and I were hiding. His entire body spasms when I peek my head under.

"Sorry, I didn't mean to startle you."

Jack looks up at me. His eyes are red and puffy. "W-What's it like out there?"

"Out there? Like in the store?"

"Y-Yeah."

This poor guy. He is clearly shaken. I mean, who wouldn't be?

Should *I* be more shaken?

"It's a mess," I say. "Glass everywhere, and—uh—*blood* everywhere."

"*Blood?*" Jack's face turns sheet white.

I don't like telling him this. But my dad always told me to tell things like they were. *Quick and dirty, like pulling off a bandage.* And I can sugarcoat absolutely nothing regarding the situation we find ourselves in.

"Yeah," I say softly. "There are a few bodies. The shelves fell on them. And there's a guy in the back. He got crushed by a fridge."

"Dave?" Jack's eyes well up.

"I don't know, maybe?"

"Long, dark hair?"

Yep. That's Fridge Guy. Or, rather, Dave the Fridge Guy. David the Refrigerator Man if we're being formal.

"I think so. He was the guy who was cleaning my phone."

"He's my supervisor. Or I guess he *was* my supervisor."

Jack cups his hands over his face and his entire body lurches. "What the *hell* is going on?"

"I don't know," I say. "I wanted to grab my phone to see if there was any news, but I couldn't. Do you have yours on you?"

I am now realizing that I should have asked about that in the first place. I'm back to being mildly annoyed with myself.

"Yeah, it's in my pocket." Jack grabs his phone and hands it to me. "The code is six-one-one-three."

"Thanks." I take the phone and enter the security code. Jack's phone background is of a dog—his dog, I'm guessing. It's a pretty dog, mostly black with a grey muzzle and paws. "Cute dog."

"Her name's Tilly."

I smirk. "Not a name you hear every day."

"It's short for Matilda."

"Ah, *well* then." I open up the search engine app and stop. Like, what do you even write in the search bar for a moment like this? Just, *what's going on? Nuclear bomb? Metro-Mall explosion?*

I don't have to ponder this dilemma too long, because I quickly notice that the phone has no service. No bars, no Wi-Fi, nothing. I hand it back to Jack.

"Whatever caused that explosion must have taken out the cell towers," I say. "There's no way to get through."

"Oh, sorry." Jack pockets his phone.

"Not your fault," I say. "I guess all we have is that announcement. Some kind of nuclear event."

"So, like, an atomic bomb?"

"I guess so. But we seem to be safe."

"Yeah, this mall was built in the fifties, at the height of the Cold War," Jack says. "The walls themselves are indestructible, and there are shields that come down over the windows and doors in the event of a nuclear detonation."

I smile. "Well, look at our MetroMall historian!"

Jack blinks. "Hardly. I just did a little research on the place when I accepted this job."

"Home from college?"

Jack blinks again. "Sort of." He pauses. "I took a gap year. Had some stuff to deal with."

"Stuff?"

"It's a little personal."

Whoops. I think I've crossed a line.

"Sorry, didn't mean to pry."

"It's okay. We did just spend two hours hiding under a table." The corners of his mouth twitch slightly. Was that almost a smile?

"True," I say. "I guess that means we're friends now."

"*That's* all it takes?" Jack's small, if restrained, grin is coming in a little clearer now.

I laugh. "Two hours hiding under a table while the world ends is at least a *start*."

Jack exhales through his nose slightly, which I'm taking as a laugh. It feels weird to be joking right now—like *really* weird—but we all cope in different ways. Gallows humor, baby. I highly recommend it.

I look around Electronix. I count five other people inside huddling under the tables.

I turn to face Jack. "Do you think we should leave the store? Maybe check things out?"

Jack furrows his brow. "Why?"

"If this mall is shielded from attack like you say it is, then it's gotta be safe outside of the store, right?"

Jack frowns. "It's a possibility."

"At any rate, we're not any safer here than we are out there. And all we have here are a bunch broken phones with no service."

"What do you mean, *all we have*?"

"I mean, we have no food, no water, nothing essential."

Jack raises his right eyebrow. "You sound like some sort of survival show host."

I shrug. "I just think it's a good idea to find something to eat. Just in case we're here for a while."

"In the mall?"

"No, in Her Majesty's realm." I smirk. "For real, though, if there was really some sort of nuclear explosion, we need to at least be prepared for the possibility that no one is coming for us. Likely not for a while."

Jack nods. "That makes sense."

"And seeing as we've now established that we're friends, you wanna come with me?" I hold out my hand.

Jack looks up at me, and a small smile finally cracks on his face. "Sure."

2

———

Jack grabs my hand and gets on his feet.

The five other people in Electronix have still said nothing. I decide to address them.

"So...hey. I'm Luke, and this is Jack." I'm very aware that my voice sounds stilted and awkward. "The two of us have decided to explore the mall and see what's going on, if any of you want to join."

The Table Huddlers are still frozen in place. There are two groups, one of three and one of two. The group of two consists of a middle-aged man in a navy suit and white shirt with a young girl in pink overalls and a striped shirt—his daughter, perhaps? The other three people in the store are teens, one male and two female. They're all wearing yellow T-shirts and jeans and were in the store taking selfies on the demo phones when I got there.

Navy Suit Dad breaks the silence. "You've got to be nuts. Do you have any idea of what's going on out there?"

I shrug. "Probably the same that's going on in here.

Nobody moving. People frozen in place. Someone's gotta check things out."

"By all means, go if you want. I'm staying right here." Navy Suit Dad clutches his daughter. "No way in hell I'm putting my stepdaughter's life in danger."

So she's his *step*daughter. The plot thickens.

"It's a free country," I say. A dark thought crosses my mind. "Or at least it *was*. Who knows now? Anyway, Jack, wanna help me get the front gate open?"

"Um," Jack says. "You may have an issue with that. I think the gate is electronic."

"So? The lights are working."

Jack shakes his head. "The lights are attached to a backup generator. The store has one so the electronics don't lose their charge in the event of a blackout. The gate is different, though." He points to the Electronix entrance. "It's on the mall's grid."

I look outside the store for the first time. The lights are off. "You have *got* to be kidding me."

"Afraid not," Jack says. "But I'm sure the mall has some sort of failsafe in place to get the gate open. I'll have to check the back room to see if maybe there's a lever or instructions or something." He turns toward the store's rear.

"Wait," I say. "Your...um...*manager* is in there."

Jack stops. "Oh. Right."

"I can look around for you."

Jack shakes his head. "No offense, but you don't know where anything is."

"Sure," I say. "Then I'll come with you."

We walk past the body of Green Hat Lady—may she rest in peace—to the back room.

Jack stops at the door. "Is it, like, gross?"

"I mean, there's some blood, but mostly all you see is the fridge on top of him."

"Fantastic," Jack says weakly. He opens the door a crack, hesitates a moment, and then walks in.

I follow behind. Should I have gone in first? My understanding of basic etiquette never covered this specific situation.

Jack stalls for a moment in front of Dave the Fridge Guy. His lip trembles, but he powers through it and starts sifting through the sheets of paper on the floor. "There must be something here about the gate."

"Would it be written down on one of these loose papers?" I scan the mountain of documents on the ground. "Or maybe on a poster on the wall?"

"No," Jack says. "I remember my manager—Dave—telling me that there was something to release the front gate in the event of a power outage, it's just...uh..."

"Just what?"

Jack looks down. "I wasn't exactly listening."

"You're kidding me."

"Listen, this is a part-time job. I don't even have health benefits. Are you telling me you would devote yourself completely to a temp gig like this?"

I think back to my job at the library, which I basically phoned in all summer. "Fair enough. But you clearly cared enough to research the mall's history before taking the job."

"I did a quick Internet search and read a few articles," Jack says. "There are some weird quirks to this mall, so I fell down a rabbit hole. My day-one orientation wasn't nearly as stimulating. Plus I figured it was information I'd never use."

"Didn't account for a nuclear explosion, did you?"

"As a matter in fact, I did not." Jack's voice is acerbic, but there's a brightness behind his glasses. He searches through the papers, giving each sheet a quick scan and then tossing it behind him. Into a pile of more sheets of paper. He suddenly jerks his right hand back from the mountains of paper. It's bleeding. "*Jesus.*"

He's cut his hand on a piece of glass from the broken coffeepot. I squat down. "Yikes. Let me look at it."

There's a pretty decent gash on his palm between his thumb and first finger. Not life-threatening, but not insignificant either.

Jack shoves his hand in my face and looks in the opposite direction. "How's it look?"

"Not great. Do you have a first aid kit back here?"

"I mean, somewhere." Jack winces. "But it's probably hidden among all this paper."

"And searching for it may yield further gashes."

"Likely yes."

I glance down at Dave the Fridge Guy. His skinny white tie may be tacky, but it could prove useful. I lean down, but something makes me pause.

If I take it, does that make me a grave robber? Probably not. This can't possibly be DFG's final resting place. He'll eventually be buried somewhere, right? Notably *not* in a shopping mall. And it's not like he's going to be needing his tie. In the grand scheme of things, I'm actually doing him a monumental favor. No man's eternal outfit should include a polo shirt and tie combo.

Then we are decided. I manage to slip the tie off of Dave's neck and wrap it around Jack's hand. The blood soaks through the white polyester—of *course* it's polyester—but it'll have to do for now.

I help Jack up. "We'll get someone to look at that when we're out of here."

"*Who* someone?" Jack asks. "It's not like this mall has a doctor's office."

"We'll figure that out. At any rate, we can't keep searching like this. You only have two hands. Do you think we could force the gate open?"

"Maybe." Jack bites his lip. "It would probably be easier if you had someone on both sides."

"Let's see if there's someone on the outside of the store, then. We can also get the other people in the store to help us."

Jack nods. "Let's try it."

We walk out of the back room and approach the front gate. "Hello? Is there anyone out there?"

Silence for a moment, but then I hear a single hesitant voice.

"Yeah."

A figure approaches from the darkness of the mall's walkway. It's Lavender Pit Stains Guy. Actually, a more fitting description at present would be "Lavender Sweaty All Over Guy."

"Hey, I'm Luke, and this is Jack. And these are five people who are also in the store whose names I haven't learned yet." I gesture to The Table Huddlers. "We're trying to open this gate. Do you think you can help us?"

LPSG shrugs. "Aren't the gates automatic?"

"Yes," Jack says. "But I don't see why we can't force them open."

LPSG frowns. "I'm happy to help. Not sure if it'll do any good."

LPSG's shirt can barely contain his bulging muscles. "It looks like you work out," I say. "Can't hurt to try."

"Sure." LPSG squats down and grabs the base of the gate. "And thanks, I guess?"

Jack and I do the same, though our technique is not nearly as refined as LPSG's. Also, completely unrelated, but I can't help but admire the size of LPSG's legs from this angle.

"On three," I say. "One, two, *three!*"

All three of us pull on the base of the gate, but it doesn't budge.

"Is there anyone else out there who can help on your side?" Jack asks.

LPSG looks around. "No one I can see. It's pretty dark."

"*Dammit.*" I look down. I was really hoping that would work.

"Wait," Jack says. "The display tables."

"What about them?" I ask.

"We can flip them over and use them as a lever to lift the gate."

"Won't that break the gate?" LPSG asks.

"Who the hell cares?" I ask. "We just need to get out of here."

"Hey, you." I point to Navy Suit Stepdad. "Can you help us with this table?"

Navy Suit Stepdad looks at me and then at his stepdaughter. He whispers something in her ear and hoists her up on her feet before crawling out himself.

"I'll help you, but I'm still not sold on leaving the store," he says.

"No one's forcing you to do anything once we've opened the gate," Jack says.

"Good," NSS says. "Because I'm not doing anything until the National Guard gets here."

"Is the National Guard coming?" LPSG asks.

"They have to," NSS says. "It's their job."

"But what if—" I begin.

"It's. Their. *Job*." NSS looks back at his stepdaughter.

She smiles back.

I decide to stop talking.

The three of us grab the display table under which Jack and I took shelter. It's heavy, but we flip it over with ease. We place it on an angle with the long side perpendicular to the gate and hook the teeth of the gate on the legs of the far side of the table. We pull our side of the table down, and the legs catch.

The gate still doesn't budge.

"You're *kidding* me," I mutter under my breath.

"We can do it," NSS says. "We just need a little more manpower to force the gate open. You three, come help us." He points to the Yellow-Shirted Selfie Teenagers.

None of the members of the YSST squad speak a word, but they get out from under the table and silently walk over to us.

"You guys stay on the left side." NSS points. "I want Luke and Jake on the right side, and I'll take the edge."

"It's Jack," Jack says.

"Like it *matters* right now."

The YSSTs take their position.

"We're all going to push down, and *you*"—NSS points to LPSG—"pull up on the gate at the same time. That should get it open."

LPSG nods, squatting. We are graced with one final view

of his miraculous thighs. Out of the corner of my eye, I notice Jack is admiring them as well.

Hmm, I wonder.

"On three," NSS says. "One, two, *three!*"

The Table Huddlers—minus Navy Suit Stepdaughter—Jack, and I all push down on our side of the table. LPSG pulls up as hard as he can. A vein pops in his neck, so I know he's working hard. We keep pushing. I'm worried that the table will break, but it holds firm. The table is moving, and the gate with it, ever so slowly.

It's working!

It takes about a full minute of pushing down on the table, but we finally get it to the ground. I look at the gate. It's only opened a little bit, but enough to slip under it.

"We'd best keep the table legs in the gate to keep it open," I say to NSS. "I know you don't want to leave now, but if you or your stepdaughter get hungry, you'll want to be able to slip out. And we now know we need at least six people on a table to get this gate open."

"I'll take my chances," NSS says. "Once the Guard gets here, we'll be able to get out of here and go home."

What home? We have no idea if any of the town survived The Boom. My gaze falls on the little girl under the table. NSS is probably just trying to keep himself strong for her sake. He may be the only person in her life now, and a child needs stability. Something normal for her to cling to.

The three teens also seem to have no desire to leave the store. They silently amble back under their table. None of them have uttered a word. I hope NSS can provide them some kind of comfort too.

"Where did muscle guy go?" Jack asks.

I look out the gate. LPSG has disappeared. "Guess he's looking for supplies, too. He must have wanted a head start."

Jack dusts off his shirt. "We'd best be on our way as well."

Jack's glasses are smudged, but a glint of fire shines in his eyes.

I crouch down. "Are you ready?"

Jack smiles. "You bet."

The two of us slip under the gate and into the darkness of the mall.

3

It becomes all too clear all too quickly that it is far too dark.

"Can you see anything?" I ask.

"No," Jack says. "I figured we'd at least get some light in from the windows, but the shields that came down must have covered them."

"Brilliant. You still have your phone?"

"Way ahead of you." Jack pulls out his phone and turns on the flashlight. "It's not much, but it'll at least keep us from running into the walls."

The tiny light emanates from Jack's phone, giving us a small perimeter of visibility. We walk for a few feet before Jack mutters some unmentionable words.

"What is it?" I ask.

"My phone. The battery's at ten percent. We won't have this light for long."

"And I don't have mine. Are you telling me you work all day in an electronics store and don't charge your phone?"

"Yes, and I'd love to take a moment to further analyze the

paradoxical nature of our situation at a later date," Jack says. "But right now, we have to find another source of light before my phone dies. Otherwise, we're stuck in the dark."

"Is there a camping goods store nearby? They'd have flashlights and stuff."

"Yeah. SportsGoods. They've got everything. Camping, recreation stuff. They even have a huge rock-climbing wall poking up through the middle of the store."

"Perfect. Let's head there, then."

Jack shakes his head. "One problem. It's on the third floor."

"That's not an issue. We can take the elevator."

"The elevator that is powered by the same electricity that powers these lights?" Jack gestures vaguely to the surrounding darkness.

"Oh, right."

"There are stairs, but they're hidden away," Jack says. "The mall's architect was all about reducing clutter. He said he wanted to mall to look like the interior of a spaceship. It was an artistic movement called *futurism*."

"Do you have enough battery to get us up there?"

"Um." Jack blinks. "*That* is an excellent question."

"Then we'll have to find something on the first floor that can last us until we get upstairs," I say.

"There aren't any other stores like SportsGoods here on the first floor."

"Could we just grab some more phones from your store?"

"Those models aren't meant to be used outside of the store," Jack says. "They have cheap batteries. They only work when plugged in. They'd last about five minutes."

Now it's my turn to mutter unmentionable words.

"Maybe we just make a run for it?" I say. "Try and get to SportsGoods before your phone dies?"

"And if it dies while we're in the stairwell? We'd be plunged into complete darkness. I can't imagine anything more horrifying."

"More horrifying than a nuclear detonation?"

"Okay, *second*-most horrifying."

I sit on the floor. *Goddammit.* Our quest is over before it even began. Our only hope at this point is someone with a flashlight finding us. I guess our next move is to go back inside the Electronix and wait. My lip starts to quiver. *Oh, God.* Am I really about to break down in front of perfect-stranger-slash-new-best-friend Jack the Technician?

"Wait. Luke, look!" Jack shines the light on the store next to Electronix.

"Oh my God," I say. "How could I be so stupid?"

Eleven letters shine back at me, mocking my obliviousness. I'd be insulted if these were not perhaps the most beautiful eleven letters in the world:

Candleworks.

"You're not stupid," Jack says. "You just got fixated on flashlights. It happens."

"This is literally my mom's favorite store, though. She used to drag me here all the time when I was little. I remember, their whole gimmick was you could get a store attendant to light your candle before you bought it to get the full aromatic experience. I hated it. The only way she'd get me to come was the promise of a ride on the big slide or a movie afterward. We were here every Black Friday."

"The three-for-ten special?"

"Yep. More mall history?"

"No. I just happen to work next door and have two functioning eyes." Jack smiles. "They do that sale once every few months."

"I, for one, am glad to be learning of this at the twilight of humanity." I get to my feet. "Can we get in?"

"Yep. Candleworks doesn't have a gate," Jack says. "Most of the shops don't. Only the Electronix and the jewelry shops have the automatic gates. I think they normally only come down in the event of a reported burglary."

"You could write a dissertation on the inner machinations of this mall, couldn't you?"

"Don't think the thought hasn't crossed my mind," Jack says. "Let's go check it out."

We cross the threshold of Candleworks. The smell hits us first. The mélange of eucalyptus, citron, and sandalwood makes for a peculiar combination. The shop is deserted and dark, but Jack's phone illuminates the floor. The light bounces off of broken glass and chunks of wax.

"Are there any candles that aren't broken?" I ask.

Jack shines his light on the walls of the store. Almost every shelf has toppled. Thankfully, there are no other people, alive or otherwise, entombed under them.

"I guess people were able to get out of here more easily without the gate coming down," I say.

"Yeah," Jack replies. "That, and the fact that there is rarely anyone in here on a Tuesday afternoon. Half the time I walk in and the cashier isn't even here."

"Low security?"

"Robbers and vandals tend to skip candle stores."

"Their loss."

"One hundred percent agreed." Jack directs his phone light to the back right corner of the store. "Look! There's a few that aren't broken!"

I examine the corner display. There are two forest-green three-wick candles, encased in unbroken glass, nestled in the edge where the two walls meet.

I walk over, instinctively remove the lid of one, and smell it. "Forevergreen. That's the name of the scent. It's my mom's favorite. It's like pine, but pinier."

Jack smirks. "You have the soul of a poet."

"Shut up. When I become a professional reviewer of candle scents in the New World Order, I'll be sure to purchase a thesaurus."

"Thank God." Jack surveys the surrounding area. "Are there any lighters?"

I grab the Forevergreens. "There should be some up by the cashier."

The two of us walk to the cashier desk. Normally the lighters would be with the rest of the impulse buys, cushioned in between the pocket hand sanitizer and the mittens—why either of these were on sale in a candle store is anyone's guess—but the display has fallen onto the floor in The Boom.

The issue of the lighters is further exacerbated as Jack's phone light flickers for a moment before going black. Darkness engulfs the two of us completely.

"You've gotta be kidding me," I say.

"I'm afraid not. Whenever my phone is on ten percent battery, it either lasts hours or a few minutes. No in-between."

"I'll be sure to write a strongly worded letter to the CEO of Electronix after all this," I say. "Assuming he's alive, of course."

Jack begins to pace slowly. "At least now we know it was the right move not to go through the stairwell without additional light."

"Remind me to be comforted by our hindsight after we're out of here."

"Deal," Jack says. "Still have the candles?"

"Yeah. And the lighters have to be around here somewhere. They're probably on the floor."

"Be careful. There's broken glass."

"You don't need to remind me. I recall dressing your wound with your dead manager's tie."

"Oh, yeah." Jack sighs. "Weird day."

"Understatement of the century." I crouch down and feel around delicately in the dark. I have a newfound respect for my late great-aunt, who was legally blind. How she managed to get through her life was a goddamn wonder. There's a lot of glass, but I manage to not cut myself.

I also manage to not find any lighters.

"Any luck?" Jack asks.

"Not so far. I *know* that they have to be nearby."

"Unless someone took them?"

"Why would someone take them?"

"People do strange things when they panic. They need something they can control. That's why people do things like hoard toilet paper during a natural disaster. The cashier probably grabbed a bunch of lighters before running out of the store. Just to have *something*."

I ponder a minute. I feel around and grab a pair of mittens—again, *why?*—from the impulse buy display, put them on, and get down on my hands and knees. A few pieces of glass crunch under me, but none pierce my skin.

"What are you doing?" Jack asks.

"The cashier might have dropped a lighter. There's no way they'd be able to carry out an entire shelf's worth while running out of the store in a panic."

"And the mittens?"

"I'd rather keep my hands in one piece."

"Fair enough."

I slowly crawl from the cashier desk to the front of the store, feeling everything in my path. Luckily, I know this store's layout pretty well from the years spent waiting on my mother to smell every goddamn candle she encountered. The fastest path out from behind the cashier's desk would be straight through the middle of the store, rounding the one central display where the Candleworks bestsellers normally stood. I make it to the entrance.

Nothing.

Well, not *nothing*. A bunch of pieces of glass and candle. And a piece of cloth near the shop's entryway. A T-shirt, maybe? I can't quite tell just from feeling. It's a little scratchy and too long to be a shirt.

I crawl back around the center display. I circle it, groping through obscurity. Nothing again except broken candles. Is this a dead end?

I think back to the piece of cloth I found. What could it be? I mean, why does it matter what it is? But why would a piece of cloth just be hanging in the middle of a candle shop? Like, who strips down when they're running for their life? Was it a tablecloth? Too small. A placemat? Too big. A towel perhaps? Why would that be in a candle shop? As far as I know, Candleworks doesn't sell non-mitten pieces of clothing.

It's the one thing I can't explain, so I backtrack to where I found it.

"Any luck?" Jack asks.

"Not yet, but I'm checking something out."

I don't know what is pulling me toward the piece of cloth,

but it's all I have. I almost dread approaching it because I know for a fact that it won't prove to be any use. What piece of cloth can be used to light a—

It's an apron.

Oh my God, it's a goddamned *apron*.

The apron that the cashiers wore. That the Candleworks cashier must have thrown off on their way out of the store. And maybe, just maybe, the cashier left a little something in the front pocket. Something that the store employees always had on them in case you wanted to test your candle before purchasing it.

I find the discarded apron and feel around for its front pocket. I take a minute before reaching in. This is it. My final prospect of light. I'm almost can't do it. If there's nothing here, then I'm officially out of ideas. Out of hope. Out of—

Yes! I pull out a small plastic tube with a long neck and a trigger. I silently praise the name of every deity I've ever heard of and press down on the trigger.

A small flame erupts from the neck. The light flickers off of every shard of broken glass in the store.

Jack jumps about five feet into the air. "You found it!"

"I did!" I get to my feet. It's stupid, but I feel incredibly proud of myself. I try to limit the amount of strut in my walk as I approach Jack and our two Forevergreens.

I light each of the six wicks. It feels like some sacred ceremony for some sorcerous cult. I make a mental note to hire a flautist to play mystical music the next time I have to light a candle.

The candles don't emit much light, but they'll give us enough to be able to walk around. And these won't run out of battery anytime soon.

"Let there be light!"

The light of Jack's Forevergreen reveals his squinting eyes and a small scowl. "That's the line you're going with?"

I give him a gentle punch to the shoulder. "Shut up. I'll hire a writer to draft my jokes ahead of time once we're out of here."

"I hope so." Jack punches my shoulder in return. "For the good of all linguistic art."

I can't help but laugh. Probably a coping mechanism, but hey, a boy's gotta cope. "Where to next?"

"Not gonna lie. I'm a little hungry."

My own stomach feels empty. I remember skipping breakfast this morning.

"We can head to the food court, then," I say. "Plus, I bet we'll find some other survivors there. Maybe we can figure out if anyone knows what's going on outside."

"Sounds like a dream."

I pause. "What kind of dreams are you having?"

Jack shrugs. "I guess the kind where I'm accompanied by a decent guy."

I'm sorry, what?

My body stiffens. I have no idea how to respond to this. I take a minute, acutely aware that my face probably looks like someone walloped me with a large herring. With no clever retort in sight, I make an asinine sweeping gesture to the front of the store. "After you."

Jack chuckles and walks out of the Candleworks entryway. I follow behind. With our Forevergreens lighting the way, we delve back into MetroMall's unrelenting darkness.

4

The Forevergreens cast a small sphere of luminosity around us, but it's not much. The best way to maximize our visibility is to walk side by side. I carry my Forevergreen in my left hand, and Jack carries his in his right. Together, we meander down the deserted walkway. We stop at a directory, just a few shops down from the Candleworks.

Jack maneuvers the Forevergreen light over the Metro-Mall map. "The food court is at the center of the mall. There are five or six little stalls surrounding the big fountain." He points at a small red X on the directory. "That's where we are. We're not terribly far, maybe a five-minute walk."

"Great. Maybe it's because you said so, or maybe it's because the existential dread surrounding my brain at all times is eating up all of my serotonin, but I'm pretty hungry now."

"Don't get too excited," Jack says. "With the power out, we won't be able to heat anything up. You may be eating some frozen hot dogs."

"I didn't eat anything before I came to the mall today. I'll take frozen cauliflower on a stick at this point."

"On a stick?" Jack squints his eyes again.

I shrug. "I don't know. I guess the joke is that I hate cauliflower, which you'd need to know for it to make sense. The *stick* part is just to add a little zest to the sentiment."

Jack chuckles. "You're an interesting guy, Luke Chesterfield."

"You have *no* idea."

But actually, Jack *doesn't* know much about me. I don't know much about Jack. It feels like we've been in the mall together for years, but it's only been a few hours. We've come together out of practicality, not necessarily out of compatibility.

"Tell me a little bit about yourself, Jack. What foods do *you* dislike, frozen-on-a-stick or otherwise?"

Jack stops walking for a moment. "You really wanna know about me?"

I turn around and face him. "I mean, I don't need a full account of your life from birth. But you know, what sort of stuff would you talk about on a first date?"

"So we're on a first date?" Jack raises his eyebrow playfully.

Why did you put it that way, Luke? "Ha ha. You know what I mean. Just tell me something about you. Give me something to think about besides the inevitable doom that awaits all humanity."

Jack smiles. "Well, I'm twenty-two."

Twenty-two? That's older than I thought he was.

"I was born and raised not too far from here. In Graham City."

"I'm familiar," I say. "My great-aunt lived there."

"Nice, whereabouts?"

"She lived right by the high school."

"Graham High? Go Groundhogs?"

"The very same! Is that where you went?"

Jack nods. "And then I was at City University, psych major."

"City University in Hampton?"

Jack nods again.

"That's a great school, congrats!"

"It was all right." The timbre in Jack's voice dims. "But I didn't finish my degree."

"You mentioned you were taking a year off."

"In a manner of speaking."

This seems like a delicate matter. I don't want to push it. *Change the subject.*

"My little brother goes to City University," I say. "But he's not in the psych program, so you probably wouldn't know him. Greg Chesterfield?"

Jack shakes his head. "I'm afraid he doesn't ring a bell."

"I figured."

"How about you?" Jack asks. "You in school?"

"Yeah. Masters in English lit at Jackson College. In between my first and second year."

"A master's in English lit, and the best you can come up with off the cuff is *frozen broccoli on a stick*?" Jack laughs.

"First of all, how dare you. Second of all, it was *cauliflower.* It's like you don't know me at all."

"Oh, I *humbly* beg your forgiveness." Jack bows his head.

"We can't *all* get scholarships to City U."

Jack's smile fades. "I didn't have a scholarship. I had some loans, and a decent amount of need-based aid."

"Oof, sorry to hear that," I say. "I know they're expensive."

We're treading dangerously close to Jack's City University history. I can tell that he doesn't want to talk about it, but in a weird way, I feel like he also *does* want to. It's a strange vibe. There is a moment of uncomfortable silence.

"And to answer your first question, I absolutely cannot stand mushrooms."

I scrunch my forehead. "What?"

"The frozen-food-on-a-stick question? It would be mushrooms."

"Oh, *that*," I say. "I'm not too keen on them either. It is my steadfast belief that the Universe never intended for us to consume fungus."

"*There's* that English lit degree," Jack says. "Anyone ever tell you that you talk like a professor?"

I laugh. "Literally every day."

"I'm glad that the people are keeping you honest."

"Well, for the sake of all that is right in the world—"

My effort to come up with something witty to say distracts me, and I'm not looking where I'm going. I trip over something solid in front of me. The Forevergreen skyrockets out of my hand. I fall.

Everything is suddenly cold and wet and dark. My forehead pounds against something hard. Pain erupts around my entire body.

I hear Jack's muffled voice. "Luke. *Luke!*"

I don't know what's going on. All I know is that I can't breathe. Icy liquid envelopes my entire body. Water. My forehead is throbbing. I'm waving my arms, trying to get my head up. But I'm not sure which way is up. I feel around. I find a hard surface. There are lots of small, unfixed pieces of metal on the bottom of whatever I'm in. I feel them more. They're flat and circular—*coins*.

I'm in the fountain. I've fallen in the MetroMall food court fountain.

The MetroMall fountain is the stuff of legend. It's the cornerstone of the entire shopping center. Normally it's lit up, and every ten minutes there's a water show. Also, it's *big*. And *deep*. And even from its bottom, I can't quite figure out which way is up. My forehead is still aching something terrific.

Is this *really* how it's all going to end? If I can't get out of here soon, I'll drown in a goddamn mall fountain.

I feel two arms around my waist. My first instinct is to struggle, and then I realize I'm being saved. One arm is wrapped around me and the other is paddling upward. After what feels like several minutes, my head breaches the water level. I take in a huge gasp—*God,* oxygen tastes good—and I look into the eyes of my savior.

It's Jack.

Jack without a shirt.

Hello.

"*Luke*, thank God," Jack says. "Are you okay?"

"F-fine." My teeth chatter. "C-can you h-help me out?"

"Yeah, one sec." Jack lifts himself out of the fountain, steadies himself, and then reaches down for me. "Take my hand."

I grab Jack's hand and he pulls me out. I struggle for a moment, but I'm able to finally remove myself from the damnable fountain.

I get out and lay my back on the ground. *Breathe in. Breathe out.*

"Geez, Luke. You really scared me."

I look up at Jack. His shirt is still off, as are his shoes and socks. He's still wearing his jeans. By the light of his Forever-green—which he apparently left at the side of the fountain before diving in for me—I can see his body. And may I say, *damn, Jack!* He's way more muscular than I thought he'd be. With his polo on, he looked much skinnier. Without his polo, I make out some nice definition in his shoulders. No discernable abs, but he's got remarkably little body fat. A moderate sprinkling of chest hair. I suddenly feel very out-of-shape in comparison.

"Man, you look good," I say without thinking.

Jack is slipping his polo back on. "What?"

Goddammit. "Sorry, I m-meant, you look good coming out of a fountain." *Stop talking, Luke.* "Like, you're a sight for sore eyes. Or rather, for the eyes of someone who almost drowned."

Jack laughs softly as he laces his shoes. "You're a weirdo, Chesterfield."

"You have no idea." I'm suddenly aware of the fact that the splitting pain in my forehead hasn't gone away. I place a finger where the pain is centralized—right between my eyebrows—and pull it back. It's covered it blood. "Um. So I'm bleeding."

Jack looks at my hairline and his eyes widen. "Yikes, so you are. Let me look at it."

He finishes tying his shoes and closes in on me. I'm still lying on the floor. He grabs his Forevergreen and places it next to my head.

"Yeah. You've got a nasty gash. Must have hit your forehead when you fell into the fountain."

Of course I did. "Is it bad?"

"I mean, it's not great. No worse than what happened to me, though." He raises his hand, still wrapped in Dave the Fridge Guy's skinny white tie. "We just need to find something else to dress the wound up."

"We're in the food court, right?" I say. "Napkins? Or something?"

"We'll need something thicker than napkins. Just a minute." Jack grabs the Forevergreen and starts to leave.

"Jack..."

He stops. "What?"

"Don't leave me."

Jack's eyes soften. "I won't be a minute. You helped me out in the back room of the Electronix. The least I can do is return the favor." He quickly jaunts off to the food court stalls.

I lie there on the cold, hard floor of the fountain plaza. I feel so helpless. Helpless and cold and alone. And Jack took the only light we had. We had two, but I was a complete moron who fell into a fountain and lost our second Forevergreen. *Just maybe watch where you're going for once in your life, Luke.*

Jack returns a few agonizing minutes later. "Not gonna lie, I've really outdone myself."

"Did you f-find something?"

"Yeah." He crouches down to where I'm lying. "The chefs at that sushi place, Rockin' Roll, apparently all wear these headbands." He gestures to a handful of black slips of fabric adorned with Japanese characters in his left hand. "These will work perfectly as makeshift bandages for you."

Jack places three of the headbands on my head and wraps them tightly. Once he's applied them, he walks back to the fountain and rinses my blood off of his hands.

"Th-Thanks, Jack."

Jack looks up from the fountain. "You okay?"

"Just a little c-cold."

"Oh, dammit." He places the Forevergreen on the floor.

"I'm so sorry, I'm not thinking. We need to get you out of those wet clothes."

I sit up. "I n-need something to wear."

Jack walks over to me and helps me up. "No duh. Need I remind you that we're in a mall? You have your pick of the latest fashion."

"That m-makes sense."

"But first, you're gonna need to get your tank and shorts off," Jack says.

No. I can't let Jack see me undressed. Not when he looks so—

"N-no. I c-can't. Not in front of—"

"In front of whom? I'm the only one here. And you just saw me with my shirt off." He raises his eyebrows.

"I'm n-not—"

"Listen, Luke," Jack says forcefully. "I understand you're uncomfortable, but this is no time to be modest. Every minute you stay in those cold, wet clothes, you're getting closer to hypothermia. It's summer, but it's getting late and the temperature is gonna drop. And the mall's heaters are unlikely to turn on."

"B-But..."

"No buts. We're close to Trixie's. That's the nearest department store to the food court. We'll get you something warm and dry. Here. I need to change my jeans out too."

Oh my God, he isn't—

Jack unbuttons his jeans and slips them off. He's wearing canary yellow briefs with bright pink hearts printed all over.

I can't help but stare.

"Interesting ch-choice of c-color."

Jack looks down. "What can I say? I have excellent taste."

I'm sure you do.

I'm trying exceedingly hard not to look at Jack's—well, at *Jack*. I peel my tank top off and slip out of my shorts. My undies are far more orthodox. Boxer briefs, gray with white stripes.

"Don't worry. We'll get you some new undies at Trixie's too." Jack laughs. "Maybe something in fuchsia?"

"Over your dead body." I wring my wet clothes out over the fountain and gather them into a bundle.

"Isn't the phrase, 'over *my* dead body'?" Jack asks.

"I know what I said."

I've gotta say, wearing nothing but my boxers and three sushi chef headbands feels like a virtuosic level of vulnerability. I'm excruciatingly aware of the soft love handles spilling out over the sides of my underwear.

Jack hands me his Forevergreen. "After you." He makes the same goofy gesture I did at the Candleworks entrance.

I give Jack a death glare. "I hate you."

5

———

The walk to Trixie's is not a long one from the food court, but the relative nature of time is well-exhibited when one is clad solely in one's skivvies, in the dark, with a single scented candle serving as the only guiding light, all under the existential umbrella of nuclear catastrophe.

I hear Jack snicker behind me.

I stop and turn around. "What?"

Jack points at the pile of clothes I'm carrying. "I just noticed your socks. They're mismatched."

I look down at my clothes. My two socks—pink and green—return my gaze.

"Yeah. I slept through my alarm this morning. Had to get dressed in a hurry to make my appointment at the Electronix."

"Oh," Jack says. "I figured you were making some sort of artistic statement."

I laugh. "Hate to break it to you, but sometimes socks are just socks."

"A *true* English lit major would strive to find the symbolism."

"To be honest, I never had any great passion for my chosen field. It just was the only thing I was good at in high school."

"Not math? Science?"

"Nope. I took chemistry my sophomore year and nearly blew up the classroom on our first lab. I took that as a divine sign that I wasn't meant to go into the sciences."

"Incredible."

"Yeah, well, what got you into psychology?"

Jack pauses a moment before answering. "My family. We have a...uh...history of mental illness. Mostly undiagnosed. I guess I wanted to do my part to help other families dealing with the same stuff."

I sense the unease in Jack's voice when he talks about his family. Something inside me wants to know more. *Why, Luke? It's none of your business.*

"Do you have any siblings?"

Jack pauses and looks down. "A younger sister, Lulu. But she died a few years ago."

I freeze. *Good job, Luke.* "Oh, God, I'm so sorry."

"It's okay." Jack looks back up at me. "It was a long time ago. I'm fine."

"Still, though, I can't imagine dealing with that."

"Yeah, it was rough. Especially on my parents." His voice cracks.

"Sorry," I say. "If you don't want to talk about it, that's fine."

"No, it's cool." Jack's voice goes back to normal. "You just have the one brother? My esteemed classmate?"

"Yeah," I say. "It's just the two of us and Mom. My dad passed a few years ago. Cancer."

"I'm sorry to hear that."

"You and me both. But he lived a good life. A short one, but a full one."

"Guess that's all we can do. Make the most of the time we've got together."

My heart skips a beat. "Together?"

Jack's eyes widen. "I mean, like, together as the human race."

"Oh. I thought you meant... Never mind. It's nothing." I look up. "We're here! Trixie's."

The Forevergreen irradiates the elegant cursive letters of the department store's sign.

"No gate," Jack says. "Good."

We enter the store. Trixie's has a few emergency lights on, like the Electronix, so we are able to blow the Forevergreen out for now.

"The men's section is on the west side of the store," Jack says. "We might want to pick up a few extra things while we're here. Sweaters or something. It'll probably get cold tonight."

Tonight. I hadn't even thought of the night. Was I really going to spend the night at the MetroMall? It sounded like some weird youth group field trip, not something I'd ever be forced to do out of necessity.

I spy a beige backpack in the section marked *Back-2-Skool* —I wonder if Trixie is making a satirical statement about the state of public education in our community—and grab it. "We can use this to carry a few things."

"Good idea." Jack grabs the backpack from me and walks toward the jeans section. I follow.

About half of the jeans are on the ground. Jack digs through the denim. "Slim or skinny, what do you think?"

I look at Jack's legs—as if I haven't been mesmerized by them the entire walk to Trixie's—and am at a loss for words.

"Uh," I say poetically. "I mean, I suppose that's a question of personal preference."

"You're useless." Jack finds a pair and slips them on. "Slim it is, I guess." They're a perfect fit, especially around his ass. Jack wears jeans well. He also wears *nothing* well.

Jack zips his fly. "How about you? We need to get you a pair."

"I'll find something." I have absolutely zero desire to reveal my waist size to Jack. I jog over to a jeans rack on the other side of the men's section. I browse through and find a pair in my size, stepping into them before Jack can walk over.

"Why so quick?" Jack asks. "You don't wanna look any further? You shouldn't underestimate the importance of a good fit of jeans. Plus those ones still have the security tag on them."

"These fit well."

They don't. But they'll do.

I can tell Jack doesn't buy it, but he doesn't press the issue. "The next thing to get you would be a shirt and some shoes. And maybe even a pair of matching socks."

Across the aisle is a shelf of comic book-themed T-shirts. I grab the first one I see—dark green with an image of some superhero with a silver helmet covering his eyes. I slip it on. No longer will Jack be exposed to the gentle curves of my upper body.

"You a big Gamma Ray fan?" Jack points at the design bedecking the front of the shirt through which I'm poking my head.

"Is that who this is?" I look down at the brightly colored character emblazoned on my chest. "It's just the first shirt I grabbed."

"It's oddly appropriate," Jack says. "There was a whole series a few years ago where Gamma Ray defeated Nucleotide, a supervillain who tried to blow up the world, basically using an A-Bomb."

"Oh, he's a *nerd*!"

"And damn proud of it. Are you telling me you never even saw the movie?"

"I guess I was too busy reading the complete works of Shakespeare."

"Certainly comparable in quality," Jack says. "Which one is your favorite?"

"Which what?"

"Work of Shakespeare?"

I rack my brain. "If I *have* to choose one, there's no beating *Macbeth*. Prophecy, witches, murder. It's got all the fixin's for a good story."

"*All the fixin's.*" Jack chuckles. "And *I'm* the nerd?"

"Shut up." I punch him on the shoulder.

"Also, isn't it bad luck to say that?"

"What?"

"*Macbeth*?"

"That's a superstition among theater people. But in a nuclear-ravaged shopping mall, I think we're okay."

"True," Jack says. "And I suppose we've had our fill of bad luck."

"Oh, God, don't say things like that. You'll jinx it."

"*Now* who's superstitious?"

"Hush up," I say. "Let's get me some shoes, and then we can head back to the Food Court."

"Sounds like a plan. Shoes are just down a few aisles."

We find a pair of sneakers in my size—black with gold lightning bolts on the side. I slip them on along with my mismatched socks.

"Don't you want some new socks, too?" Jack asks.

"Mine are pretty dry at this point. Plus, I kind of like the different colors. Gives me an edge."

"To each his own." Jack grabs a few hoodies hanging nearby and stuffs them in the backpack. "I think we're good now."

"Looks like it," I say. "Back to the food court? I think it's close to lunchtime."

"Already?"

"I mean, I have literally no way of knowing the time. Without my phone, I'm totally helpless."

"Spoken like a true child of the twenty-first century."

"Hey, *my* phone was charged. It just happens to be in the pocket of a guy currently under a refrigerator."

"Like I haven't heard that excuse a million times."

I laugh. Jack's a pretty funny guy. Plus, he's handsome. The whole package. I can't help but wonder if—

"Onward?" Jack asks.

I look up. *Bigger fish to fry, Luke.*

I grab the Forevergreen and relight it. "Let's roll." We stroll up to the entrance of Trixie's. We're about to walk back into the mall walkway when—

Waaaaa! Waaaaa! Waaaaa!

I almost drop the Forevergreen. It's the store alarm. The damn tag on my jeans has set it off. It's not as loud as the alarm that went off before The Boom, but this one is closer to my ears and it's not pleasant.

"Just keep walking, Luke," Jack says. "It'll go off eventually."

"But now people will know we were here."

"So?"

I pause. "Guess it doesn't matter."

I continue to walk out of the store, but I stop when I feel a tap on my shoulder.

"What is it *now*, Jack?"

But it isn't Jack tapping my shoulder. I turn around to see a woman with long brown hair wearing a pale-yellow sweater and a green skirt.

"Sir, you're going to have to pay for those."

6

———

"I'm sorry. What?"

"Your jeans," Yellow Sweater Saleswoman says. "They set off the alarm. You're going to have to pay."

"Um..." I say. "I don't know if you're aware, but the entire mall is on lockdown because of a nuclear detonation. Did you hear the alarm? Did you hear The Boom?"

"Of course I heard it." The woman wrinkles her forehead. "That doesn't mean you can just take whatever you want. Trixie's has several anti-shoplifting policies in place, and—"

"And what?" Jack asks. "You're gonna call the cops on us?"

"When the mall reopens—"

"*If* the mall reopens," Jack says. "We have no idea what's going on outside. All I know is it's not good and we're lucky to be alive."

"Will you stop interrupting me?" YSS asks.

"Will you stop insisting we pay for our post-apocalyptic pants?" Jack asks.

"If my manager finds out—"

"Is your manager here? In the MetroMall?"

YSS shakes her head. "No. He usually isn't in until after noon."

"Then he's probably dead," Jack says coldly.

YSS recoils.

I step forward. "What my friend means to say is, this mall has some incredible shields in place, and the only way we're getting out of here is if the National Guard saws through them. My name is Luke. This is Jack. I fell into the fountain and needed to get a pair of dry pants."

"You fell into a fountain?" YSS wrinkles her forehead further.

"Hey, it's dark in the walkway area," I say. "Don't judge me."

"Wouldn't dream of it." She crosses her arms. "Fine. Take the pants. But if we do reopen you better come back and pay for them."

"If the mall reopens, I'll come in and perform an interpretive dance in a skintight pink unitard to celebrate," Jack says.

Woof. I wouldn't mind seeing that.

Focus, Luke.

"*Anyway*," I say. "We're headed to the food court. Trying to find some other people. You wanna come with us?"

"I'm not supposed to leave the store," she says. "I was the only one on duty when the alarms went off. My coworkers were supposed to get in at ten, but—" She buries her head in her hands. "Oh *God*. They're *never* getting in!"

She starts to cry.

Jack awkwardly pats her on the shoulder. "I'm sorry. I lost some coworkers too."

"It was my friend, Jane. She was running late, so I told her I'd cover for her. And now she's probably—"

"Hey," I say. "We don't know what's going on. For all we

know, the whole mall lockdown was just some elaborate prank. Something to make the governor look stupid."

"And that big Boom?" YSS wipes her eyes.

I have no response to this. *Change the subject, Luke.*

"Was there anyone else in the store with you when the alarms went off?" I ask.

YSS looks up from her hands. A few more tears streak down her face, but her composure has solidified. "A few people, but they ran out. No idea where they went. As far as I know, I was the only one in the whole store until you guys came in."

"Then our best chance at survival is to find more people," I say. "Come with us to the food court. I'm sure you could use something to eat. This is Jack."

YSS wipes her eyes. "Polly. Polly Featherstone."

Jack's forehead wrinkles. "Polly, like a parrot?"

"Yes." Polly rolls her eyes. "And congrats for being the first person ever to make that incredibly clever and innovative joke."

"Sorry. Not trying to make fun. Just a unique name. You don't hear about many Pollys anymore."

"My mom had old-fashioned taste," Polly says. "Just be glad you didn't have to get through elementary school with my name. *Especially* paired with a surname like Featherstone."

"My last name is Chesterfield," I say. "It's not much better."

"And mine is Jay," Jack says. "We've all been there."

I look at Jack. This is the first time I've heard his last name. *Jack Jay.* It's a funny name, no doubt, but it's also kind of hot. Fitting name for a well-toned, handsome guy. *Ugh.*

Why does knowing his full name make me even more attracted to him?

Polly laughs. "Your parents really didn't give you much of a chance, did they?"

"You have no idea." Jack looks down for a moment—this is a sensitive subject—but soon recovers. "C'mon. Let's head to the food court. I've heard the chicken tenders are exquisite."

"Exquisite, even?" I smile. "I guess I missed the article about them in this month's *Gourmet Digest*."

Polly is silent for a moment. Gears are turning behind her eyes. "Fine. Let's try it. And who knows? Maybe Jane somehow got in and is down there."

Not likely.

"You never know," I say.

"Do you have a flashlight or something?" Jack pulls out the Forevergreen. "All we have is this candle. We both lost our phones in the chaos."

"I've got this," Polly pulls a pen out of her pocket. It has an LED light on the top of the cap.

"That's pretty small," I say.

"It's brighter than it looks," she replies. "And it's notably not a scented candle."

"Excellent point. We'll take what we can get."

"Eventually we'll make it up to the SportsGoods and get something heavy duty," Jack says. "But first, the food court. It's not far from here."

"And try not to fall into any fountains." Polly raises her eyebrows at me.

"Luke can't make any promises." Jack elbows me playfully. "We can't all have the exceptional poise it takes to walk around things."

"Great." I crack a small smile. "Now I have *two* critics."

We exit Trixie's. I have the Forevergreen, Polly has her flashlight pen, and Jack follows close behind us. The walk back to the food court only take a few minutes—turns out it's a lot faster when one is completely clothed—and this time I very gracefully manage to walk *around* the giant fountain.

"So where are these chicken tenders I've heard so much about?" I ask.

Jack points to a nearby stall. The words "Cluck Hut" are written in big, bubbly red letters on the sign above. Underneath, the company's slogan: "*The best fricken' chicken.*"

Poetry.

"Let's try it out," I say.

Polly stops. "This may not be the best time to tell you this, but I'm a vegetarian."

"No matter. There's a Salad Gardens two stalls down." Jack walks into the Cluck Hut and starts foraging.

Polly leans over to me. "How much does he know about this mall?"

"A lot. He works—*worked?*—in the Electronix and apparently did quite a bit of research before taking the position."

"Gotcha," Polly says. "And how long have the two of you been together?"

I stop. I blink. "Oh, we're not—I mean, that is to say—*I'm* not, uh..." My brain has lost its capacity to string words together. "We're friends. That is, rather—we just met. I was in the Electronix store when everything happened."

"You *just* met?" Polly places her hands on her hips.

"Yeah, why?"

"I don't know. You two just have a chemistry. Like you've known each other for years."

She's right. She's so right. *But—*

"I hadn't thought about that," I say. "The last few hours have been pandemonium. I guess we just fast-forwarded to friendship out of necessity."

"Still, though," Polly says. "There's something. I can see it. You two were meant to be in each other's lives."

I laugh. "Well, if global nuclear devastation is what it took for us to meet, I'm not sure if I can say it was worth it."

"Hey, you two!" Jack calls across from the Cluck Hut. He's behind the counter. "You gonna eat, or what?"

I walk over to the stall. Jack is sitting on the floor, next to the Cluck Hut freezer, holding a large plastic bag.

I sit down next to him. "Find anything?"

Jack looks up. "I have good news and bad news. The good news is there's a ton of frozen tenders and fries."

"And the bad news?"

"No power, so we can't heat them up."

"So we're gonna have to eat...?"

"Frozen chicken tenders? Yes."

I wrinkle my nose. "Are they safe to eat frozen?"

"The meat is already cooked through." Jack snaps a frozen tender in half and shows me. It's all white inside. "All the Cluck Hut people do is toss them in the fryer to warm them up. Same with the fries."

"Still, though." I glance over at Polly, who's already fixed herself something green at Salad Gardens. "Frozen chicken tenders? Is there any way we could heat them over the Forevergreen or something?"

Jack stares blankly. "Are you legitimately asking if we can use a three-wick scented candle to cook a frozen chicken tender?"

"I mean... Okay. That was a stupid question."

"Now, if we had a *four*-wick candle, that'd be a different story." Jack simpers.

"Shut up."

"We can wait for them to thaw out. Then we'd simply be eating room-temperature wet chicken tenders."

"That's seems somehow worse." I say.

"Well, you can leave a scathing online review of the mall's frozen food catalogue when we get out of here," Jack says. "In the meantime, I think it's chicksicles for lunch."

"*Chicksicles?* That's the best you can come up with?"

"There aren't many chicken-related words that blend well into 'popsicles,' okay?"

I think of something. I grin. *Don't say it. Don't say—*

"How about *cocksicles?*"

You're a goddamn twelve-year-old, Luke.

Jack's mouth opens but no words emerge. He stares at me a minute but then laughs. "I'm gonna let you figure out why that one doesn't work."

He's playing it cool, but I notice a little bit of blood relocating to his cheeks.

"Fine, for lack of a better term, we'll stick with *chicksicles* for now," I say.

"Probably for the best."

"Have you tried one yet?"

"No. I figured we could embark on the Great Chicksicle Journey together." He grabs two frozen tenders—*chicksicles,* rather—from the bag in his hand. He hands one to me.

We clink our chicksicles together.

"*Bon appetit,*" I say in my best Julia Child voice.

Jack snorts. I bite into the chicksicle.

It's weird. It doesn't taste *bad*. It tastes like a chicken tender, just if it were hard and cold. But it's weird. And difficult to chew. I swallow and look at Jack. Based on the grimace on his face, he seems to be having a similarly unpleasant experience. I can't help but laugh.

"We've gotta find a way to heat these up, Luke," he says. "This is no way to live."

"Chicksicle's not doing it for you?"

"Not at all. You?"

"I've had worse." I slowly chew through a second bite and force it down. "I've also had much better."

"How's it hangin', boys?"

I look up. Polly is back, standing in front of the Cluck Hut counter.

"Just eating frozen chicken tenders," Jack says. "Basically salt in the wound. How was your salad?"

"Pretty good. I guess that's a point to the vegetarians."

"I guess so," I say. "There's no way we can keep eating frozen chicken tenders. There's gotta be something we can do."

Jack's face brightens. "SportsGoods! I bet they have a propane stove in their camping section!"

"Good idea," I say. "It would be smart to see what else they have. Sleeping bags and the like. Stuff to get us through the night."

"Why didn't you two go there first?" Polly asks.

"It's on the third floor," I say. "And we didn't have any light at the time to get us up the stairwell. But now we do!"

"We can get some stuff and then set up camp here at the Cluck Hut," Jack says. "That way we'll have easy access to the food, and a safe, secure location behind the counter if any more Booms hit us."

"I love it," I say. "Looks like we make a good team!"

I look back up at Polly. She's smiling at us. A knowing smile. A telling smile.

Shut up, Polly.

Jack and I throw what's left of our chicksicles away. I grab the Forevergreen and lead the way *around* the fountain and toward the stairwell.

7

<hr>

"*For emergency use only,*" Jack reads the sign on the door to the stairwell.

"I would think a complete nuclear cataclysm qualifies," I say.

"I think the folks who designed the mall were thinking more along the lines of a fire." Jack opens the door. "But *tomato-tomahto.*"

"You two sure do joke a lot." Polly enters the stairwell, her pen light in hand.

"Coping strategy," Jack says.

"Did I mention that Jack here is a psychologist?" I ask Polly.

"Bravo," Polly says. "Maybe we should call you Jacklov!"

Jack looks at Polly. "What?"

Polly frowns. "You know, like Pavlov? The ring-a-bell, feed-a-dog guy?"

"The joke doesn't really work. Pavlov worked in the field of classical conditioning. He didn't conduct any research regarding the human processing of trauma."

55

"Yeah, *God*, Polly," I say.

"Never mind." Polly starts climbing up the stairs. "Guess I shouldn't have tried to get in on your bit."

"You'll catch up soon enough." Jack follows her but looks over his shoulder and raises an eyebrow at me.

I return a confused smile.

"Third floor, you said?" Polly asks.

"Yep," Jack says. "Should be the next door we see."

We arrive at the top of the third-floor flight. A door awaits us. Inscribed on it is a large number three spray-painted in red. Polly grabs the handle.

"Uh...Doctor Freud?" She looks over her shoulder. "Door's locked."

Jack stops. "You're kidding."

"Wish I were," Polly says. "You wanna try it?"

Jack walks up and jiggles the handle. It doesn't budge. "Why would it be locked? They're supposed to unlock these at opening."

"They?" I ask.

"Mall security. They lock the doors at nighttime once everyone's out. Then they unlock them in the morning at the start of the workday."

"Around nine in the morning?" I ask. "As in right when The Boom happened?"

Jack frowns. "Yeah, I guess it's possible they may have been otherwise occupied."

"Wait a minute," Polly says. "Does that mean that the door we came in also locked behind us?"

Every ounce of blood seems to drain from Jack's face. He grabs the Forevergreen out of my hand and flies down the stairs. From two floors below I hear, "God*dammit*."

Probably not a good sign.

"Jack," I call down. "Are we locked in the stairwell?"

Jack traipses up the stairs. "Well, floors one, two, and three are locked. It's entirely possible that floor four is open."

"And if it isn't?" I ask.

"Floor four will be open," Jack says. "It has to be, it just *has* to."

Floor four is not open.

Jack wrings the door handle as if for dear life, which, I realize in retrospect, is kind of the case. "You have *got* to be kidding me."

"There are more stairs," I say. "Is there another floor?"

"Just the roof."

"And we can't go on the roof, right?" Polly asks. "If a bomb really went off, it wouldn't be safe to go outside."

"Likely no." Jack hangs his head.

"Anywhere else we can go?" I ask.

"I don't think so." Jack closes his eyes. "Our best bet is to go back to the first floor and pound on the door. Someone may hear us."

"Who?" I ask. "We've barely seen anyone since we left the Electronix. There was the guy in the lavender shirt and Polly. I don't think there are that many people in the mall."

"Do you have a *better* suggestion?" Jack snaps.

I don't respond. Did Jack really just raise his voice at me? He must see the hurt bewilderment in my face, because he immediately eases his tone.

"Sorry." Jack sits down on the steps and places his head in his hands. "This is my own damn fault. I'm upset and I took it out on you."

I sit next to Jack. "It's okay. You had no way of knowing that we'd get locked in here. How about we split up? Polly and you stay at the third-floor entrance, and I'll go down to the first floor. We can split our pounding and yelling efforts. Someone will hear us and let us out."

"Shouldn't someone be on the second floor?" Jack asks.

"Well, we only have our two lights." I stand. "I don't want you all alone in the dark."

Jack doesn't counter. He just stares blankly at me. I feel like he's trying to silently communicate something to me, but I can't get a read on him.

He sighs. "Okay."

I take the Forevergreen down to the first-floor door. I'm about to start beating the door, and then I see a small half-flight of stairs just beyond it. Jack must have missed it when he went back down to check. What the hell, let's check it out. It's probably nothing. Jack and Polly begin to yell for help up on the third floor.

I walk down the half-flight. It doesn't seem to lead to anywhere important, just a small storage area where the custodians keep their supplies. Two yellow mop buckets on wheels, a push broom, and a slightly unsettling white container full of dried scum sit on the floor. A shelf of cleaning chemicals hangs over everything else. Guess I should just head back up to the—*wait.*

It's easy to miss, but there's a door behind the yellow mop buckets.

Don't get your hopes up, Luke. Probably just more storage.

But I have to at least check. I push the mop buckets out of the way and place my hand on the handle. *It's gonna be locked.*

It's not. It opens! The Hallelujah Chorus blares inside my head.

I'm still not sure what it is. But it's bigger than a storage closet. I prop the door open with one of the mop buckets and walk through. I immediately inhale a pound of dust and cough my lungs out for a minute. I hold the Forevergreen in front of me. It's a long hall. A tunnel?

Why on earth would the MetroMall have an underground tunnel? It's so...*cultlike*. Is this where some secret society of lizard people made sacrificial slaughters and drank blood out of a lamb's skull? Or is it—

Nope, turns out that's not the case. I walk to the end of the tunnel and a small room greets me. In it, a couch, two twin bunk beds, a small kitchenette, two refrigerators, and a table. A shelf full of canned goods. A small battery-powered lantern sits on the table.

Oh my God, it's a fallout shelter.

It makes sense, I guess. The mall was built in the fifties. Probably just a routine part of architecture at the time. What takes me back most is the shelter's diminutive size. It really could only accommodate two, maybe three, people. Certainly not an entire mall's worth of people. It must have been reserved for one person. Maybe the MetroMall owner.

I suppose it explains why the mall architects wanted to minimize use of the stairs. Probably why the mall security's job included locking the stairwells at closing, too. Whoever built this wanted to keep people from finding it.

At any rate, it's a dead end. Unless—

Building codes—even in the fifties—would have required that a building this size contain more than one stairwell. For emergencies. MetroMall definitely has at least two separate stairwells. This couldn't possibly be the only path that would lead to this shelter. What if the owner—or whoever—was on the other side of the mall when an attack occurred?

No, there's gotta be another tunnel. And maybe this one would lead to an unlocked door. But where? There's only so much space in the shelter. Could there possibly be a hidden door?

I settle my gaze on the refrigerators. Their plurality gives me pause. Why would a nuclear shelter only built for a few people need two of them? I had three roommates at my grad school apartment and we were able to share a fridge pretty easily. Well, except Rob, who had all manner of health shakes taking up my diet soda real estate.

There's no way one of these fridges is a secret door. That's just way too *Scooby-Doo* to be true.

Then again, today's events *have* been cartoonishly bizarre to say the very least, so I may as well try. I open the first one—closest to the shelf of canned foods—and it is very much a refrigerator on the inside. The light inside even works. It must be connected to the emergency generators. I eye the second fridge. This one looks much more dilapidated, and slightly bigger than the other one. Big enough to walk into, even.

I open it. The light inside the fridge is brighter than I anticipate. My vision goes black for a second, but when my eyes adjust, my suspicions are confirmed. A second tunnel extends through the refrigerator.

"My God," I mutter out loud. What the *hell* kind of mall is this?

I need to get Jack and Polly. Even if we can't get out, at least there's food and shelter down here. And maybe a way out through the secret fridge door.

Taking no time to contemplate how ridiculous that thought is, I quickly run through the tunnel, making sure to not let any doors fully close behind me. I arrive at the third floor. Jack and Polly are still battering away at the door, but their energy has clearly diminished since I left them. Jack's face is red from the yelling and his eyes look swollen.

"Guys," I say upon arriving. I take a second to catch my breath. I haven't run this fast in quite some time. "I have *got* to show you something."

8

———

"What. The hell." Jack's mouth is agape.

"Is that a reaction to the secret tunnel, the fridge door, or just the shelter at large?" I ask.

Jack runs his fingers through his hair. "D. All of the above."

"Why on *earth* would they build something like this under a shopping mall?" Polly asks.

"The mall *was* built in the fifties." Jack sits down at the table. "There was a looming threat of nuclear war. Still, though, this is weird. People built fallout shelters like these in their basements, not under commercial buildings."

"That's what I thought." I sit across from Jack. "My theory was that it was for the mall owner or something."

"That *could* be it," Jack says. "MetroMall's highest-ranking employee is its CEO. The current holder of that title is Maxwell Stride."

"Sounds like the name of a senator's kid," I say.

"The Strides have owned the MetroMall for a few generations," Jack says. "Jacob Stride built the mall. He was Maxwell's grandfather."

I laugh. "Are you telling me MetroMall has a *dynasty*?"

"In a manner of speaking." Jack stands and paces around the bunker. "There does seem to be a certain primogeniture around the position. And I *guess* it makes sense that the elder Stride would build himself a fallout shelter in his own mall. He was a vocal supporter of McCarthyism during the Second Red Scare. The family has some serious political connections, too. It stands to reason that his paranoia was rooted in a deep-seated fear of the Soviets' ability to initiate a nuclear strike."

"That would explain why the mall has such great defenses," I say. "He must have spent a fortune on the barricades that went up this morning."

"Guess it turned out to be worthwhile." Jack smiles. "For us, anyway."

"What about the door in the fridge?" Polly asks. "Did you figure out where *that* goes?"

"Not yet. I wanted to grab you guys first. Figured it'd be safer to go as a group."

"That, or we all get killed at once." Jack laughs weakly.

"I mean, six in one."

"In all likelihood it just leads to another stairwell." Jack looks down the dark walkway. "Which is likely also going to be locked."

Polly looks over his shoulder and then faces me. "Well, someone has clearly been here recently."

"What makes you say that?" I ask.

Polly gestures to the lantern on the table. "That can't have been on long. Those battery-powered lanterns don't last forever."

A chill runs down my spine. "We should maybe get out of here, then. Stride—or whoever this belongs to—can't be happy we found their shelter."

"Agreed." Jack scans the shelter. "This was clearly meant to be kept secret."

"Through the fridge, then?" Polly asks.

"Yeah, I think that's our best move. Hopefully it leads to a way out." Jack grabs the lantern off of the table. "And we have a third light now!"

"Should we really take that?" I ask. "Whoever it belongs to will know someone was down here."

Jack sets the lantern back down on the table, mulls a minute, and then picks it back up. "Yes. We've already lost one of our candles, and this lantern is better than our other two light sources combined. I'm not *not* taking it."

Something doesn't feel right, but I don't argue. It's not a bad idea to have another light source. Plus we could all be murdered by another nuke at any moment, which gives the situation some perspective.

Lantern in hand, Jack walks through the fridge door. Polly and I trail behind. This tunnel is much longer than the first one, and a *lot* creepier. There are quite a few more cobwebs and the ground has a slight dampness to it. Not exactly a Sunday stroll in the country.

We turn a corner. I assume this will be the mall's second stairway, but it isn't. It's more tunnel. But a small glint of light glimmers ahead of us, maybe thirty yards away. I feel another knot form in my stomach. We pause.

"What do you think that is?" I ask.

"Not sure," Jack responds.

"Is it maybe another lantern like the one we found?" Polly suggests.

"I doubt it." Jack squints. "It looks too bright. Like an entire lit room."

"How is that possible with the power down?" I ask.

"Well, there were emergency lights on in the Trixie's," Jack says. "And in the Electronix. There are probably quite a few working off of emergency generators. At the very least, it's something not dark and not damp."

"That's reason enough for me to go for it." Polly forges ahead.

"Are you guys sure?" I ask. "It just seems weird."

Polly pauses and turns toward me. "What's the worst that could happen?"

I clap my hands over my ears. "Oh, God, don't *ever* say things like that. That's what the characters in movies say right before everything goes to hell."

"Well, this may be news to you"—Polly places a condescending hand on my shoulder—"but we're not in a movie. We're in a mall. And our best bet for getting out of here is that room up ahead."

"I've gotta agree with Polly," Jack says. "We know there's nothing waiting for us in the stairwell, spare the miraculous coincidence of someone opening the doors for us."

"Fine, *fine*." I take a few steps in the light's direction. "You're right. I'm just being paranoid. This whole underground lair thing just gives me the creeps."

"I mean, that's fair." Jack catches up with me. "It's weird. But it's also like the fifth weirdest thing we've dealt with in the last three hours, so I'm just rollin' with it."

I look up at Jack, and I can't help but be in awe of him. A few hours ago, he was this skinny, freaked-out kid hiding under a table with me as the world ended. Now he's some sort of valiant, unexpectedly hot cavalier leading us into the unknown. *What a world.*

We amble slowly toward the light. We're almost there now. I can't help but wonder if this is the last moment I will spend on this plane of existence.

We cross through an entryway. It's a door that's been left open. Jack is right. The space is illuminated by emergency lighting. We're in a large room, surrounded by fluffy couches, big-screen TVs, and a billiards table. The door closes behind me. I look over my shoulder and see that it blends in with the rest of the wall. I shift my focus. Four words are printed on a placard above one of the TVs:

Jacob Stride Memorial Lounge

"Jack." I point at the sign. "Mall history lesson, please."

"Glad to be of service." Jack walks toward the center of the room. "I think this was Jacob Stride's office when he first built the mall."

"This was his office?" Polly asks. "It's huge."

"The elder Stride wasn't known for his humility. When they built the mall, he had a huge office. When he died and his son, Jacob Junior, took over, he moved the offices to a more practical corner of the mall and turned this space into an employee lounge. They also rent this space out for events."

"Makes sense, though." I lean on the edge of the pool table. "The original office has direct access to the tunnel leading to the shelter."

"Yep." Jack gestures to a picture of Jacob Stride hanging underneath the lounge's sign. "I'm guessing the second Jacob was unaware—or just didn't care—about the shelter. By the time he took over in the early eighties, the looming threat of nuclear war had dwindled substantially."

"Until today," Polly says.

"Indeed." Jack gives a half-shrug and then turns toward the north side of the room. "But look. There's our way out!"

He's right. There's a door leading back to the mall walkway.

"We did it!" I punch my fist in the air.

"Nah." Jack looks me dead in the eyes. "*You're* the one who found the shelter. I'd still be clawing at the third-floor door if it weren't for you, Luke."

He flashes me a brilliant smile. I can't help but smile back. My cheeks warm.

Polly places herself between the two of us. "I hate to interrupt this precious moment, but we should get out of here before anyone realizes we were somewhere we shouldn't be."

"Right." I look around. "What floor are we on?"

"The lounge is on the first floor," Jack says.

"All that trouble, and we're still on the first floor?"

Jack laughs. "Yessir."

"And the stairwell is locked." I sit down on one of the couches. "Even if we propped the first-floor door open, we wouldn't be able to open the third-floor door from the inside."

"Yeah." Jack sits down next to me. "Until we somehow make contact with people on the third floor, I don't see any way of getting up there with the elevators down."

"Wait," Polly says from behind us.

Jack and I turn around.

"What is it?" I ask.

"Okay, I have an idea." Polly circles the room. "But bear with me, it's a little...*whimsical.*"

"Getting to the SportsGoods store is gonna improve our quality of life exponentially," Jack says. "I'm willing to do most anything to get there before nightfall."

Polly hesitates a few seconds. "How good are you at climbing?"

Jack and I look at each other and furrow our eyebrows in tandem.

I stand up. "You can't seriously be suggesting scaling the walls of the mall to get to SportsGoods."

"No."

"We can't climb up the elevator shafts, either," Jack says.

"*No.*" Polly stomps her foot on the ground. "May I speak?"

"Sorry," I say. "What is it?"

"Did you guys ever come here as little kids?" Polly asks.

Is Polly suggesting what I think she's suggesting? There's no way. It couldn't possibly work. Or could it? I look over at Jack.

He's smiling. "Oh my God. Why didn't I think of it before?"

"Well, to be fair, stairs were the far more practical option at the time," Polly says.

"Still, though." Jack is pacing—almost hopping—around the room. "I never would have thought of it in a million years."

Polly laughs. "How is it that I'm the oldest one here, and I'm the one who thought of it?"

"I suppose Jack and I are mature beyond our years," I say.

Polly rolls her eyes. "Oh, yeah, *that's* it."

"*Anyway.*" Jack points out the door. "It's just down the hall from here. Not even a minute walk."

"Let's go, then!" I get on my feet.

The three of us walk—*jog* is actually more accurate—and reach our terminus. We behold the multicolored majesty before us. A huge wave of nostalgia hits me, and a childlike sense of wonder that hasn't stirred in years awakes within my soul. I feel a small lump developing in my throat.

"Here we are," Polly says. "The famous MetroMall Mega-Slide!"

A single tear runs down my face.

9

The MetroMall Mega-Slide has been the delight of children across the county as long as I can remember. A trip to the mall with my mom was not complete without at least one ride down the plastic behemoth before going to see a movie. A stunning rainbow-colored spiral, it stretches all the way down from the third floor of the mall before spitting its riders out through the mouth of a large unicorn into a pit of soft foam blocks on the first. An elevator is located right next to the slide entrance for parents—or nervous siblings—to ride down to meet their children at the conclusion of their journey.

Of course today, the elevator isn't an option.

"Do you really think we can climb *up* the slide?" I ask. "It's probably slippery."

Polly shrugs. "I'm just the idea person. I'll defer to you two on the actual execution of the ascent."

Jack wades into the pool of foam blocks and gently kicks the slide. The twisted monolith shakes slightly but doesn't falter.

"It's stable." Jack hoists himself onto the ride's exit—the last few feet of the slide serve as the unicorn's tongue—and feels around. "It's definitely slippery. We'll need something with a little grip to it."

"Like what?" I ask.

"Cleats, maybe?" Jack shrugs.

"There's only one place that would sell something like that," I say. "And it's the very store that we're desperately trying to reach."

"Hiking boots, then? Anything with a grip." Jack jumps back into the foam pit and wades back to us.

"That's all gonna be on floor three." Polly looks around the mall. "Trixie's doesn't carry anything like that. I don't think any of the other department stores here do either."

"Well then," Jack says. "Perhaps our passage has ended before it even starts."

"There's gotta be something here on the first floor." I try to remember which shops we've passed.

A lot of stores by the edge of the slide cater to kids—a thinly-veiled marketing strategy. There's *Nutcracker's Toy Shoppe*—oddly *not* a seasonal store. *Fluffystuffies*—personalized stuffed animals. *Doctor Sweetz*—a candy shop with a vaguely threatening dentist mascot. Nothing helpful here.

I walk a little farther down the walkway and spot a small store burrowed in the corner. An anthropomorphized statue of a dolphin wearing a backwards baseball cap stands guard outside. Above is the store's moniker. *Flipper's Slippers*.

"Hey," I call back to Jack and Polly. "What about slippers? Would those work?"

Jack looks back. "Wouldn't slippers just *slip* more?"

"I don't think so." I walk toward the store's entrance. "Most of the slippers I had growing up had non-slip grips on the bottom. I remember being annoyed that I couldn't use them to slide around the hardwood floor."

"Worth checking out," Polly says.

We enter. A display of pink bunnies greets us.

"Are there any, like, *normal* slippers here?" Jack asks.

"I don't think so." I pick a pair off of a shelf and stare into its bulging eyes. "It's a kids' store. I think all the slippers here are supposed to be animals."

"Will we even find something in our size, then?" Polly asks.

I point to the sign behind the cash register. "*Matching pairs for Mom and Dad,*" I read aloud.

"Oh, thank God." Jack rolls his eyes as he approaches the *Mom and Dad* shelf. "It *is* possible to get bunny slippers in a men's size twelve. God bless us *all.*"

"Not just bunnies." I survey the selection. "Looks like there's sharks, hippos, dinosaurs...the whole animal kingdom is represented. Maybe you'd like something from the *Big Boy Collection?*"

Jack doesn't respond.

"I like the zebras myself." Polly grabs a pair.

"No dolphins, though," I say. "Ironic, considering the store's name."

"Dolphins must be seasonal," Jack says.

I examine a nearby piglet. "That, or there's a terrifying implication that Flipper is the head of an organized crime family that turns all other animals into slippers."

Jack stifles a laugh.

Polly stares at me. "What the hell, Luke?"

Jack puts the Trixie's backpack down and browses. "I'm gonna go with my theory. It *is* summer, after all. Marine mammals are really more apropos for autumn, don't you think?"

"Gotta keep the people on their toes," Polly replies. "That's just good business."

In the end, Jack selects the sharks, and Polly takes the zebras. I grab a pair shaped like rubber ducks. I notice a bin of slipper socks to the side of the store.

"Jack," I say. "These may suit you better. They've got the same grips, but they're just socks."

Jack looks over. "I've kind of already committed to the sharks."

"Oh, wow," I say teasingly. "Careful. It almost sounds like you're actually enjoying yourself."

"Shut up."

Polly is at a mirror, admiring her zebras. "Grab some of the slipper socks anyway. We can put those over our hands for the climb."

"Good idea." I grab three pairs—all green-gray—and toss them into the backpack.

"I hope this works." Jack picks up the Forevergreen. "If it doesn't, we're officially out of ideas to get up to the SportsGoods."

"I'm sure you'll think of something." Polly walks over to where we're standing. "It seems like you two make a good team."

A good team. *That's* a way of putting it.

I grab the lantern and we walk back to the slide.

"How're we going to hold our lights?" Jack asks. "If we're gripping with both hands, we'll have nothing to illuminate our passage."

"Well, the candle won't work," Polly says.

"Right, good call." I blow the Forevergreen out, put the lid on, and place it in the backpack.

"I can go first and hold my pen light in my teeth," Polly continues. "Luke, what about the lantern? Can you clip it to your jeans or something?"

I look at the lantern. It's big. "Uh...maybe? I can fasten the handle to a beltloop. It'll be clunky, though."

"Well, with you in rear, and me in front, that should give us enough light to get up." Polly jumps into the foam pit and pulls herself onto the unicorn's tongue. "Unless one of you has another option, I think the lantern is our only choice."

"Don't you have a phone on you?" Jack asks Polly.

Polly shakes her head. "I'm afraid my battery died while I was hiding out in the Trixie's. I kept trying to figure out what was going on."

"Does *no one* charge their phone in this mall?" I ask.

"Lantern pants it is." Jack dives into the foam pit. "Side note, that's a good name for a band."

Polly and I do not dignify this with a response.

Jack shifts gears. "Tough crowd. I guess I'll go in the middle. Polly, you ready?"

"As I'll ever be. You have the socks?" She bites down on her pen light.

I take the slipper socks out of the backpack and toss a pair to her and to Jack. Polly puts her pair on her hands. The Mega-Slide is about four feet wide, with edges curving up another two feet. Polly spreads her arms and grips the sides. Her feet follow behind. She seems secure.

My heart starts to accelerate. This just got real. "Are you able to grip safely?"

Polly looks over her shoulder and I realize she can't talk

with the pen light in her mouth. But she nods and keeps climbing.

I turn to Jack. "I guess you're next." I attach the lantern to my rear belt loop, praying that it won't damage the family jewels during my ascension.

Jack nods. He puts his slipper socks on and trails Polly by a few yards. *Damn, he's fast.* He must have incredible upper body strength. His climb looks effortless. And, not gonna lie, I don't hate this view of his ass.

I am once again feeling incredibly out of shape. I lift myself onto the tongue of the unicorn. The lantern clangs about behind me, but I'm able to establish a steady grip. Not nearly as steady as Jack's seems to be, but I'm able to move up.

The climb is mostly uneventful. We take a few breaks to catch our breath but soon reach the final section of the slide. Or rather, the slide's entrance. It's the steepest bit—clearly designed to give the children riding it a boost of momentum at the beginning. And unlike the rest of the slide, which is open, the ultimate segment is a fully circular tube.

This doesn't slow Polly down in the slightest. She's able to keep her grip and she reaches the top. She climbs out and takes the pen light out of her mouth. "I made it!" She shines her small beacon down, guiding Jack's climb to its conclusion as well. They've both made it up.

I'm several yards behind. Now that Jack is looking back at me, I can't let him see me struggling. I accelerate my climb. I'm almost there.

But the lantern catches on the upper edge of the slide as I enter the tube section. I'm moving too fast to react in time. The clip on the handle breaks off from my belt loop. The lantern falls behind me and I lose my grip. My face hits the smooth plastic.

"*Luke!*" Jack shouts.

I manage to reestablish my grip, but now I'm completely enveloped in darkness. And something feels off.

Oh, God.

The slide. It's *swaying.* It wasn't as stable as we thought. And I just slammed my entire body onto it. It's going down.

"Luke, the slide is shaking!" Jack yells. "Hurry!"

I feel the unsteadiness below me. My vision blurs. My heart is on the verge of bursting out of my chest. There's no way in hell I'm making it out of this. "I don't think I can."

"*Luke,*" Jack says. "You *have* to."

I look up. Jack is on the edge. I see his face. He isn't far. I can make it. Jack grabs the pen light from Polly and gets on his knees at the slide's entrance. He shines the light down and reaches out with his right hand.

I climb a few feet. The shaking is getting worse now.

"Now or never, Luke," Jack says. "Come on, you're almost there!"

"Hurry!" Polly calls.

I'm so close. I can almost grab Jack's hand. But then I feel it. My stomach drops.

The slide is *falling.* And I'm going down with it.

"*Luke!* Grab my hand!" Tears stream down Jack's face.

He's just a few inches out of my grasp. But it's too late. I'm not gonna make it.

"I'm sorry, Jack," I say quietly.

"The hell you are," he growls. "Polly, hold my legs."

Polly plunges to the floor. Jack drops the pen light and jumps headfirst into the slide, reaching both arms out. He grabs my wrists right as the slide slips from under me.

We hang suspended in the air. For a brief moment, everything is still. All I feel are Jack's hands and the blood pumping into my wrists.

"I've got him," Jack calls up. "Pull us out!"

Polly groans as she strains to pull us up. She manages to pull Jack up far enough for him to get his knees behind the slide's entrance. He lifts me up over the edge. I collapse on top of him and take a huge breath in.

Behind me, the slide crumples. I turn my head around just in time to see the iridescent plastic monstrosity tumble onto the first floor with a muffled *boom*.

I turn my head back around. Jack's face is so, *so* close to mine. Our noses are touching.

"Hey," he says softly. "You made it."

It's too much for me. A resonant sob escapes my body. "*Jack*. You saved my life."

Jack smiles. "You got us out of the stairwell. We're even."

We are *so* not even. I found a tunnel. Jack grabbed me out of the air. In fact, that's twice Jack has saved me now. First the fountain, and now this.

I have no idea what to say. I just stare into Jack's eyes. They're a gorgeous shade of green. Like two emeralds twinkling back at me with incredible warmth, piercing my soul.

Also, Polly is here.

Right.

I get up, dust myself off, pick up the pen light, and return it to Polly. "And thanks to you, too. How the hell did you lift both of us up?"

Polly smiles. "As soon as I got up, I noticed some velvet rope they used for when there's a line. One end is attached to the wall. I grabbed the other end and wrapped it around my waist in the event I had to rescue one of you. When Jack jumped for you, I grabbed his legs and used the rope to keep me from falling in after him."

"You foresaw me falling?" I hang my head. "I don't know if I should be insulted or relieved."

"Both, I suspect." Polly laughs. "But that doesn't matter anymore. We're here, on the third floor."

"With no way of getting back down to the first, thanks to me." I look down at where the Mega-Slide once stood. The great rainbow monstrosity looks like an exploded circus tent.

"Oh, hush." Jack stands and brushes something off of my shoulder. "You very well may have saved all our lives. The slide wasn't as stable as we thought. If we had gone down it normally, it may have collapsed with all of us on it. All that matters is that we're all okay. And like Polly said, we make a good team."

He smiles at me. This smile is different from the ones I've seen before. His eyes are softer, his face warmer.

I smile back.

"I guess you're right." I grab my backpack and pull out the Forevergreen. "But we're down to two lights again."

"Hey, thanks to you, we're finally going to get to Sports-Goods." Jack beams at me. "They've got *walls* of flashlights. I think we're okay on that front."

Thanks to *me*? Now he's straight-up lying to comfort me. The slide was Polly's idea, and he's the one who rescued me. But I don't argue. The sincerity radiating from Jack's eyes is something I could never disagree with.

10

———

It will come as no shock whatsoever to anyone who's spent more than two minutes with me that I've never been inside the MetroMall SportsGoods. The store's enormity engrosses me. Like Trixie's, a few emergency lights are on, so I can blow the Forevergreen out. Immediately in front of us are rows of fishing rods, line, and nets. A cardboard cutout of a man in a khaki hat proudly holding a fifteen-inch bass stands idly by.

Polly's eyes widen as she beholds the store's immensity. "You could fit two football fields in here."

"I'll have to take your word on that," I say.

Jack walks in and admires the selection of fishing equipment. "I think this is the biggest store in the mall. The movie theater's bigger in terms of actual area, but this is the biggest single room."

"You *really* should give tours of this place when this is all over," I say.

Jack turns around and shrugs. "*If* this is all over."

"Also that."

Jack points to his right. "I believe camping stuff is in the east quadrant. Right now we're in the fishing section. Not a lot of use to us right now."

"Unless a tsunami hits us and floods the mall," Polly says.

Jack laughs. "One catastrophe at a time. Our first goal is to get out of these slippers."

Right. I look down at the yellow ducklings on my feet. They're cute, but not incredibly practical for the apocalyptic hellscape in which we have found ourselves.

The camping section turns out to be quite the jaunt. We pass athletic wear—where we stop briefly to trade our slippers out for sneakers—a large row of bicycles and tire pumps, and finally a children's play area simply called "Ball World." The juvenile part of my personality that invented the word *cocksicles* can't help but laugh.

"What?" Polly asks.

"Did you see the sign?"

Polly looks up, reads the moniker, and sighs. "Are you five?"

"Come *on*, you have to admit, whoever green-lit the name choice didn't fully think it through."

Polly rolls her eyes. "It's a bunch of giant sports balls that kids can climb on. What would you have called it?"

I pause and ponder. "*Sphere* world?"

Jack laughs. "Ah, yes," he says in a faux academic voice. "The American pastime. Base*sphere*."

"I was a basket*sphere* girl myself," Polly piles on.

"Ha ha, very funny." I ponder a moment. "It could have just been the 'SportsGoods play area,' then."

"I'm sure there's a suggestion box at the front where you can leave your critiques," Jack says. "We're almost at camping goods. Let's go."

Between Ball World and the camping section is an array of hunting knives and crossbows. I can't help but notice something that unnerves me slightly—there appear to be quite a few empty spaces on the shelf.

They probably just didn't have a chance to restock yet this morning. I'm sure that's it.

But I look around the store and most of the other shelves and displays seem to be well-stocked. Should I say something to Jack and Polly? They're already searching through the camping stuff. I decide not to, but I do grab a knife—at the very least, we can use it for food prep. At the very worst—no, it won't come to that. *You're in a mall, Luke. Calm down.*

I saunter over to where Jack and Polly are browsing. Jack's found some decent flashlights.

"Do you want to get some batteries for those?"

Jack is comparing two flashlight models. "There's a big rotating display of batteries by the checkout. I'll grab some when we leave."

I give a thumbs-up. "Sounds good. What else are we looking for?"

"A propane stove," Jack says. "Maybe some dry goods if they have any here."

"Like, food?"

"Yes, dry goods." Jack returns to the shelves and continues perusing. "There isn't a grocery store in the mall, but I'm pretty sure they sell freeze-dried meals here. The kind that backpackers use. We can use those for sustenance until we figure out how to get back down to the food court."

"Love it. Anything else?"

Jack pauses a moment. "Sleeping bags for sure. Maybe a space heater for when it gets cold?"

"Where are we even going to sleep?"

Jack wrinkles his forehead. "Guess we have to figure that out too."

"Cool beans."

Jack turns around. "Only if you find a can opener."

I laugh. "Glad you haven't lost your sense of humor."

I wander up and down the aisles of the camping goods section. There's so much stuff that we have no use for—bear spray, hiking sticks, feeding bowls for dogs. I spot and pocket a small first-aid kit that could prove useful. I see a few more things we could utilize—a pair of binoculars and an emergency blanket—and I toss them into the backpack.

And here we are. The dried-food aisle. A row of silver envelopes with pictures of food on them greets me. "Just add water!" they shout at me collectively.

A lot of the options—beef stroganoff, cheese omelet, and crème brûlée—make me want to gag. There's no way those taste good freeze-dried and rehydrated. I spy some others that appear *slightly* more palatable. I grab a few packets of spaghetti and meatballs, chicken fried rice, and chili mac. I suddenly realize that I have no idea what kind of food Jack likes.

Or Polly.

Right. I don't know what either of them like.

To ensure nutritional egality within our ranks, I grab a couple of other options. There are also two giant bins full of granola bars and bottles of water. I stuff a half dozen of each into the backpack. The zipper barely closes. We're gonna have to add a second backpack to our list.

What else did Jack want? A propane stove. Right. I didn't want to admit this to him, but I have no idea what I'm looking for. In my mind's eye, I'm picturing a four-burner stove, like what my mom has in her kitchen, but miniaturized. That can't be it.

Whatever it is, it should be near the food. I walk up and down a few aisles with no luck. I could be walking right past it without knowing—I've never gone camping in my life and am really out of my element here.

I decide to return to where Jack and Polly are and see what they've found.

"I found a ton of dry food." I walk up behind Jack and open my pack. "A cornucopia of delicacies both foreign and domestic."

"Wish I could say the same for sleeping bags." He looks down at his own bounty. "I could only find two of them."

"Maybe we could sleep in shifts. You never know if there's someone weird out there." I remember the hunting knife in my left pocket. I place my hand inside and lightly handle it.

"I'm sure we'll be fine." Jack crouches down and unrolls one of the sleeping bags. "There are only two of them, but one is a double."

"Like, for a couple?" My throat tightens.

Jack's eyes connect with mine. Just like they did at the top of the slide. "Well...a couple of people, yeah."

"And the other one is a single?"

"Yeah." Jack doesn't break eye contact.

"Well." I pause. I am choosing my words very carefully. "I suppose it would be the...*chivalrous* thing to offer the single to Polly."

Jack smiles shyly. "What a gentleman."

I bow goofily. "I do what I can."

"And then, I guess, we'll...share the double?"

I strain every muscle in my body in an effort to try and play it cool. "I mean, if that's okay with you."

"Fine by me." Jack smiles. "I guess you've already seen me in my underwear, so what's the difference?"

I laugh. "Well, there wasn't much underwear to see."

"*Luke!*"

Polly walks up to us with a smallish box in her hands. "Look what I found!"

Jack examines the box. "*Pro Bro, the pocket stove of the future*," he reads. "This is perfect, Polly, thanks!"

"I found a few quarts of fuel too." Polly puts the box down. "But I'm gonna need a second pair of hands for those. Luke, wanna help me?"

"Sure."

Jack walks back to the shelves. "I'll browse for other supplies in the meantime."

"Sounds good." Polly crosses toward the dehydrated food. "They're just a few rows down."

Polly and I walk over. As soon as we're out of Jack's earshot, she pulls me aside.

"You've gotta tell me. What is going *on* with you and Jacklov?"

I freeze and blink a few times. My jaw drops open, but words don't come out immediately.

"What do you mean?"

Polly laughs. "Every two minutes, I catch the two of you staring at each other. Staring and smiling. Smiling and staring. Exchanging some tacit communiqué."

"He *did* just pull me out of the slide. We were both in shock for a few minutes."

"And what did he pull you out of just now next to the sleeping bags?" Polly smirks. "Face it, you two have got it *bad* for each other."

I frown. "Oh come *on*, Polly. I don't even know if he's, you know—"

"What?"

I struggle. "If he's *into* guys. Or into *me*, at least."

Polly laughs. "Well, he's not into me. Neither of you are."

Again I struggle. "Well, that's not to say that you aren't a *lovely* woman—"

"Luke. I am an attractive woman. I am very aware of that fact. Your sexuality does not offend me."

How does she talk so matter-of-factly about this? *Damn, Polly.*

"At any rate, you don't have to put a label on him to know that he digs you. It's clear as day."

I don't respond. I think Polly can tell that I'm not entirely comfortable with this conversation.

"Here." She points to her right. "There's the propane."

I eye the metallic-red cylinders in front of me. "How many do you think we should bring back?"

"No idea. Let's grab a few each, that should hold us for now."

I grab four containers, Polly grabs three. A wall of backpacks hangs nearby. I snag one—this one is an army green—and stow our finds inside. We return to Jack, who has the two sleeping bags in tow.

"Is that everything?" I ask.

Jack is rolling the sleeping bags up. "I'd *like* to find a space heater, but I don't think they sell those until fall. We can use the stove for warmth if we have to."

"Awesome. You need help carrying those?" I motion toward the sleeping bags.

"I'm good." Jack eyes the new backpack. "Oh, great thinking! Another backpack will do us some good."

"I'm more than just your damsel in distress," I joke.

"There's no denying your merit in that field as well." Jack smirks. "But I concur wholeheartedly."

Polly places her propane canisters on the floor. "Where to next?"

Jack finishes rolling the sleeping bags and stands up. "Our next step is to figure out how to get back down to the first floor. I'm hungry, and our chicksicles await!"

"Any ideas?" I ask.

Jack laughs. "Not a one. Save parachuting down."

"Let's put a pin in that for now." I hold up the beige backpack. "How about we take a moment, cook up some of the definitely-not-disgusting freeze-dried food, and regroup from there?"

"Oh, yeah," Jack says. "I guess we still haven't eaten."

"I could certainly use a break." Polly takes a seat on the floor. "Maybe a whole thirty minutes without something horrifying happening?"

Jack chuckles. "Best I think we can do is fifteen."

"Where should we set up?" I ask

"How about Ball World?" Jack asks.

I laugh. "You're kidding."

"I mean, why not?" Jack ties the two sleeping bags together. "Name aside, it's an open space, out of the way. We can sit down in the parents' area."

"I believe it's called *the dugout*." I gesture to a sign overhead.

"Of course it is." Jack examines the Pro Bro. "Let's fire up the grill! What's on the menu?"

I unzip the backpack. "We have a quite an abundance at our fingertips this evening," I say in my best snooty waiter voice. "May I interest you in some freeze-dried pad thai? Or dehydrated chicken and dumplings?"

Jack grimaces. "Neither of those things should come in a bag."

I laugh. "There's more. Those are just what's at the top."

"My guess is it all tastes like salty mush." Polly rises. "So surprise me. I'm gonna explore the rest of the store, stretch my legs, see if there's anything else we can make use of."

"You sure?" I ask. "It shouldn't take more than ten minutes to whip this up."

"Yeah. You two spend some *quality* time together. I'll be back in a bit."

She walks off, leaving Jack and me alone.

Alone. In Ball World.

———

11

The *dugout* section of Ball World is really just one long silver bench surrounded by a chain-link fence. This dugout is cleaner than the ones I've seen in actual baseball games—the ground thankfully devoid of sunflower seed shells and saliva.

Jack removes the Pro Bro from its box and places it on the bench. We sit on either side of the stove. I grab a quart of propane out of the green backpack.

I handle the propane delicately. "I have no idea where this goes."

Jack laughs. "You never went camping as a kid?"

I shake my head. "Nope. My family couldn't really get behind the idea of camping. My dad always said he didn't understand why rich people would spend all that money on gear just so they could pretend to be homeless for a weekend."

Jack frowns. "My family was far from rich. In fact, camping was really the only way for us to have a quote-unquote vacation. My parents inherited all the gear we had from my grandparents. You don't have to break the bank to have a decent time."

"Alternatively, you can just steal the gear from a sporting goods store in a mall ravaged by nuclear devastation."

"Also an option."

I grab a packet of food out of the beige backpack. Spaghetti and meatballs—seems harmless enough. Jack screws the red fuel container into the bottom of the stove and twists a small lever on the side. A tiny blue flame erupts from the top of the Pro Bro.

I instinctively jump back at the sight of the flame. "Jack! That's incredible. How'd you do that?"

"It's literally the easiest thing in the world. But I'm flattered that you're so impressed."

"Do we need a frying pan?"

"Got one right here." Jack pulls it out of the smaller sleeping bag beside him. "Figured we could use these for carrying stuff, too."

"Your ingenuity never ceases to amaze me."

I pour the freeze-dried spaghetti and meatballs onto the frying pan. It looks like dried dog vomit.

Jack does not appear to be fazed. He's used to camp food.

"Do I just pour the water on top?" I grab one of the bottles of water out of the beige backpack.

"Yeah," Jack says. "Careful, not too much. You can always add more—"

"But you can't take it away." I smile. "My dad may have foregone teaching me about camping stuff, but I did learn a thing or two from him about the culinary arts."

"Good thing too, because there is nothing more culinarily artistic than this meal."

I laugh. "Too bad that camp doesn't have freeze-dried sprigs of rosemary. A meal is *nothing* without a garnish."

I pour a half-cup or so of the bottled water in the pan.

"A little more," Jack says.

"Okay." I splash a little more of the water in, and the meal is actually starting to gain some semblance of normal spaghetti and meatballs. The smell is even pretty good—for a brief moment I forget that I'm on a bench in the dugout in Ball World in a SportsGoods in a quarantined post-nuclear shopping mall. It feels nice to do something so ordinary.

A few minutes pass. "I think it's done," Jack says. "You're a real natural!"

"Thanks." I feign a chef's kiss. "I just really feel like a chef has to pour his soul into his cooking, you know? Every dish is a work of art."

Jack laughs. "You're a funny guy, Chesterfield."

"Backatcha, *Jack Jay*." I glance at the sleeping bags. "I don't suppose you have some silverware in there?"

"As a matter in fact, I do." Jack reaches into the smaller sleeping bag again. He pulls out what looks like a pocketknife. Upon closer inspection, I realize that it's a fork, spoon, and knife combo.

I'm genuinely impressed. "Will wonders *never* cease?"

"Campers like to buy things that are compact and light. Packing your grandmother's best silver usually isn't the way to go."

"What about plates?"

"We'll just eat off of the frying pan. You mind sharing?"

"What about Polly?"

Jack looks up. "She's clear on the other side of the store. We'll make her a fresh batch when she returns."

"Guess that's fair." I grab one of the utensil combos. "Dig in."

I take a bite. It's not bad. A little *al dente* for my taste, but it *was* in an unrefrigerated package just minutes ago. I try a meatball. It's salty, and the texture leaves a lot to be desired. But it's sustenance. I take a second bite. While I chew, a bizarre thought crosses my mind.

Is this, technically speaking, my first date with Jack?

We had that brief flirtation right before I fell in the fountain. But we were just joking around then. Now we're sharing dinner. We're even sharing a plate, for God's sake. Is it too cheesy that I hope we end up sharing a single noodle like in the movies?

Unfortunately, these noodles are too short. *Dammit.*

Jack finishes a bite. "So, tell me more about your dad."

I'm silent. Dead-dad talk is a third-date conversation. And this is just our first—*it's not a date, Luke!*

I place my silverware down on the edge of the pan. "Like I said, he died a few years ago. And he was sick for the last year and a half of his life."

"Before that. You said he taught you to cook?"

I smile. "Yeah, that was our thing. We used to watch cooking shows every Saturday afternoon. We would argue for hours about the appropriate amount of garlic in a dish. Stuff like that."

"How much garlic did you think was appropriate?"

I laugh. "It is my personal belief that the limit does not exist. I'd put an entire bulb in a recipe that called for half a clove if I had it my way."

Jack smiles. "Sounds like you were close."

I nod. "Yeah. Closer to him than I was with Mom."

"So you weren't close with your mom?"

"No, it's not like that." I shake my head. "I just had more in common with Dad. We had more we could talk about. My mom loves me. I never doubted that."

Jack's posture collapses. He's quiet for a moment. "I'm glad you had such a good relationship with your parents."

There's a brief moment of silence. I get the same feeling I did earlier when we were talking about college—that Jack wants to talk about something but also doesn't want to. This time I decide to go for it.

"How about your family?"

Jack sighs. I can't tell if it's in anguish or relief—or some combination of the two. After what seems like an eternity, he finally responds.

"My family is...*complicated.*"

Oh, God. The most dangerous C-word.

"If you don't want to talk about it, it's fine."

Jack looks up. I can see a mix of pain and light in his eyes. "No, it's cool. I figured you might ask. Maybe that's why I brought the subject up in the first place."

I don't say anything. Jack can see that I don't know how to respond, so he keeps talking.

"Like I said, we didn't have a lot of money. But we were close when I was younger. We were tight-knit, did everything together. And I didn't have a lot of friends in school, so my family was my main support system."

I nod. "Go on."

"Then, Lulu died." Jack's voice cracks slightly. He takes a moment and continues. "She died, and obviously that changed everything."

"I'm so sorry."

Jack brushes a small tear from his eye. "It was years ago. Car accident. She was with a friend and her mom, driving home from school. The vehicle was side-swiped right where Lulu was sitting. Hit-and-run. They never caught the bastard who did it."

"Oh, God."

"Yeah, it was horrible. The friend and the mom were fine. They were on the driver side of the car. My parents were obviously crushed. She was the baby of the family. They cried for months. I thought it would never end."

"Yeah, my Mom was the same when my dad passed."

Jack frowns. "I'm sure she was. But here's the kicker. One day the crying *did* finally stop. And it made everything so much worse."

"How so?"

"It was like a shadow had fallen over our house. Mom and Dad were just *empty*. Numb. They went to work, came home, watched TV for a few hours, and went to sleep. Day in and day out. Nothing changed. They had this *routine* and they never deviated from it."

"Depression?"

Jack nods. "Oh, it was textbook. That's part of the reason why I decided to study psychology in school. My parents simply turned the faucet of mourning off. I knew something wasn't quite right. I wanted to learn about how all those mental processes worked so I could help other people avoid what happened to my mom and dad."

"I'm so sorry, Jack." I lay a hand on his shoulder. "That can't have been easy."

Jack recoils a bit at my touch, but doesn't remove my hand. "It wasn't. But when I went to school, things got better. I was away from the darkness, away from the emptiness of our house. For the first time since Lulu was alive, I felt like a normal guy."

"Well, that's good."

"It was, for a while." Jack lowers his gaze. "I was finally able to explore parts of my personality that I had buried for years. My...uh...sexual preferences and the like."

Three hundred jackhammers are quarrying directly into my brain, but I manage to nod. Again, trying to play it cool.

"My family was pretty religious growing up," Jack continues. "They weren't like fanatics or anything, but we went to church every Sunday. Before Lulu died, we were super involved. So I was never really comfortable with being—how did my mother so sensitively put it?—*queer as a three-dollar bill.*"

There it is.

"And I knew—or at least I *thought* I knew—that there was something wrong with me. But when I went to school, I realized that it wasn't something wrong, it was just a slice of who I am. A slice of Jack Jay."

I, for one, wouldn't mind a slice of Jack Jay right now.

"So, middle of junior year, I called my parents and came out."

"And?"

Jack's eyes droop. "Suffice to say they weren't in love with the idea. With Lulu gone, I was their last shot at grandchildren, and the way they were raised, they thought it was a choice. Like I could be straight if I just *tried* a little harder."

"But that's not how it works."

"I'm well-aware." Jack laughs softly. "They still loved me, but the whole dynamic of our relationship was different. Like I think that they always *knew* about me, like deep down, but once it was all out on the table it couldn't be taken back. *Can't put the toothpaste back in the tube,* I think that's how Dad put it."

"But you still went back home?"

Jack's smile vanishes. "I came back to town. Never said I went home."

"Oh."

"Yeah." Jack pauses and looks down. "Unfortunately, my financial aid package was conditional on me maintaining a 3.5 GPA at school. The whole coming-out fiasco drained me emotionally and my grades slipped. I ended up drinking a lot, missing class. It was my own damn fault. So I had to take a year to save money to pay for my last year of tuition. My parents never explicitly stated it, but it was clear to me that they didn't want me back in the house when I came home from college."

"I'm so sorry, Jack."

"It's okay," he says. "I got a little studio apartment in a cheap neighborhood and I got the job at Electronix. The pay there actually isn't bad, for a greedy corporate conglomerate."

"I'm sure."

"Yeah, it was nice." Jack looks back up at me. "And it's not like I never saw my parents. They didn't, like, *shun* me. I just needed my own space. Because I knew that I could never bring a guy back to their house. They wouldn't be able to handle it. And if I ever got married, I don't think they could find it in themselves to come to the wedding."

Jack's face twists. His body gives a slight heave.

"Here." I hand Jack a napkin—the spaghetti and meatballs packet came with two.

"I'm sorry." Jack blows his nose. "Unloading all of this on you."

"No, *no*, Jack." I scooch a little closer to him. "Don't you feel bad for a second. You are more than welcome to share this kind of stuff with me. After all, we're apocalypse buddies."

Jack sniffs. He looks up at me. His beautiful emerald eyes meet mine.

"Thanks, Luke."

Neither of us says another word.

The only thing I can hear is the soft rumble of the stove. I can't help but notice how gorgeous his lips are. And they're so close to mine.

And getting closer…

A piercing shriek across the SportsGoods shatters our trance.

My heartbeat—which was already pounding at full speed for unrelated reasons—quickens.

"Is that Polly?" I ask.

Jack snaps up. "I think so." He shouts across the store. "*Polly!*"

No response.

"Oh, God." My legs tremble as I stand. "Do you think she's okay?"

"We'd better go check." Jack turns the flame of the Pro Bro down. I grab the green backpack. "No, leave it. We'll come back for it later."

Jack starts to walk towards Polly's scream. I reach into my pocket. The hunting knife I grabbed earlier is still in there.

I pray I won't have to use it.

12

We find Polly spreadeagled on the floor of the electronics section. An upturned shopping basket lies next to her.

I rush to her. "Polly!"

She doesn't respond.

"Is she breathing?" Jack asks.

I fall to my knees and place my left ear next to her mouth. I hear a very stilted shudder of air. "Yeah. But it sounds uneven. And shallow."

Jack gingerly lifts her right shoulder. "She's injured." A small pool of blood trickles out from under her. Jack's face turns a pale green.

"What is it?"

"She's been *stabbed*. There's no other explanation for this wound on her back shoulder."

"How can you tell?"

"The wound is too precise to be an accident." Jack gently lowers Polly's shoulder. "We need to wrap her up."

I pull the first aid kit out of my right pocket. I didn't think I'd have a chance to use it so soon. It's mostly small bandages, but there is a small roll of gauze. I pull it out. "Will this help?"

Jack nods. "Better than nothing. What she really needs are stitches."

"Maybe there's a sewing shop nearby."

"Luke." Jack looks up. "You realize that needlepointing thread and life-threatening injury thread are different, right?"

"Right," I say. "Just trying to think of something useful."

Jack rips a hole in Polly's blouse above her right shoulder and begins to dress her wound. "Luckily, it looks like Polly is a good clotter. And the wound is smaller than the pool of blood indicates."

"She'll be okay?"

"We'll know more if she wakes up." Jack rips the gauze with his teeth and finishes dressing the wound. "It's not deep. Whoever did this was just trying to incapacitate her, not kill her."

That brings up a separate but gruesomely crucial point. The uncomfortable question we've avoided thus far.

"Who do you think *did* this?" I ask.

"No idea." Jack eyes the basket next to Polly. "She must have been collecting some supplies. Looks like someone attacked her from behind and grabbed what she had."

"What on earth could she have had that was so valuable?"

"I have a better question," Jack says. "Do you think whoever did this to her is still in the store?"

"God." I shudder and look around SportsGoods. There are so many places for people to hide. Every shelf is over eight feet high. The store is full of huge objects—rafts, tents, even a rock wall in the center of the store. An entire army could be hiding in plain sight and we wouldn't be any the wiser.

Like, I *knew* Jack, Polly, and I weren't the only people in the mall. There was Lavender Pit Stains, the people in the Electronix—the mall wasn't particularly crowded on a Tuesday morning, but it would be foolish to think we were completely alone. I just figured most of the other survivors were still too freaked out to explore. It never occurred to me that any of them might have some sort of malintent. After all, we're all in the same boat, right?

Right?

But now that I think about it, there was always something lurking in the back of my mind. Some feeling of uneasiness. Why else would I have grabbed that hunting knife in the first place?

I pull it out.

"Woah!" Jack steps back a bit. "You didn't tell me you were packing, Chesterfield!"

My fingers tighten around the knife handle. "I grabbed it earlier. Thought it may come in handy. At the time I figured it would at least be useful for cooking."

"And now you can use it to kick some ass!"

I shrug. "I'm more interested in protecting our collective ass."

"A valiant mission indeed." Jack laughs uneasily.

Despite our unconscious, recently wounded friend on the floor, I can't help admiring Jack's continued commitment to our flirtatious back-and-forth. Something about that makes me feel a little safer. I return the knife to my pocket.

Jack refocuses his attention to Polly. "How's her breathing?"

I lean down and listen again. "Better now. Still shallow, but it's a little more even."

"She'll be okay." Jack holds up his right hand—still clad in the white tie of Dave the Fridge Guy—and points to my forehead with his left. "And now we're three-for-three on injuries."

"Polly does have the distinct honor of being clad in actual medical bandages." I fiddle with my sushi headbands.

Jack laughs for a second, but then stops. Our bit is over. "So, what's our plan with her?"

"How do you mean?"

"I mean," Jack says, "do we wait for her to wake up, or do we do our thing?"

"Our *thing*?" My heart flutters.

Jack pauses. "Not our *thing*, whatever that is." He looks down. "I just meant do we try to find a way back down to the first floor? She may be out for a while."

So we have a *thing*. Good to know. I can't help but crack a tiny smile before returning to the task at hand. "I really don't think we should leave her. She wouldn't leave us."

"Do we really know that?" Jack asks. "We barely know her."

"She helped save my life, in case you need reminding," I say forcefully. "No, we stay until she wakes up."

Jack frowns, but then nods. "I guess you're right. We can at least grab our stuff from Ball World and bring it over. We should have something ready for Polly to eat when she comes to. You stay with her."

"No." I rise. "I don't want you going alone and getting stabbed. Buddy system."

"But then we're leaving her behind." Jack gestures toward Polly. "And *she* can't defend herself. Most recently injured party gets the benefit of company. And as second-most recently injured party, you should be the one to stay with her. I won't be five minutes."

I don't argue. He has a point. "Fine. But please be careful."

"I'll be okay. Just keep Polly safe."

"There's a wall of knives close to Ball World." I point in the direction of the children's area. "Grab one for yourself before you pick up our stuff."

"Good idea." Jack's putting on a confident air, but underneath his handsome armor he's shaking slightly. Who wouldn't be? "I'll be back before you know it."

He walks off, disappearing behind the shelves.

I don't like this. Not one bit. Jack shouldn't be alone.

But he's right, we need to help Polly.

I still don't like it.

Also, this seems less urgent, but did we almost kiss in Ball World? *Damn.* We were so *close.* And now what if something happens to him? I'll never know what those lips feel like.

It's a selfish thought, but I can't help but wish that Polly had been stabbed a few minutes later.

Or better yet, not stabbed at all.

Where is Jack? He said he'd be right back. I reach for my phone.

Oh, *right.*

Time is weird. Without a watch—or cell phone—keeping track, I have no idea if it's been five minutes or not. I look around. Is there a clock on the wall in SportsGoods? I don't see anything. Even if there was, I didn't log the time of Jack's departure.

It feels like it's been a while.

It's definitely been at *least* five minutes. Probably longer.

But how much longer? A few minutes? An hour? A

decade? My heart races, and my breathing accelerates. *Where the hell is Jack?*

God, I feel like I'm choking. I look down at my fingers. They're trembling, but I also can't feel them. And I can't seem to catch my breath. Air is stacking in my lungs. I can't fight the thought that Jack is lying dead somewhere in the store. That I'll never see him again.

That *I'm next.*

My vision blurs. Am I crying? Or have I too been stabbed and this is what it feels like to have the life drawn out of you? I hear a distant sound. A metallic rattling. I strain every muscle in my body to regain control. The rattling slowly swells in my ears. It's getting closer. *Closer.*

This is it. The cold hand of Death is clutching me by the throat. I hear it whisper, almost seductively, into my ear. *Just accept it, Luke. You got more time on this plane of existence than anyone outside of the mall. You're the lucky one. All your problems will soon be over.*

The rattling sound is right next to me. I can't see anything. But I beseech that it be swift and painless.

Goodbye, Jack.

"Luke!" someone shouts. The voice is ethereal. As if I'm hearing it from within a dream.

Dad, is that you?

"*Luke!*"

My vision pulls back into focus. I see the face of a blond-haired, bespectacled angel.

Wait. Do angels wear glasses? Surely there's access to decent eyecare in the heavenly realm. If it's not an angel, then it has to be—

"Jack!" I cry out. It's him. It's *him.*

"Luke!" Jack breathes a sigh of relief. "Are you okay?"

I pull out of the daze slightly. My body has fallen back to Earth. My heartrate and breathing stabilize. I raise my head off of the floor. When did I lie down?

"I'm okay, Jack." I smile weakly. "Now that you're here."

I lay my head back on the floor. Everything goes black.

13

I stir.

I'm still alive. And we're still in the SportsGoods. The Pro Bro is sputtering.

I hear a female voice. "Oh, that's awful, isn't it?"

A male voice responds. "Yeah, the spaghetti was a lot better. Not a fan of the chicken and dumplings."

I sit up. Jack's face pulls into focus.

"Hey, sleepyhead," he says. "Nice of you to join us."

I raise my head. Jack is handling a frying pan over the stove. Next to him is a shopping cart full of all our stuff. Across from the Pro Bro is Polly. She's awake, and she seems okay. She's scowling at the taste of whatever ungodly rehydrated pigswill she has placed in her mouth.

"Polly, you're okay!"

"In a relative sense." She tenderly handles the bandages on her shoulder. "How about you?"

"I'm fine." I rub my temples. "At least I *think* I am. What happened?"

"I came back from picking up the stuff," Jack says. "I had

to grab a shopping cart from the front of the store. Too much stuff for one trip."

"*That's* what took you so long."

Jack raises his right eyebrow. "I mean, it added a few minutes, I suppose."

"It felt like you were gone forever." My voice cracks. "I thought they got you."

"They?"

"Well, whoever got Polly."

Jack smiles. "*They* didn't get me. But something got *you*. I came back and you were curled up next to Polly in a fetal position. Hyperventilating and shaking."

"Sounds like a panic attack," Polly says.

I sit up. "A *panic attack*? No, that's not me."

"Maybe not normally," Polly says. "But this is an extraordinary situation we find ourselves in. It's perfectly natural. You're fine."

I still don't like the sound of that. "Did I faint?"

Jack smiles. "It was actually kind of cute. I rolled the cart up and I saw you on the floor. Polly wasn't awake yet. I turned you over to check out what was going on with you, and the moment you saw me, you stopped shaking. Almost instantaneously." He laughs. "Guess I don't have to finish my psych degree anyway. It looks like I'm a brilliant therapist already."

"But then I fainted?"

"It wasn't really a faint." Jack grins. "It was something more akin to a puppy falling asleep."

"You must have tuckered yourself out," Polly says. "That can happen."

"You were asleep for about fifteen minutes when Polly came to." Jack adjusts the flame on the Pro Bro. "And now, it's been—what? An hour or so?"

"About," Polly says.

I straighten my spine. "I was out for an *hour*?"

Jack smiles. "Well, an hour-fifteen if you want to be precise."

Polly smiles at me. "Jack told me that you stayed with me. It seemed only appropriate to return the favor."

I stand. My legs are shaky. I gesture to Polly. "So what happened to *you*, then?"

Polly frowns. "I wish I knew. I was collecting stuff. I had a basket with me." Her gaze shifts to the upturned shopping basket we found lying next to her. "I had just found this incredible AM/FM long-range radio. Figured we could try to tune in and see if there were any reports of what was going on. Then I heard something fall behind me. I turned around —thinking it might be one of you—and then I felt a sharp pain in the back of my shoulder and I fell. Last thing I remember seeing before I lost consciousness was a pair of black patent leather shoes right by my head."

"Did they steal everything?"

Polly shakes her head. "Just the radio. It was the last one in the store."

"Yeah," Jack says. "I checked. They were cleared completely out."

I frown. "Of *course* they were."

"Yeah." Polly takes another bite of the chicken and dumplings. "Then I wake up and Jack's cooking this absolutely *elegant* meal. Then you woke up. And now you're all caught up."

"And no one else is here now?" I nervously glance around the SportsGoods.

"As far as I know, the store is empty," Jack says. "And they got their radio. I'm not sure what else they would want."

I eye the basket. "What else did you find?"

"I found some interesting things in the climbing section." Polly turns the basket right-side up. "I was trying to think of ways for us to get up and down the floors of the mall, since the slide is no longer an option." She pulls out a harness and some other equipment I can't identify. "Have you ever gone rappelling?"

I shake my head.

Polly laughs. "I figured not. Jack told me about your aversion to the outdoors. It's a descent, usually down a vertical mountain face using a double rope, which is belayed at a higher point for security."

"Basically, it's all the fun parts of falling off a mountain minus the splat at the end," Jack says.

I breathe in. *What?* "And people do this for fun?"

"They do," Polly says. "I used to do it all the time when I lived in the Rockies. It's actually a pretty good time and quite safe."

"How fortunate that we have an expert," I say. "But you can't seriously be considering repealing—"

"*Rappelling*," Polly says.

"Right—*that*—down the walls of the mall?"

"No, of course not," Polly says. "There's very little wall to rappel down. And even if we did manage to get down without accidentally murdering each other, there'd be no decent way to get back up."

"Then what are you suggesting?"

Polly smiles. "You do know that this SportsGoods has a giant rock wall in its center?"

I nod. "Jack and I passed it when we ran over here to save you."

"Thanks again for that, by the way." Polly takes another

bite of food. "What you don't know—what most people who aren't avid climbers don't know—is that this particular rock wall *doesn't* belong to SportsGoods."

"What, like a separate company rents out the space?"

"You haven't been near the rock wall, have you?" Polly asks.

"Nope. Just ran past it."

"Then you wouldn't have noticed that SportsGoods doesn't have a rock wall," Polly says. "SportsGoods is built *around* a rock wall."

Jack stands and points to the center of the store. "Yeah! The top of the rock wall ends up in SportsGoods. But it actually stretches to the first floor of the mall."

I frown. That's almost *too* convenient. "But then why didn't we just climb up that to get up here? Why did we go up the Mega-Slide instead?"

"The thought crossed my mind. But we didn't have harnesses," Polly said. "And the rock-climbing gym on the first floor definitely has all their equipment locked up. We would have been free climbing the whole way up. One misstep and you'd be a goner."

I scoff. "Need I remind you I was nearly killed on the slide?"

"Listen, you *almost* died on the slide. You *definitely* would have died on the wall."

I cross my arms. "Try not to inflate my ego too much."

Polly rises and crosses to where I'm standing. "I'm not trying to insult you, Luke. Unless you're harboring some secret past as a brilliant climber, there's no way you would have made it up the whole way. I don't even think I could have. But with this equipment, we can safely get down and get back up pretty easily. And safely."

"And this way, we can bring all of our stuff with us," Jack says. "We can toss the sleeping bags down with some of our unbreakable supplies, but I can carry the stove by its handle in one hand. We'll each take one of the backpacks. And look what I found!" Jack pulls three turquoise straps out of his pocket, each one wrapped around a small light. "Headlamps! Hands-free light! Goodbye Forevergreen!"

I laugh. "I mean, will your headlamp invoke the aromas of a woodland cottage?"

Jack smiles. "I believe they have an update coming out in the next fiscal year to fix that particular bug."

I smile back at him. "When are we gonna try it out?"

"As soon as Polly finishes her chicken and dumplings."

Polly crosses back to the Pro Bro and turns the flame off. "Which is right now. I couldn't possibly eat another bite. I'll eat at the Cluck Hut."

I look at her discarded meal. "I thought you were a vegetarian!"

"First of all, there is absolutely no way *that* contained any actual meat." Polly points to the frying pan. "And Jack just informed me that Cluck Hut has a very nice impossible-chicken menu."

"They *are* a very progressive company," I say.

"Truly," Polly says. "Let's pack up, then?"

"Way ahead of you." Jack's been silently packing the Pro Bro away while Polly and I talk and throws the frying pan and utensils into the double sleeping bag—right, *that's* still a thing—and kicks it in Polly's direction.

"Can you roll that up? I'm finishing up our backpacks." He tosses the beige backpack at

me.

I catch it.

"If Luke takes the beige backpack and Polly takes the green, that should evenly distribute the weight of all our stuff," Jack says.

Polly nods as she finishes wrapping the double sleeping bag. It's quite lumpy—how much stuff did Jack cram in there?—but it's secure. She grabs the green backpack. Jack grabs the handle of the Pro Bro in one hand and the sleeping bags by their drawstrings in the other. He leads us to the center of the store, where the rock wall peeks through the SportsGoods floor surrounded by four guardrails.

"There's an entrance right over there." Polly gestures to the far side of the rock wall. "Well, I guess technically it's the exit. I think SportsGoods had a deal where anyone who climbed to the very top and exited into the store got a ten-percent discount on anything they bought that day."

I see what she's talking about. There's a small platform for people to get off the wall once they reach the top. Or get *on*, in our case.

I think back to the Mega-Slide. "I hope it hasn't escaped you that this is the second time today we're using something in the wrong direction."

"Not at all," Polly says. "But when the world turns upside down, you have to stand on your head to make sense of things."

"Fortune-cookie levels of wisdom." Jack elbows me in the ribs. "You could learn a thing or two from Polly's poetic nature."

I roll my eyes. "I'm laughing on the inside."

Polly attaches her harness clip to the belay on the Sports-Goods exit platform. She runs a rope through it and pulls on it to test its security. It doesn't budge.

"I'll go last," she says. "I'm the most experienced, and I can help guide you two down."

"And hold onto our ropes?" I ask.

Polly nods. "Yep. So if you lose your grip, you'll have someone holding one end of the rope to catch you."

I look down the rock wall. It's a long drop. "But then who's going to hold your rope?"

"No one," says Polly. "But I'll be fine. I've done longer climbs and not fallen."

"But you always had a harness."

Polly purses her lips. "Yes, so this time I have additional motivation not to fall. Even if I do lose my grip, the belay will in all likelihood catch me."

"*In all likelihood* doesn't sound very certain," I say. "What if the rope snaps under the weight?"

Polly's face darkens. "Then you and Jack will have the intrinsic pleasure of dealing with that. But that *won't* happen. I'm sure of it. We have to keep my harness in the belay anyway. That's our only way back up to the third floor if we need more supplies."

"Are you sure there's no other way to get down?" I look around the store. "We haven't explored any of the other shops on the third floor."

Polly shakes her head. "The only other stores on this floor are hobby stores. Jack and I discussed it while you were out cold. We *could* try to get back in the stairwell and go through that basement shelter, but that again leaves us no way of getting back up if we need additional supplies. The door to the lounge shut behind us anyway, so we'd have no guarantee of that working again. With the slide gone, I'm afraid we're out of options unless the elevators magically spring back to life."

"Okay," I say. "And you're sure you'll be fine?"

Polly pulls on the rope. "I'm sure. The rope is stronger than it looks. Just like you are."

I can't tell if Polly is being condescending or compassionate. "I hope you're right. In case you haven't noticed, I'm not exactly in prime physical shape."

"First of all, shut up, you look great. Second of all, you'll be fine." She cracks a sly smile. "I promise it's as easy as falling off a mountain."

"That does absolutely nothing to calm my nerves."

Polly laughs. "Sorry, couldn't resist."

I slip on the harness.

Jack, who has been standing by watching Polly and me argue, steps up next to me. "Sure you wanna go first?"

I gaze at Jack. Jack, who has saved me twice—thrice if you count the panic attack—and who has proven himself to me time and time again since this whole mess started. Jack, who has been the source of all the information we need about this mall, and who has constantly taken the lead. I smile at him. For some reason, this activity that would normally terrify the living daylights out of me doesn't daunt me in the least. Not with him at my side.

I step a foot closer to him. "This reminds me of a joke I learned in elementary school. What was the name of the second guy to ever go skydiving?"

Jack rolls his eyes. "I know I'm gonna regret this, but what?"

I grin. "*Hugo First.*"

Jack rolls his eyes so hard he must have seen his brain. "God, Chesterfield, you're the Hugo *Worst.*" He's barely restraining a grin, though. I think—just *maybe*—he might return the feelings that have begun to boil over in my heart the last few hours. We stand there for a few seconds of dead air. I think he wants to say something. But he doesn't. He just steps forward and places his arms around me.

This is the first time Jack has hugged me. He's so warm, so safe, so *toned*. I hug him back, squeezing his waist gently but firmly.

"Be careful." His voice is soft as he lets me go.

I smile. "I will be. See you when you get down."

Jack nods. I clip myself into the harness. I look over to Polly, who gives me a thumbs-up. Everything is secure. With Jack's last whispered words to me echoing inside my ears like cannon fire, I slowly step off of the platform.

14

My climb down the rock wall goes off without a hitch. Which is nice, considering the incredibly hitch-filled nature of the day. It ends up being a lot easier than I thought it would be. Foot, foot, hand, hand. Rinse and repeat. I slip a few times, but Polly is holding onto the rope, and I recover easily. The headlamp is extremely helpful, especially once I'm outside of the faint glow of the SportsGoods lights. I stop briefly when I hit the second floor—this part of the rock wall just juts through the mall walkway—to catch my breath.

"Everything all right down there?" Polly calls down.

I readjust my grip on the climbing hold. "Yeah, just taking a quick breather."

"You need to take a break from falling down?" Jack teases.

"Shut up," I say. "I've done more falling today than a person should experience in a lifetime. I think I deserve a break."

I hear Jack chortle. I can't see it, but I know Polly is rolling her eyes at our banter.

My plunge continues. I cross down into the first floor, and I'm inside the rock climbing gym. It's a medium-sized room with high ceilings. Bright primary colors bounce off the light of my headlamp. Other smaller rock walls adorn room's edges. The main wall, the one I'm climbing down, stands at the very back of the space.

My feet touch the floor and I unclip my harness. "I'm down!"

Polly yells something down, but it's hard to hear her from two stories below. Something about moving out of the way, I think. I move a few yards to my left. The rope I was hanging on falls in a pile right next to me. The double sleeping bag follows. The clang of the frying pan inside it reverberates through the gym.

I look up. A figure jumps into the void above me. *Jack.* His succession has begun. I move the rope and sleeping bag out of the way. I watch as Jack's body slowly increases in size. I can't help but envy how easily he descends the face of the rock wall. And he's only using one hand since he's carrying the Pro Bro in his right hand, which I should mention is still injured. He slips only once, and Polly's steady hold of the rope spares him.

"*Woof.*" He approaches the floor. "Doing this one-handed is not the simplest task."

I walk over as he steps off. "You only slipped once. Pretty damn remarkable if you ask me."

Jack puts the stove down and stretches his fingers up towards the ceiling. I catch a fleeting glimpse of his midriff as the bottom of his shirt rises slightly.

"Still, though, it takes its toll."

I take a moment to recover from the sight of Jack's abs

before I speak. "You're gonna wanna move out of the way. Polly's gonna drop the rope."

"And her sleeping bag." Jack walks with me to the side. "How'd our bag come out?"

"It's fine. I didn't hear anything break. Polly's bag-rolling abilities are as flawless as your one-handed rappelling abilities."

Jack smiles. "Guess I'd better add that to the special skills section on my CV."

I hear a small *poof* behind us. Polly's sleeping bag has made its way down. There's nothing inside this one, so I just kick it out of the way.

Oh, God. This is it: the moment of truth. Polly is climbing down without a safety net. I swallow nervously. Even Jack slipped once. Polly doesn't have that option.

Jack looks over at and notices my tension in my body. "She'll be fine."

"I'll believe it when she's safely down with us. She doesn't have someone to grab her out of the air like I did."

"Are you talking about the slide, or the fountain, or the rock wall?" Jack nudges me gently in the ribs.

I don't smile. "Remind me to laugh about that after she gets down."

Jack chuckles softly, but his eyes are wide. He's anxious too. Polly may be a better climber, but she also has a signifi-cant handicap in her injury. The two of us fixate on her silhouette as it slowly descends.

But Polly's stature doesn't waver. She is slow but steady. *And* she's doing this wearing a skirt. She stops briefly at the second floor. She's close enough now that I can see her wince slightly. But she continues down and reaches the gym floor.

I exhale a huge sigh of relief. "Welcome back."

Polly says nothing.

Jack walks over to her. "You okay?"

She stands up and grips her shoulder. She pulls her hand away and it's covered in blood. Oh, God. A lot of blood.

"Holy shit." I run over. "She must have reopened the wound on her climb down."

"*She* has a name." Polly cringes.

"*You* conserve your strength," Jack orders. "Lie down right here, Polly. We'll wrap you back up nice and quick. Luke, do you still have that first aid kit?"

"I do," I pull it out of my pocket. "But we used up all the gauze on the initial wound."

"Dammit." Jack helps Polly lay herself onto the floor. "Look around the store. They've gotta have something. Surely the rock gym has dealt with injuries before."

I pull the emergency blanket out of my bag, unfold it, and place it over Polly. I look around the store, and sure enough, there is a box hanging on the wall behind the front desk. The words "First Aid" shine across it like a beacon. I jog over and try to open it.

Naturally, it's bolted shut.

"You have *got* to be kidding me." I look over to Jack. "It's locked."

"Find something else, then." Jack returns his attention to Polly. The bleeding is getting worse. "You're gonna be fine, Polly."

I scour the gym. The majority of the space is empty. Minimalism will be the downfall of humanity.

Well, it would be, were it not for the nuclear blast that started all of this.

"Luke, *hurry!*"

I rush over to the desk by the first aid box. I open a drawer. Pencils, sticky notes, a personal calendar. Nothing helpful. I open the drawer below it. Files on the gym's clientele and employees. Exasperated, I close the drawer. A small *thud* echoes.

Huh? There's something more solid than file folders inside the drawer. Something I may have missed. I reopen it and pore through its contents. Then I see it. Our dazzling silver savior.

"Will duct tape work?" I pull the roll out of the drawer.

"Oh my God, brilliant," Jack says. "Bring it over here."

I run back over to Polly. Her face is a lot paler than it was when we first found her lying in the SportsGoods, and her eyes are half-shut. A pool of blood expands slowly beneath her shoulder. I hand the duct tape to Jack.

"Okay, Polly, stay with me." Jack rips open the original hole he tore in Polly's blouse. Ardent crimson obscures the entire right side of Polly's body. Jack throws the original gauze —now soaked in blood—away and rips a few feet of duct tape off of the roll. He attempts to wrap it around her shoulder, but it doesn't stick. Too much blood.

Jack looks around the gym. With no other options in sight, he removes his Electronix polo and sops up the blood.

I can't help but silently curse the fact that someone's life has been in immediate danger every time I've seen Jack shirtless.

Jack tosses his blood-soaked polo to the side and reapplies a fresh strip of duct tape. This time it takes. He wraps nearly half the roll around Polly's shoulder. Blood leaks through the first layer, but by the second or third coat, it has stopped.

Polly is conscious, but motionless.

"It's okay." Jack wipes his forehead. "You're gonna be okay, Polly. Just rest." He looks over to me. "Do you have anything she can eat? She needs energy. She's lost quite a lot of blood. The twists and turns of the climb down ripped her wound to pieces."

I grab the beige backpack and pull out a few of the granola bars I found in the SportsGoods. "Here." I toss a few to Jack.

Jack unwraps the granola bar. "I know you probably don't feel like it, but you need to eat this."

"Th-Thanks." Polly takes the granola bar with her left hand and takes a bite. She chews slowly.

"You're gonna be okay," I reassure her. "Jack's the best caretaker in the world."

Polly says nothing. She finishes the granola bar.

"Another one." Jack grabs the second granola bar from the floor next to him. "Then you can rest."

Polly follows Jack's instruction. She finishes the second bar and lays her head back on the floor. She closes her eyes but doesn't fall asleep.

"Just relax," Jack says. "You'll feel better in an hour or so."

I sit down next to Jack. "Now what?"

"We wait until she's okay to move around," Jack says quietly. "You ever donate blood? She'll be woozy for a bit, but she'll be able to move soon enough. Until then, we stick together."

"Right. No more splitting up. All for one and one for all?"

Jack smiles. "Finally, that English lit degree is coming into use."

I chuckle softly and sit down next to Jack at Polly's side.

I'm right next to Jack, so close I can hear his heart beating. He places his naked arm around my shoulder.

I almost gasp.

He's so *warm*.

15

———

Jack is so close to me that when he finally speaks, I can feel his voice resonating in my chest.

"It's been an hour."

An hour? *Damn.* It feels like we've been cuddled up to each other for only a few minutes.

"Are you sure?"

Jack points at a clock on the opposite wall. "Yeah, we got down from the climbing wall right before two. It's almost three now."

Huh. Three o'clock. That means that Jack Jay has only been in my life for six hours. Time is weird.

I lean down to where Polly lies. "Hey."

She rouses. Her eyes flutter open and squint at the bright light of my headlamp.

"Sorry." I maneuver it to the side of my head.

Jack walks over. "How do you feel?"

Polly slowly sits herself up on her elbows. "Weak. But okay."

"Strong enough to walk over to the food court?" I ask.

"I think so."

Jack and I each grab one of her arms and help her to her feet. She walks a slow lap around the gym. She's limping.

"You hurt your foot?"

Polly turns to me. "No, it's just asleep. A little numb."

"Keep moving," Jack says. "That'll help your circulation. You're working with a lot less blood, but your body will adapt."

Polly looks at her blouse. The shoulder is torn clean off, and her bra—a delightful purple—peers through. She eyes Jack's bare chest and laughs. "Guess we've gotta schedule another appointment at Trixie's. New shirts."

Jack smiles. "Yep."

Polly turns to me. "I bet you're enjoying the view, right?" She winks.

Polly!

I chuckle nervously. "I mean, the gym is nicely decorated."

"Decorated with cute shirtless guys."

Dammit, Polly! What *are you doing?*

No one says anything until Jack finally breaks the tension. "We should all be so lucky. The only one of us fully covered is Luke."

"As much as I'd love to join the shirtless brigade, I couldn't possibly let down the fans of Gamma Ray." I gesture to the superhero emblazoned on my t-shirt.

"Yeah, that'd be a damn shame," Jack says. "Polly, are you feeling good enough to walk back to Trixie's and get some new shirts?"

"Trixie's is so far from here." Polly gingerly massages her legs. "And as much as I'd love to traipse across the entire mall with my boobs on full display, there's a novelty T-shirt store just a few stores down from here."

"Oh, *that* should be fun. Luke, you game?"

Not gonna lie, I'm not exactly rooting for Jack to put a shirt on. But I acquiesce. "Yeah, let's get moving. Polly, you need any help?"

"I think I can walk fine." Polly's paces the gym. Her stride is a little more even now. "If I feel like I'm gonna faint, I'll give you two a shout. You lead the way, I'm right behind you." She adjusts her headlamp and turns it back on.

We exit the rock-climbing gym and begin the short walk to the T-shirt store. Jack carries Polly's sleeping bag in one hand and the Pro Bro in the other. I hold the double bag.

Jack leans down and whispers into my ear. "So that was nice."

"What was nice?"

Jack nudges me slightly. "That hour snuggled up to you."

My heart accelerates. "Thanks."

Thanks?

I can tell from the look on Jack's face that he wasn't looking for gratitude. My brain recalibrates. "I mean—uh—it *was* nice."

Jack smiles. "Wouldn't mind spending a few more hours like that."

My brain is literally on fire. "I'll be sure to pencil you into my day planner sometime."

Dear God, was I absent the day we were taught how to flirt like a normal human being in school?

Jack laughs. Whether it's because what I just said was ridiculous or if he actually likes my joke is anyone's guess. Probably some pitiful combination of the two. He looks me dead in the eyes.

"I like you, Chesterfield."

I freeze. There's no way that those four glorious words just escaped Jack Jay's beautiful mouth. I must still be unconscious from that panic attack. This is a dream. A phantasm brought on by the trauma of the day. There is no other logical explanation.

My mouth stands agape for a moment before I can form some semblance of a sentence. "Um...me too. I mean, I also... you...*like* you. I also like you."

Spoken with the articulation and eloquence of a toddler.

Jack smiles. "I guess it's the second year of the English lit master's degree when they teach you how to speak in full sentences."

"Shut up." I can't help but smile. And it's a big smile. We're talking Cheshire Cat level. *Jack Jay just said he likes me.*

"Hey smiley, we're here," Jack says.

We stop outside the store. The marquee across the entrance depicts a stereotypical mustachioed British man sipping from a teacup. Next to the man are the words *T-4-Two.*

I observe the sign. "Well, that doesn't make much sense. Obviously, it's a pun on the word 'tea,' but the man is sipping actual tea. But it's *T* as in T-shirt."

"Let's save the literary critiques for next month's *Mall Fancy Digest*," Jack says. "In case you haven't noticed, I am still lacking a shirt."

"Oh, I am *quite* aware." I playfully poke Jack's nude shoulder.

"*Luke.*" Jack takes a step back. "Aggressive flirtation is *my* thing. You're supposed to just stand there and babble."

"Sue me for intellectual property theft, then."

"Wait for me." Polly is about ten feet behind us. "And

please know that I'm one hundred percent supportive of whatever this is." She gestures at the two of us. "But please let's get some shirts on first. I'm freezing."

"Right," Jack says. "Let's check it out."

We enter the storefront. It is very evident that, unlike Flipper's Slippers, T-4-Two is *not* a store for kids. A wall of profane shirts greets us—*assaults* is a better word, actually. I'm no prude, but even I'm a little shocked. These vestments are certainly not something I'd wear in front of my grandmother. Or *anyone's* grandmother.

Jack finds a black shirt—on it a skull with three gold teeth wearing a backwards fitted cap and smoking a joint. "I think this is it." He holds it up to my headlamp. "Lucas, have you ever seen a more divine piece of art in your life?"

"Beatific," I say. "The skull is clearly a metaphor for humanity's futile march toward death, and the joint and gold teeth indicate that hedonism is the only true answer to life's great question."

"And that hat?" Jack slips the shirt on—it's a perfect fit.

"I think that's just to look cool."

Jack laughs. "If English lit doesn't work out, I think you have a place in the field of Arts Journalism." He turns to the back of the store, where Polly is browsing the ladies' section. "Find anything?"

Polly holds up a white shirt with the words *Wine First, Ask Questions Later* printed in pink cursive. "I think we have a winner. The rest of them are just bad jokes about penises."

"Our brand of humor is far more cultured and intellectual," Jack says. "Just ask Mr. *Cocksicles* over here."

I raise my hands in defense. "I withdrew that suggestion and you know it."

Polly laughs. "Look away, you two. I'm gonna put this on."

Jack and I turn around while Polly changes her shirt.

Jack leans down and whispers into my ear again. It tickles. "I assume that you don't really need to turn around."

I smirk. "No, not really. Just being polite."

"And *what* a gentleman." Jack leans in and kisses me on the cheek.

It is at this moment that every synapse in my mind goes haywire. I feel all manner of dopamine soaring through my headspace. Every ounce of blood in my body diverts to my cheeks. Well, not *every* ounce. A fair amount diverts in the other direction.

"*Jack*. Polly's right there!"

"And she's changing her shirt. Her eyes are focused on other tasks. I just wanted to take advantage of the first private moment we've had since Ball World."

I hate the fact that our first pseudo-romantic encounter was in a place called "Ball World," and that knowledge will undoubtedly haunt me for the rest of my life, yet I smile.

"Besides, it's not like I grabbed your ass or something."

I would very much like Jack to grab my ass sometime.

Polly's voice shatters the silence. "You can turn around now."

"Think you can make it to the food court?" Jack asks.

Polly nods. "Yeah, as long as I don't move too quickly, I should be in good shape."

"Perfect," I say. "Onward, then!"

We depart *T-4-Two* and walk toward the food court. This time, Polly leads and Jack and I follow with our SportsGoods supplies in tow.

"So, what's our first move once we get there?" I ask Jack.

"Now that we have all the supplies we need, we can set up

camp. The food stalls are kind of perfect for setting up a safe, secluded space."

Not gonna lie, I'm looking forward to playing house with Jack. Even if it is this bastardized, post-apocalyptic version. And having our own space means we'll get to spend more time together in private. Never a bad thing. I really want to hold Jack's hand as we walk to the food court, but he's busy carrying the Pro Bro and sleeping bag. Never mind. There'll be time for hand-holding—and perhaps more—later.

We return to the food court. I feel like a soldier who's just come home from war. I breathe an audible sigh of relief. "We're here."

"Yep." Jack motions toward the Cluck Hut. "Shall we?"

Polly is already sitting on the counter as we walk up. "Nice of you to join, slowpokes. How is it I beat you two and your fully-blooded bodies?"

"Need I remind you we're carrying all our supplies? Including *your* sleeping bag?" Jack places the Pro Bro on the floor and arranges the sleeping bags around them.

Polly looks down. "I see there's only two bags."

I swallow. "Guess we never told you, Jack and I are gonna...share the double."

"Of *course* you are."

Jack and I laugh. We're back at the food court. After climbing up and down the mall, we're here, with food and supplies. We're together. And we're safe.

For now.

16

The Pro Bro has turned out to be worth its weight in gold. I found some peanut oil in one of the Cluck Hut cabinets and we've fried up several of the frozen chicken tenders. The *Chicksicle's* reign of terror has come to an end.

I take a bite and turn to Polly. "How's the impossible chicken treating you?"

"It's not bad." She dips a misshapen tender in a carton of barbecue sauce and then a carton of honey mustard. "The sauce adds a certain *je ne sais quoi*."

"Love to hear it," Jack says. "Because we'll be eating nothing but this for a while."

"We have the camping food," I remind him.

"Let's save that for emergencies. Not only because it'll last longer than the food here, but also because it's disgusting."

I swallow my bite of chicken. "Wait. How long will these freezers last? Almost everything here in the food court is perishable."

Jack walks over to the freezer. "They're on emergency power. There was a big blackout in the eighties and the mall lost hundreds of thousands of dollars because all the food spoiled. So these babies should have power for at least a few days. Maybe longer."

"And after a few days?"

Jack frowns. "We'll cross that bridge if and when we come to it. Besides, by then, certainly someone will have saved us." He grabs another tender.

I can't help but wonder—what if there's no one else out there to save us? None of us really knows what happened after The Boom. For all we know, we could be the only ones left.

The only ones left. I hadn't thought of it that way until now.

Oh, *God.* That means my mom, my brother. Everyone I ever knew. There's a good chance they're gone. Blown away.

I take a shaky breath in.

Jack looks up. "You okay?"

I can't speak. If I do, I'll start sobbing.

Everyone.

There's a good chance that every single person I love is dead. I remember studying the devastation of Hiroshima and Nagasaki back in school. And nuclear weapons have gotten so much deadlier since then.

I never even said goodbye to my mom. I ran out of the house so quickly this morning. I robbed myself of that final moment because I slept in. It was all so *stupid.*

I stand. "I need to run to the bathroom." My voice is painfully uneven, and my lower lip is quivering with the placidity of a jackhammer. I'm not fooling anyone.

But I can't break down here. Not in front of Jack and Polly.

They're practically strangers. I turn my headlamp on and practically sprint across the Food Court. I look around. Is there any true privacy here? There are five food stalls total, and it's an open floorplan.

My entire body heaves. The floodgates are opening.

I fall to my knees. I'm at the fountain. Right next to where I fell in earlier. I breathe in. All control is lost. I weep.

My howls reverberate through the entire food court. Possibly the entire mall. I can't regulate it. It's all just pouring out at once.

My mind keeps flashing back. The weight of the last six hours is hitting me all at once. The Boom. The tables in Electronix. The Electronix technician crushed under the fridge. The frosty cold of the fountain. The brief moment where it was all over as the slide crumpled beneath my weight. The helplessness I felt as I watched Polly bleed uncontrollably at the bottom of the rock wall.

I have no control over anything here. The fact that I'm still alive right now is through an incredibly fortunate sequence of random events. I'd be dead if one small thing had gone wrong.

Dead. *Dead.* Like those poor people crushed under the shelves at the Electronix. Green Hat Lady. Polly's friend Jane. Everyone outside of the mall—my family and friends. *Mom and Greg.*

In a weird way, I resent them. Their struggles are over. They don't have to worry about what's coming next. I gasp for air between sobs. My entire face is dripping with tears.

I hear a voice behind me. "Hey."

It's Jack. *Oh no.* He shouldn't see me like this.

I wipe my eyes. "I n-need a moment alone."

Jack sits down next to me. "I think you need the exact opposite."

"Please, I'm just—"

I can't finish the sentence. I'm keening again. Loudly. I strain to regain my composure, but my efforts are in vain.

"It's okay." Jack puts his arm around me. "You've been through a lot. We all have."

I look up. I'm well-aware that I'm an ugly crier. I must be the least attractive person in the world in this moment. And to have Jack—attractive, unbelievably resolute Jack—seeing me like this is too much to handle.

"I don't see *you* breaking down."

"Are you kidding?" Jack laughs softly. "I've fallen apart several times. Once in the stairwell while you were busy saving our asses. And when you left me under the table at Electronix."

I think back. Jack's eyes *were* bloodshot when I returned from the basement shelter. "I'm sorry I left you." I let out another cry.

"You've held it together so long." Jack tightens his hold around my shoulders. "You've coped as long as you can. It's *okay*. We're not exactly in a normal situation. Let it out. You'll feel so much better."

"Me crying isn't going to help us survive."

"Attempting to put on a brave face won't either. We all feel helpless. We *are* helpless. We have no idea what's going on outside right now. It could be the end of the world. Grief is a natural, *healthy* byproduct of what we're going through. The acknowledgement of our lack of control."

I look up at Jack. I'm not buying it.

"Even if you *did* break down, at least you haven't let it stop you from helping me and Polly." My body quakes. "I've provided *nothing* to the group effort from the beginning. You and Polly have. All I've done is put the group in danger. Falling in the fountain, breaking the goddamn slide—"

"Are you kidding me?" Jack squeezes my shoulder. "Luke, I'd still be hiding under the table in Electronix if it weren't for you. I was lost, and *you* were the one who moved first. I was too afraid to even go with you into the back room. You showed me that I could be brave." He grabs my face with both hands. "Everything we've accomplished, I owe to you."

I'm once again face-to-face with Jack's striking verdant eyes. I'm still shivering, but a warm sense of peace cloaks my body. In this moment, there is no chaos. There is no mall.

I lean my face toward Jack's.

His lips meet mine.

They're so soft.

Fireworks erupt in my head. The Fourth of July times infinity.

Our kiss begins soft, but slowly crescendos into a symphony. Tubular bells are clanging in my ears, and yet all is still.

Jack gently breaks away. "Believe me now?"

My mouth opens, but I'm incapable of forming words. All I can do is behold the wonderful, beautiful man in front of me.

I'm finally able to whisper one word.

"*Jack.*"

He smiles. I grab him by the shoulders and reel him back in. The second kiss is stronger, more passionate. *Hotter*. I slowly lower my body to the floor, bringing him with me. Our chests make contact and our legs intertwine.

Absolute, utter perfection.

Either hours or seconds pass—I can't tell.

Jack's lips depart from mine—*no*—and he sits back up. "I hate to be *that* guy, but we really need to check on Polly. Make sure she's okay."

Polly. Right. She's a person who exists. Who is injured. Badly. And shouldn't be left alone.

But all I want is to kiss Jack again. Surely Polly can wait a few more minutes. "I'm sure she's okay."

But the moment has passed. It's over. Jack is getting to his feet and dusting himself off.

"I'm sure she is too. But she's part of our team, and we can't abandon her. No matter how pleasant the alternative is."

"Oh, you enjoyed yourself?"

"*Very* much. Like I said, I like you, Chesterfield."

I'm smiling. "I like you too, Jack."

Jack offers me his hand and helps me up off the floor. He looks at the fountain. "This is right where you fell in, isn't it?"

I nod. "Yeah, it's all very poetic."

"Almost like you planned it."

"I *am* a candidate for a master's degree in the literary arts. In case you weren't aware."

"You may have mentioned it three or four thousand times," Jack grabs my hand and squeezes it. "C'mon, Polly will start wondering what we're up to."

I know full well that Polly is acutely aware of what Jack and I have been getting up to. But Jack's right. We should be with her.

"How long were we...*away*?"

Jack laughs. "Away? We were *away* for at least half an hour. French *away* at that."

"*Jack.*"

"*Luke.*"

I still haven't let go of his hand. We walk back over to the Cluck Hut.

Polly is right where we left her. Sitting on the floor, next to the Pro Bro. The frying pan is next to her, empty except for a splash of oily residue. But I stop. My heartbeat, which had finally slowed down while I was with Jack, picks up the pace again.

Polly is not alone.

17

———————

Jack lets go of my hand. My arm falls to the side of my body like a dead fish.

"Uh...hi," he says.

Three new faces look up at me from around the Pro Bro. Two women—one middle-aged wearing pink horn-rimmed glasses and an orange turtleneck, the other a teenager with a blond ponytail wearing a red and blue plaid school uniform, and a middle-aged man, wearing a blue-striped golf shirt and a gold watch, more salt than pepper in his disheveled hair.

"Where have you two *been*?" The twinkle in Polly's eye shows that she knows exactly where we've been and what we've been doing.

Jack eyes the newcomers and laughs nervously. "Nothing. Luke ate something that didn't quite agree with him and I went to check on him. All's good now, though."

"Oh, I'm *sure*," Polly retorts.

Silently thanking Jack for implying to a group of strangers that I was diarrheal, I step behind the Cluck Hut counter. "Hi,

135

I see Polly has found a few more survivors. I'm Luke, and you are?"

Golf Shirt Man stands up. "Sorry if we startled you. I'm Don. I was in the food court when the alarms went off and I've been hiding away in the Burger Palace ever since."

"And I'm Kathy," the horn-rimmed glasses woman says. "With a K. And this is my daughter Brooklyn. We were also here, running a quick errand before taking Brookie in for a doctor's appointment—"

"*Mom*," Brooklyn says.

"Oh, sorry, sweetheart." Kathy pats her on the head. "She doesn't like people to know she goes to the doctor. Even though everybody goes to the doctor."

Brooklyn buries her face in her hands.

"Anyway, we also took refuge in the food court. At the Taco City stall. We were there until Polly found us. She was circling the perimeter of the food court, seeing if there was anyone around."

"You were?" Jack crosses his arms. "Are you sure you should be up and about so much with your shoulder?"

"I literally did one lap of the place," Polly says. "It took five minutes. These were the only people I could find."

"A lot of people were in the food court when the alarms first went off," Don says. "But there's an exit nearby. They got out before the safeguards came all the way down. They're either free outside, or, you know—"

"Dead," Brooklyn finishes for him.

Don's nostrils flare. "Yeah, that."

I snap my fingers. "So *that's* why we haven't run into many others. We've been wondering why the mall was so deserted."

"Yeah." Kathy straightens her back. "There was a huge

rush. But I remembered my mother telling me about nuclear drills in school. They were trained to get under something solid. Taco City looked like our best bet, so we ducked under."

"We were too afraid to come out," Brooklyn says. "We weren't sure how stable the rest of the building was."

"Valid concern." Jack gently pounds the wall of the Cluck Hut stall. "But the shell of this mall is pretty solid. Some of the stuff inside is a little rickety, though. A certain slide comes to mind."

"The Mega-Slide is gone?" Don asks.

I nod. "We used it to climb up to the third floor. Long story short, it fell as we got to the top."

Kathy gasps. "Heavens! Are you all right?"

Jack smiles. "We've been to hell and back, but it was worth it to retrieve the supplies we needed. We decided to set up our base at the Cluck Hut. It's out of the way, and there's obviously plenty of food."

"And you have a stove." Don fiddles with the Pro Bro. "Smart guys. I ate a few raw burgers while I was hiding. I don't recommend it."

"Weirdly enough, that's a perfect segue to a conversation I wanted to start," Polly says. "Assuming we're in this for the long haul, we should establish control over the food court. It's easily the most important space in the mall."

"Establish control?" I frown. "You sound like an army general."

"And is this not war?" Polly rubs her shoulder. "I seem to remember getting stabbed."

My stomach turns. I hadn't thought of it like that. *Woof.*

"Plus, if a nuke really hit us, I think it's safe to say there's a smidgeon of conflict around us."

Jack crosses to where we're standing. "Well-reasoned. Go on."

"I've been thinking about this ever since I woke up in the SportsGoods," Polly says. "Obviously the six of us aren't the only people in the mall. Most people are scared for their lives and are likely still hidden away. Some people are dead. And I'm guessing a small number—small, but significant enough —are taking advantage of the free-for-all."

"At least one person," Jack says. "Whoever stabbed you in the SportsGoods."

"Yeah." Polly walks to the counter. "But if we have control over this area—the main source of nourishment in the mall —we have a bargaining chip. People need to eat, and the only other foodstuffs people can get in this mall are the camping meals at SportsGoods and maybe candy from *Doctor Sweetz*."

"There are a bunch of restaurants on the second floor too, but we don't have access to those," Jack says. "Even if we took the rock wall, there are barriers around it until you reach SportsGoods."

Polly crosses the stall. "Ergo, if we have control of the food court, we have control of the mall. Or at least of the first floor."

I wrinkle my nose. "I guess that makes sense. Basic supply and demand."

"Right." Polly's face darkens. "And no human need trumps hunger."

Jack furrows his brow. "And you worked at *Trixie's*?"

Polly shrugs. "Guess I'm more complicated than I look. I was an army brat growing up. My parents were both in the Marines. I may have picked up a few pearls of wisdom from them."

"How do you expect us to defend ourselves?" Don asks.

"The guy who attacked you at the SportsGoods clearly had a knife. Without weapons, we're just sitting ducks."

I pull the hunting knife out of my pocket. "I have this. I think Jack got one too, right?"

"Yeah, mine's in one of the packs."

"And I grabbed this while you were out cold." Polly riffles through the sleeping bag where we threw the frying pan. She pulls out a crossbow.

Jack gasps. "*Polly!* When the hell did you grab that without me noticing?"

Polly grins. "I grabbed it when you were attending to Luke, and I packed it up when I rolled the sleeping bag. I didn't want to mention anything in case it broke when we threw it down the rock wall."

Jack's mouth opens. "Was I *that* distracted?"

"You were...*fixated* on the task at hand." Polly fidgets with the trigger of the crossbow. "Anyway, with this baby and the boys' knives, we've got a nice little arsenal. Plus there's some cutlery in the Rockin' Roll stall that our new companions can make use of."

My head is spinning. All this talk of weapons has taken a minute to get through my skull, and the gravity is just now hitting me. "Wait wait *wait*. Are we really sure that this is necessary?"

"We know that there's at least one person in this mall with the capacity to stab someone from behind." Polly motions at her shoulder. "And they might not be alone. Crisis brings out the best and the worst in people."

Jack runs his fingers through his hair. "Polly has a point. It can't hurt to be prepared."

"And again, we have something that people need," Polly

says. "They may have things that we need. We can provide food as a sort of currency."

Brooklyn speaks up. "Can't we just use money?"

Polly laughs. "Money isn't real. At least not in here. My guess is we'll end up using a barter system. If it worked for cavemen, it'll work for us."

"Let me see." Don quickly counts the heads in the stall. "There are six of us, and five stalls. Burger Palace, Salad Gardens, Rockin' Roll, Taco City, and Cluck Hut. I guess we could split our efforts pretty easily. And two of us can double up."

"I'll take Salad Gardens," Polly says. "I'm the vegetarian anyway."

"I can take Taco City and Brookie can run the sushi place," Kathy says. "It's basically one big stall, with an empty doorway connecting them. That way we can stay close." Her eyes fall on my headbands. "Unless *you'd* rather take the sushi place."

"These are a makeshift bandage, so go ahead. I hold no claim to Rockin' Roll." I shift my gaze towards Don. "I suppose you'll want to take Burger Palace, since that's the stall you're most familiar with?"

"Fine by me."

"And then Luke and Jack can double up at Cluck Hut." Polly raises her eyebrow. "Funny how it worked out that way."

Jack shrugs. "Well, we *were* the original settlers of the Cluck Hut. And all our stuff is here. It makes sense."

Don looks at the Pro Bro. "What about the stove? This is the only one we have. The stoves in the stalls are connected to the mall power grid, which is still down."

"I suggest we leave it at a neutral location, and people can cook as they need," Polly says.

"Why not just keep it here at the Cluck Hut?" I ask. "Since there'll be two of us in here, that will keep us from running off with it."

"At least keep it in eyeshot of the rest of us," Polly says. "I trust the two of you, but the other three have no reason to."

"Very well." Jack turns the Pro Bro off and grabs it by the bottom. "We'll keep it on the counter."

"And we'll all just bring our food over and cook it?" Brooklyn asks.

Polly nods. "Eventually, when my shoulder has healed a bit, I'll make a run up to SportsGoods and grab a few more."

I frown. "Eventually? How long do you think we'll be doing this?"

Polly shrugs. "As long as it takes."

That was a stupid question. *Of course she doesn't know, Luke.* No one does.

But I have other, more pressing concerns. "And what happens if—or *when*—the guy who attacked you comes down and demands that we give him food?"

Polly laughs lightly. "Bold of you to assume it was a man. But if that esteemed individual makes an appearance, we'll put up a fight. There's six of us. Maybe we'll pick up a few more stragglers. We'll be fine."

"What if there's more than one?"

"And what if they're wearing top hats made of pastrami?" Polly's voice is sharp. "I don't *know*, Luke. This mall is huge. There are so many things we don't know. All we can do is prepare for the worst and hope for the best."

Prepare for the worst and hope for the best. My internal organs ossify at those words. But Polly's right. It's all we can do.

Still, though, the thought of all the people hidden away in

the mall unsettles me. Jack, Polly, and I have been wandering around for hours across two floors and haven't encountered a soul. But there *must* be others. Shrouded in the shadows. And at least one of them has a knife and isn't afraid to use it.

I swallow. These thoughts aren't going to get me anywhere. All I can do is focus on the present. And for now, I'm in the Cluck Hut, next to Jack.

Jack. I almost forgot.

We kissed!

We were making out by the fountain not twenty minutes ago. All this talk about weapons and murderers and crossbows almost made me forget how nothing else in the world mattered in the moments we were connected.

And tonight we're going to share a sleeping bag.

Ahhh!

Yeah, I'm gonna be fine.

18

D ay One is coming to a close.

Has it really only been a day? *God*. My appointment at the Electronix was a little over twelve hours ago. I mentally catalogue everything that has happened since then. The Boom. The Electronix gate. The fountain. The stairwell. The Mega-Slide. Ball World. The rock wall. The *kiss*.

We've all been at our posts in the food court for the last few hours. No one has come down. Polly said we likely shouldn't expect any people to show up until morning. According to her, most people, in the face of our collective trauma, would have suppressed appetites, at least for the first twenty-four hours. Something to do with the fight-or-flight reaction. Jack explained the psychology of it all afterward.

I *may* have been more focused on the lecturer than the lecture.

There was quite a bit of cutlery in the kitchen behind the Rockin' Roll. We found some vegetable knives in the back of the Salad Gardens, too. Between those and the weapons we brought back from the SportsGoods, we are well-armed.

Of course, if Polly's SportsGoods aggressor shows up, we'll have no way of knowing, since Polly didn't see her attacker. Hell, one of our three new comrades could be the assailant. None of them are wearing patent leather shoes, though—our only clue to the SportsGoods Stabber's identity.

Then again, they could have changed. There are plenty of shoe stores around.

Let's not think about that right now.

Jack and I have been at the Cluck Hut standing guard. We haven't gotten any real time alone, though, because the other four Food Courters have been in and out cooking things up on the Pro Bro. We've talked a little bit but haven't touched any of the more intimate topics we brought up while we were in Ball World.

I guess that's to be expected, though, right? We ripped off the bandage of our vulnerability while we were at the fountain. It stands to reason that we're both feeling a little exposed, especially with all the new blood in our group.

But it's getting later now. Soon we'll be heading to bed.

In our shared sleeping bag.

Polly swings by Cluck Hut. "Everything all good here?"

I nod. "Don was just in here cooking up a burger, but he took it back to his stall."

"We haven't seen Kathy or Brooklyn in a while," Jack says.

"I just saw them," Polly says. "They're fine. Apparently they had some stupid argument about something insignificant. That Brooklyn is a piece of work."

I laugh. "Aren't all teenagers pieces of work?"

Polly grins. "You're not wrong there. I think she's too

young to truly grasp the magnitude of our situation. I remember when I was her age. I thought I was immortal."

"A couple of near-death experiences will even her out." Jack meets my gaze. "Right, Luke?"

I laugh softly. "Yeah, that definitely changes your outlook a tad."

Polly rolls her eyes. "I'm glad it hasn't affected your weird-ass sense of humor."

"If Luke ever loses that, then the terrorists truly have won."

"God willing, it never comes to *that*." Polly's voice is imbued with faux gravity. "Anyway, when I was talking to Kathy and Brooklyn, I floated the idea of sleeping in shifts. Since there are so many of us now, it makes sense."

I nod. "I guess that tracks."

Jack sits at the counter and places a hand on the Pro Bro. "Are you sure we can trust those other three? I mean, what if, while we're sleeping, Don straight-up pilfers the stove and rides off into the sunset?"

I raise my eyebrows. "The sunset in the middle of the night?"

"Shut up," Jack says. "It's an expression."

Polly walks inside the stall and sits next to Jack. "Way ahead of you. I suggested that one of the three of us pairs up with one of the three of them for each shift. That way we have accountability until we can trust each other a little more."

"Oh." I realize that means I won't have Jack as a lookout buddy. Or Polly, for that matter. The idea of making small talk with one of these new strangers is almost as terrifying as drowning in a mall fountain. The logic is airtight—that's undebatable—but that still doesn't mean I like it.

"Don't worry." Polly spins around and faces me. "You'll have plenty of private office hours with Professor Jacklov when it's my turn to keep watch."

"I mean—um—that *wasn't* what—"

Jack covers for me. "You'll have to pardon Lucas. He still has one more year of study in his advanced English lit degree."

I roll my eyes. "You already made that joke."

"I made a joke in a similar vein. And Polly didn't hear it, so this one still counts."

"Oh my *God*." Polly runs her fingers through her hair. "*Anyway*, I'll take the first shift with Don, and then Jack will pair up with Brooklyn, and then Luke and Kathy will round out the evening."

I stand up and walk to the counter. "How long are these shifts gonna be?"

"Three hours each, starting at ten o'clock." Polly takes a gold timepiece out of her pocket. I recognize it as the one Don was wearing. "We'll use this to keep track of the time. That way everyone should get about six hours of sleep."

"I'd prefer eight if I can get it," I say.

"And I would prefer to not have a gaping wound in my shoulder." Polly pockets the watch. "Things change, Luke. Roll with it. Adapt."

"Fine." I'm not going to argue too much. After all, this still means I'll have three hours of sleeping bag time with Jack.

"Great," Polly says. "Don and I will be at the fountain if you need us. Our shift starts in about fifteen minutes. Jack, I'll come and wake you when it's your turn."

"Sound good," Jack says. "Thanks for taking so much initiative, Polly. You're really kicking ass."

Polly smiles. "I know. Now you two get some shuteye.

You're gonna want to get as much sleep as you can. God only knows what fresh hell awaits us in the morning." She blows us a kiss.

Once she's out of earshot, I glance down at the floor of the Cluck Hut. "So...how do you want to go about sharing the sleeping bag?"

Jack looks at me. His expression falls. His eyes now look tired and sad. Not what I was hoping for.

"Hey, Luke, can we talk?"

Can we talk? Jack just uttered the three most unequivocally horrifying words in the English language.

"Sure. What's up?"

Jack smiles in the way you smile at a dying pet. "About that kiss..."

That kiss? You mean the glorious thirty minutes we spent interwoven at the foot of the fountain? The moment where it felt like everything in my life had aligned perfectly? *That kiss?*

"I just—" He pauses and bites his lip before continuing. "Let's not make a big deal out of it, that's all. I was caught up in the moment. We both were. There's so much going on. And I don't want you to get the wrong idea."

"The wrong *idea*?"

"It's just...um...I just want to make sure we're clearly communicating what we *are* to each other. And I don't want the craziness of today to make us rush something that shouldn't be rushed."

"So you want to take things slow?" *That's fine.* I can do slow.

Jack sighs. "If by slow, you mean no movement at all, yeah."

What?

I'm trying not to let it show, but I'm kind of pissed. "I'm confused. I thought you were into this?"

"I was—*am*. I just—let's not *do* anything tonight, okay?"

I blink.

"At least for now. I just need to get my head around everything. It's not you. It's just, *everything*." He gesticulates wildly.

Okay. I guess that makes sense. *At least for now*. I can live with that. But how long is *for now*?

Is it because he thinks I'm unattractive? Out of shape? There was less light by the fountain, but with all our headlamps combined in the Cluck Hut, maybe Jack's having second thoughts and he's trying to let me down easy.

"Is that cool?"

I blink again. "Yeah. I mean I guess that's fine. It's not like I was picking out china patterns or anything. And I don't want to feel like I'm pushing you into anything you don't want."

Jack smiles. "You're the best, Chesterfield. Thanks for understanding."

"Are we still sharing the sleeping bag? Or is that too weird?"

Jack shakes his head. "That's fine. It's huge. There's plenty of room for us to be...uh...for us to have plenty of room."

I hate everything about this. But if Jack really means it when he says it's a temporary pause, then *fine*. "Okay. So I guess we should get ready for bed, then?"

"Cool if I sleep in my underwear?" Jack's cheeks turn a light shade of pink.

I'm sorry. Is Jack Jay really asking me if it's okay if he strips down to practically nothing while sharing a sleeping bag with me and I'm not even allowed to cuddle with him?

Is this a test? Am I supposed to call his bluff?

"Uh...I guess it's fine with me as long as you're cool with me *also* being in my underwear."

Jack furrows his brow. "Really? Your demeanor sort of gave me a T-shirt and pajama bottoms vibe."

Nail, meet head. I've literally never slept in just my underwear.

"No. I like to go *au natural*."

Jack's eyes widen. "You'd rather sleep naked?"

With you, yes.

"Oh, God, no. Sorry, just trying to sound cool. *Au natural avec* undies."

Jack laughs weakly. "I'll never get used to you, Chesterfield."

And apparently you'll never get the chance to.

"Guess we'd better get ready for bed, then."

I remove my shirt and my love-handles spill over my jeans. *Ugh.*

Meanwhile, Jack strips down. His skin is practically glowing. His sculpted ass is falling out of his teeny-tiny undies. I can't even bring myself to look at the other side. That would be torture.

He slips inside of the sleeping bag and shifts to the left edge, leaving me plenty of room. Far too much room.

God. I've been looking forward to sharing this sleeping bag with Jack the last several hours, but now it's about as tantalizing as a vermin-infested grotto. I slowly climb inside, making sure not to accidentally graze Jack's body, lest he misinterpret it as an unwelcome proposition.

"Good night, Luke." Jack turns off his headlamp.

"Good night, Jack."

I can't help but laugh inwardly at myself. It's not going to be a good night. I won't be getting a wink of sleep. The buzzing voice of my own anxiety has already confirmed I'll be questioning Jack's actions all night. Couple that with the fact that I'm sleeping in my underwear out of sheer spite.

And lest we forget, the literal world as we know it has ended.

Goddammit, it's cold.

19

────────

As predicted, I don't sleep. I spend most of the first three-hour sleep shift dissecting every single action I've taken that day, trying to pinpoint the exact moment I ruined Jack's and my relationship. As of now I've narrowed it down to about two dozen different instances, each one more innocuous than the last.

I look over at Jack. So close to me physically, yet so far from me emotionally. I think he's asleep. It's hard to tell. At the very least, his breathing is steady and his eyes are closed.

How is he able to sleep? And why can't I? It's not as if we haven't been through the same day. I've been exhausted the entire day. And now, when rest is more important than ever, I'm extraordinarily alert.

I keep replaying the conversation Jack and I had before we went to bed. "It's not you. It's just *everything.*"

Okay, that's a fair point. The world as we know it could be over. Important to process.

Or maybe you're just a bad kisser.

No, *stop.* I grit my teeth. Why doesn't this stupid little voice have an off-switch?

I hate this. Normally I fall asleep streaming TV on my laptop. Without the distraction of some sitcom subduing my inner demons, I am defenseless against insomnia.

Some time passes. I hear a rustling nearby. It's Polly. She walks in and gently wakes Jack. She's whispering. I pretend to be asleep.

"Morning, sleeping beauty."

Jack shifts around. "Already?"

Polly yawns. "Not soon enough. Here, Don found some sodas in the Burger Palace. They'll help wake you up."

Jack slowly slithers out of the sleeping bag. His body makes brief contact with mine as he exits. I relish this moment as long as I can. Probably the most I'll get for a while.

"How was *your* night?" Polly clearly thinks that Jack and I got up to some trouble in the night. Joke's on her.

And me.

"Fine." His tone is curt. I can tell from his tone he doesn't want to bring Polly into the weirdness between the two of us. Polly takes the hint and changes her tune.

"Brooklyn's already up by the fountain. She has Don's watch. Your shift goes until four."

"Perfect." Jack's voice is groggy. He still hasn't fully woken up. I hear him shamble around in the dark for a moment, and then he slowly walks out of the Cluck Hut. Polly follows behind, leaving me alone.

And alone isn't bad.

Without Jack next to me as a constant physical reminder of the night that could have been, I'm a little more relaxed. Maybe I actually will get a little sleep tonight.

I'm able to stretch out a little more in the sleeping bag. Before, the two of us were crammed at either end of the double bag, maximizing the distance between our bodies.

My eyelids get heavy. This is nice. This is how it should be. I don't need *Jack* to be happy. I didn't know him from Adam until yesterday morning. We're just two people who happened to be in a store when all manners of hell broke loose. Two extremely compatible people whose chemistry rivaled that of any alchemist.

No. Stop thinking like that, Luke.

I'm right. My mind is racing again. I need to unwind. Something to distract me.

I'm thinking back to my job at the library. I fell asleep on the job there all the time. I try to place my mind there—pre-Boom, pre-mall, pre-Jack. I can almost smell the dusty books surrounding me. It's calm. It's peaceful.

I'm going, going.

Gone.

I wake. It's nice. I feel well-rested.

Hold on.

A little *too* well-rested.

My eyes snap open. I don't know what time it is, but Jack hasn't woken me up for my shift. I grab my headlamp and shine it around. The Cluck Hut is empty, save for our pile of equipment.

Surely three hours have passed. At *least* three hours.

I get out of the sleeping bag and throw on my *Gamma Ray* shirt and jeans. It can't hurt to check things out. Jack and Brooklyn have our only timepiece. Maybe it's really only been an hour and I have more time to sleep.

But I can't shake the feeling that something is wrong.

I walk out of the Cluck Hut and toward the fountain. I see a small light. *Okay, that's them.* They're fine.

It's not Jack's headlamp, though. It's not nearly bright enough. *Maybe he's saving the battery?* I walk forward a little farther as I trace the imprint of the hunting knife in my pocket.

It's the Forevergreen. Jack must have brought it out with him. The scent would have given him something to help keep him awake. The candle is almost spent. One solitary wick remains lit.

Jack isn't here. Neither is Brooklyn.

They're probably patrolling the area. But why would they leave the candle? That's a fire hazard. The last thing we need right now is a fire.

The light of the Forevergreen reflects off of something metallic. A small golden glint a few yards away. I walk toward it. Probably a penny from the fountain, or—

Don's watch. I pick it up. It's been stepped on, but the hands are still ticking behind the fractured crystal. I hold it up to my headlamp and squint.

Six o'clock.

Six o'clock? Jack and Brooklyn's shift should have ended two hours ago. No one came to wake me up. *Where is Jack?*

I race over to the Salad Gardens. Polly is inside—*thank God*—curled up in her sleeping bag. I lean down and shake her by her uninjured shoulder.

"*Polly.* Wake up!"

Her eyes slowly open. "What? Your shift up already?"

"No, it never started. Jack and Brooklyn are *gone.*"

Polly yawns. "They're probably just strolling around."

I grab Don's watch and shove it in her face. "It's six a.m., Polly. They should have finished their shift two hours ago."

Polly processes this information for a moment, then her eyes widen. "Oh, God. Have you checked on the others?"

"Not yet. I came to find you first."

Polly slinks out of her sleeping bag—she is still fully clothed—and stands. "My headlamp."

I spy it on the Salad Gardens counter and grab it. "Here."

We quickly sprint over to the Burger Palace. Don is there, asleep against the wall. Kathy is also accounted for in the Taco City, sprawled out across the floor.

"Okay," Polly says. "Let's calm down. They may have just wandered off and gotten lost."

"And left the watch behind?"

"Let's go look around the fountain." Polly crosses in front of me. "See if there's any sign of struggle. No reason to wake Don and Kathy up unless we have reason to alarm them."

Sign of struggle? "Do you think they were *taken*?"

"I know as much as you, Luke."

"I thought you said we wouldn't see anyone until morning."

"Once again, I'm *famously* not a fortune-teller." Polly quickens her pace. "C'mon, we're wasting time."

I leave the watch on the counter of the Cluck Hut. We rush to the fountain. "This is where I found the watch." I gesture over to where the Forevergreen—still flickering—lies.

"Look around. See if there's anything else. They may have just dropped the watch."

I have my doubts, but Polly's right. No reason to panic until we have proof of foul play. I flash my headlamp around. Nothing. It occurs to me that this is right where Jack and I shared our first kiss, just a few hours ago. How quickly circumstances change.

I continue to wave the headlamp around haphazardly. I

stop when I spy a couple drops of water on the floor, but those probably came from the fountain—

Wait. The drops are too dark to be water. Oil from the Pro Bro, maybe? I inch closer and shine my light. My stomach turns over.

The drops are a deep shade of unmistakable red-brown.

Blood.

20

I dry-heave at the sight before me.

Polly runs over. "What is it?"

I point my headlamp at the small scarlet droplets speckling the ground. Polly squints at them for a moment before realizing what it is.

She inhales slowly. "Okay, don't freak out. I know it doesn't look good, but if something *really* bad happened, there'd be more than a few scattered drops of blood."

"Still, though, *something* happened."

"It could easily be a nosebleed. All we *really* know is that they were here at one o'clock, and now they're not."

"That leaves *five hours* unaccounted for, Polly."

"Maybe one of the others knows what's going on." Polly shines her headlamp across the fountain. "No other clues?"

I shake my head. "No."

We walk over to Taco City.

Kathy is just beginning to wake.

"Is it time for our shift, Luke?"

I have no idea how to answer. How do you tell a woman

you barely know that the most important person in her life is missing? I'm at an utter loss for words.

Luckily, Polly takes over. "Kathy, don't panic, because there's no reason to suspect anything is wrong, but Brooklyn is missing. Jack too. Do you know the last time you saw her?"

The blood drains from Kathy's face and her eyes widen. "*What?*"

"Brooklyn is missing." Polly voice is calm and even. "We think she's okay, but the last I saw her was when she started her shift with Jack. That was at one in the morning. Now it's a little after six."

"Oh, God." Kathy's eyes fill with tears. "My baby! She's *gone*?"

"No, no, not *gone*," Polly says. "All we know is she and Jack didn't wake you or Luke for your shift."

"I'm sorry, what *other* word would you use for *not here*?" Kathy begins to sob. "Because that sounds like *gone* to me."

I grab some napkins from the front counter of the Taco City and hand them to Kathy. "We're both missing someone we care about. We need to know if you saw Brooklyn at any point after her shift started. Something that may help us find her."

Kathy wipes her eyes. "I think she passed by an hour or so after they started. I always wake up when I hear her walking nearby. It's a mother's instinct."

"Okay." I sit down at the Taco City counter. "We know they were okay for the first hour of their shift. And whatever kept them from coming back would have happened before four when their shift ended."

Kathy lets out another cry. "It should have been *me*! I told her I'd take the middle shift so her sleep wouldn't be interrupted. But she wanted to be with Jack. I think she thought he was cute."

I suppress a laugh. *Wrong tree, Brooklyn.*

"We haven't woken Don up yet," Polly says. "He might have seen them before they left too."

Before they *left*? I admire Polly's optimistic use of language.

Kathy wipes her eyes with the napkin and grabs her pink glasses from the floor near where she was sleeping. "Let's find my girl."

We quickly walk over to the Burger Palace to wake Don. He's still fast asleep, leaning up against the side wall.

Polly gently pokes his shoulder. "Don. Wake up!"

Don's eyes slowly open. He looks down at his wrist and realizes he doesn't have his watch on. "What time is it? I just got back to sleep."

Polly crouches down to his level. "*Just* got back to sleep? When did you last wake up?"

"I don't have my damn watch, so I can't tell you exactly." He rubs his eyes and surveys the three of us. "What's with the wakeup crew? Gonna play me a morning reverie?" He laughs, clearly thinking his joke is funny. His eyes are still half-closed.

"Jack and Brooklyn are...*missing*." I'm trying to avoid using the G-word for Kathy's sake. "Any chance you saw them when you woke up?"

Don opens his eyes a little wider. He strains to be as alert as the situation requires. "Christ. I think I heard them wandering around when I woke up. No idea when that was, though."

"Did they say anything about where they were going?"

Polly asks. "We're thinking maybe they wandered off and got lost."

Yeah, right. Jack knows this mall like the back of his hand. There's no way he's lost. I'm pretty sure Polly knows this too. But we're both trying to keep Kathy calm.

Don closes his eyes. "I think the girl said something about a candle? She liked it and wanted to get one for herself." He frowns. "That couldn't be it, though. Why would she be talking about a candle?"

"The Forevergreen!" I say. "Jack brought it with him for his watch, and maybe they ran over to the Candleworks to find one for Brooklyn."

"Guess we should start there," Polly says. "That's our only lead."

I look at Polly. "You still need to take it easy. I'll go. Jack's my...erm—"

My *what*? Clearly not a romantic interest, at least not any longer. Would I even call him my friend? *You just met him, and he's already shattered your heart.* My apocalypse buddy? That just sounds dumb.

"Jack's my *responsibility*." Not perfect, but it's accurate.

Polly purses her lips. "So *that's* what the kids are calling it."

I shoot her a dirty look. "Plus, someone has to hold down the food court. All our stuff is here, and we need someone keeping watch. And you have your crossbow. No one else is gonna get taken."

"*I'm* coming with you." Kathy grabs two of Don's sushi knives from the Burger Palace counter. "This is my daughter we're talking about."

I catch a spark behind her pink glasses. Kathy means business.

"Of course," I say. "And Polly and Don can stay at the food court. Don can stay here, and Polly can take over the Cluck Hut. Between those two vantage points, you should be able to keep an eye on the entire food court."

"Good plan." Polly runs over to the Salad Gardens and grabs her crossbow. She brandishes her weapon as she returns to the group. I can tell she feels *really* badass right now.

Don gets to his feet and grabs his own knife. "Good luck. And be careful. Whoever's out there isn't screwing around."

"I'm well aware." I feel around in my pocket for my hunting knife. It's still there. "Kathy-with-a-K, shall we?"

I offer her my hand with stately grandeur. In this moment, I've taken over Jack's role in this group as the charismatic, quippy leader. Maybe I *can* do this.

Kathy's eyes are like two flames. "Let's go save my girl."

We begin our march toward the fountain.

"Stay safe!" Polly calls out behind us.

I give her a thumbs-up. The Forevergreen's final stubborn wick is still burning as we approach the fountain, even though all the wax has melted. Might as well puff that out. No reason to risk adding a fire to our list of trepidations. I approach the candle and spot something I missed before. Right by the little bloodstains is a series of scuff marks, the kind left by a dress shoe. Jack was wearing sneakers from the SportsGoods, so those can't be his.

I kneel down to get a better look. "What kind of shoes was Brooklyn wearing?"

"Her school shoes. Sensible flats."

"Do those leave marks on the floor?"

Kathy frowns. "I don't think so. Why?"

I show her the scuff marks on the floor by the fountain.

"Has she ever left marks like this from her shoes at your home?"

Kathy moves forward and squints through her cat-eye glasses. "No. And she's running up and down our hardwood stairs all day. Never left a mark like that."

"Then we have another clue. I'm pretty sure whoever made these was wearing dress shoes. And they may be related to Jack and Brooklyn's disappearance."

Kathy kneels down next to me. "How do you know they weren't just there before? A lot of people were running out of the mall when the alarms started. There are probably scuff marks all over the floor."

"Not here." I flash my headlamp around the immediate area. "Jack and I spent a lot of time near this fountain. I'm pretty well-acquainted with this area. The floors were spotless, besides some debris from The Boom. At least in this spot, where they were standing guard."

"Oh, God." Kathy's voice cracks. "That means there *was* some kind of struggle."

"We don't know that yet." I don't think I can handle Kathy breaking down without Polly nearby. "But we can at least assume that someone was wearing dress shoes—likely men's dress shoes."

"Lots of men wear dress shoes, though," Kathy says. "Yesterday was a Tuesday morning. Lots of people were here picking something up on their way to work."

"I realize that. But it's *something*. Let's see if there's anything at the Candleworks. It's not far from here."

We move through the mall's walkway. I shine my headlamp in every direction to see if maybe Jack and Brooklyn left a clue to where they went. Lots of potted plants overturned, but that's likely damage from The Boom.

I pause. *This is a fool's errand, Luke.* There's so much destruction in the mall from the explosion, and anything out of place could be attributed to that. There's no chance we'll find something definitively related to Jack and Brooklyn's whereabouts.

At the same time, we can just do *nothing.* I keep moving.

Something cracks under my foot about five shops away from the Candleworks. I've stepped on something. Something glass? No, plastic. I point my headlamp toward it. A small teal strap with something plastic—the part I've stepped on—fixed to the middle.

Jack's headlamp!

My stomach drops. There's no way Jack would voluntarily part with his headlamp. As far as I'm concerned, this and the scuffs by the fountain are all the evidence we need that Jack and Brooklyn didn't just wander off. There's an element of criminality afoot.

And here we are, walking into the lion's den.

I flick the small switch on the headlamp. It still works, even with the plastic casing around the light broken. "Here." I offer it to Kathy. "This was Jack's. If we both have headlamps, we'll be able to cover twice the ground."

"This was *Jack's?*" Kathy's face twists and I know she understands the grim implications of our discovery as well as I do. "Oh, no, I couldn't possibly—"

"*He's* clearly not using it." I force the headlamp into Kathy's hands. "So you may as well get some use out of it."

"Fine." Kathy wraps the strap around her forehead and tucks it under the arms of her glasses.

I sigh. "Sorry. I didn't mean to snap. I'm just worried about Jack."

"You two are close, aren't you?"

I frown. *Maybe not as close as I thought.* "Sort of. We just met yesterday morning. We were both in the Electronix when the alarms started. He's a technician, and I was getting my phone fixed. We've just been through a lot together."

"So *that's* where your phone went." Kathy turns her headlamp on. "I was wondering why you didn't have one. I never see a young person without one. Brookie had hers, but it died in the first hour after. This mall has horrible reception. Drained her battery quick. And I left mine at home."

The idea of leaving one's house without one's phone is repugnant to me, but I don't comment on the matter. Kathy is talking a lot, and fast. I figure that's her way of coping with stress. Can't blame her. If she keeps talking, her brain won't have time to think about atrocities that may be befalling her daughter.

Huh. I guess I *was* listening when Jack was delivering his psych lecture.

"So now we know Jack lost his headlamp," Kathy says. "But he or Brooklyn clearly made it back to the fountain. Or else those scuff marks wouldn't be there."

"Whoever got Jack—if Jack *got* got—must have gotten him first."

Kathy stops. "What?"

I frown. "Sorry, I got *no* sleep last night. What I mean is that Brooklyn may have made it back to the fountain before someone—the guy in dress shoes—got her."

Kathy's eyebrows furrow. "Didn't Polly say that whoever stabbed her was wearing patent leather shoes?"

I slap my hand to my forehead. "Jesus, *yes*. I can't believe I didn't put those two together. It could very well be the same person."

"Or there are two deranged men in this mall wearing

similar pairs of shoes." Kathy's face reddens. "Oh, *God*, and one of them has my daughter!"

She almost lets out a cry, but I throw my hand over her mouth. "Listen, we shouldn't be too loud. They could be hiding in any corner. I get it. You're upset. I am too, and no one understands the benefits of a good cry better than I do, but I'm gonna need you to not make any loud noises for the time being. That or you're gonna have to go back to the food court. Cool?"

A single tear falls out of Kathy's eye, but she nods.

I take my hand off of her mouth. "Again, sorry. Rescue missions are new to me."

"No, you're right." Kathy exhales slowly. "I'll be strong. For Brookie."

I advance down the walkway. "Right now, our objective is to whittle down who the patent leather shoe guy could be. Problem is, I haven't seen anyone else in this mall, except for a few people in the Electronix store before Jack and I took off. And you guys, of course."

Kathy brings her hands together and twiddles her thumbs. "We haven't seen anyone at all. Brookie and I were hiding in the Taco City stall all day until Polly found us."

There's a bench nearby. I sit on it, deflated. "Then we're officially out of leads. The trail runs cold here."

"We could go inside the Candleworks and see if there's anything there." Kathy waves her headlamp around for a moment. Then her eyes light up. "*Wait*."

"Wait what?" I stand up. "You see someone?"

"Not some*one*. At least, not technically."

She walks over to a nearby directory. It's the same one that Jack and I used when we first left the Candleworks. But the map of the mall is only on one side of the sign. There's another side facing a nearby entrance.

Plastered on the opposite side of the map is a full-length photo of a man in a sleek, tailored charcoal suit, no tie. Perfectly coiffed brown hair and a smile that could blind an army. His arms are crossed as if he's trying to say, "I may be rich and powerful, but I can also be casual and down-to-earth, just like you!" Underneath, the following text:

CEO Maxwell Stride welcomes you to MetroMall!

I shrug. "It's Maxwell Stride, so what? He's the head honcho of the mall. Third in his family to take the position. Guess he put these tacky signs up so people would know who he was. Gotta feel important."

"Look at his feet." Kathy points her headlamp downward.

Weird suggestion, I think. But I'll humor Kathy, she's been through a lot. Stride is wearing black dress shoes. Shiny black dress shoes.

Patent leather dress shoes.

21

I stand there with my mouth open for a solid thirty seconds before I speak. "No. There is *no* way that Stride is the one responsible. That's a *moon-landing-was-faked, earth-is-flat* level of bananas."

"It does seem a little neurotic." Kathy crouches down to get a closer look at the shoes. "But think about it. He's enjoyed a life of opulence, and in one flash of a moment, money no longer matters. The playing field is completely leveled for everyone in the mall."

"So?"

But my mind flashes back to something Jack said earlier: *The Strides have some serious political connections.*

Kathy may have a point.

"All I'm saying is, that guy is trouble," Kathy says. "If he was in the mall when the alarms started, he would immediately feel the loss of his privilege. And he'd panic. And when people panic, they do outrageous things."

"But stabbing a girl in the back is a *touch* beyond desperate."

"Perhaps. Still, though..." Kathy lowers her voice. "You're too young to remember this, but a while back there was a big scandal about the MetroMall working conditions. A lot of custodians, especially, came forward with these horrifying accounts of how they'd been treated by the upper management. Jacob Stride the second was in charge then. There was a big exposé. All the papers picked it up. One thing became very clear: this family doesn't care about people beneath them. As far as they're concerned, the lower classes are nothing but a necessary inconvenience—a foundation upon which they can build their wealth."

"Really? Jack didn't mention that when he was talking about the mall."

Kathy shrugs. "He may not have known that part of the story. The Strides did everything they could to keep it quiet. This was before the Internet, so the story was pretty easy to suppress. People forgot, or they just didn't care enough. MetroMall didn't lose any business. They cleaned up their act just enough to get the press off their backs. Jake Junior also gave up his office so it could be turned into an employee rec area—an empty gesture to quell the qualms of his critics."

"Yikes."

"That's just how the Stride family is," Kathy says. "And I'm willing to bet the youngest one is the worst. There was a rumor going round that he wasn't supposed to inherit the mall upon his father's death. That it was supposed to go to someone else. But then Jacob Stride died very suddenly. It was fishy to say the least. The executors never found his will, so Maxwell inherited the mall by default. People were suspicious, but because of his status and wealth, he got away with it. I have zero difficulty believing that he may have a hand in everything that's been going on."

"That's *nuts*, though," I say. "Then again, how many people wear patent leather dress shoes on a trip to the mall on a weekday morning?"

"A lawyer picking something up on the way to the office, perhaps?"

I shake my head. "No, normal dress shoes I could see. But patent leather is such a specific vibe. It's flashy. Not everyone can pull it off."

"Fair point."

"That said, we have no definitive evidence that Stride is our culprit, so we shouldn't be jumping to any conclusions, right?"

"No, we shouldn't. But let's keep it in mind. Figuring out what Stride is up to may very well lead us to Brookie."

I sigh. We have no other leads on Jack and Brooklyn's location, so we might as well humor this notion.

Then it hits me. "The shelter! The Strides had a small shelter built into the basement of the mall. Jack, Polly, and I stumbled on it earlier yesterday."

"Do you think that's where Brookie might be?"

"Maybe. There was a lit lantern inside when we first discovered the shelter. It couldn't have been on long, so someone had to have been using it recently. Stride, or someone very close to him. If he's really our perpetrator, that's our best place to start."

Kathy nods. "Sounds good. And where is it?"

"There's an access through the stairwell. But the door locks automatically behind, so we could be stuck inside."

"Why not just put a wedge in the door?"

I shake my head. "I don't think that's a good idea. If Stride is really as evil as we're thinking, we should leave no evidence that we were in his special bunker."

"Fair point."

"There's another entrance, though. Through the rec area. The one that used to be the CEO's office."

"Of *course* there is." Kathy crosses her arms. "Papa Stride would have wanted easy access to it. I bet his son didn't even realize the shelter existed when he moved the offices."

"Well, someone told *someone*. The shelter was accessed at some point yesterday." I motion past the Candleworks. "The Rec Room is this way, near the pile of rubble formerly known as the Mega-Slide."

The walk to the Rec Room—sorry, the *Jacob Stride Memorial Lounge*—is short. It's amazing how fast we can traverse the mall when we have proper lighting.

Kathy walks about ten feet ahead of me. She's fearless. A tigress forging into the dusky cave to save her cub.

We enter the lounge. The door to the shelter is hidden. I remember it closing when we first exited the shelter.

I approach a wall and knock gently. "The entrance blends into the wall. Feel around until something clicks."

Kathy goes to work. We walk the perimeter of the room, banging on the walls. I find the spot where I *think* we entered and knock softly. The wall doesn't budge.

Kathy doesn't appear to be having much luck either. "How did you open it before? Maybe there's a lever or something?"

"No. It was open when we got here. And we came from the inside, so I have no idea how to open it from this side."

Kathy frowns and places her hands on her hips. "There has to be a way. Stride would want easy access to his foxhole."

Everything in the lounge is modern: the flat-screen TVs, the couches, the pool table. There isn't anything that could have been a relic from when the mall was first built in the fifties. I eye the black-and-white photo of the former CEO at his desk in the office underneath the lounge placard. I close in on it.

Jacob Stride looks a lot like his grandson. The same hair and smile. He's wearing a white suit, bolo tie, and a ten-gallon hat—like a wannabe oil baron—but, other than that, he could be Maxwell's twin. He's sitting at a huge wooden desk with the MetroMall insignia draped over the front. One large M towering over a lowercase, cursive M. I can't help but feel like the Big M is the Stride family looming over us—the little Ms—as we struggle to make our way through the chaos.

"Based on this photo, the desk was placed right by where the pool table is now," I say.

Kathy surveys the area. "I don't see anything. Certainly not anything that could trigger a door to open."

Dammit. I really thought I was about to pull a Jack and save the day.

Ugh. *Jack.*

Everything going on, while terrifying, has been a glorious distraction from my thoughts about him. And here I am, putting my life on the line to save this guy who doesn't even want to be with me. Or maybe he does. Feelings are dumb, and also how am I supposed to find this damn door to the shelter that may or may not contain the person that I—

"Luke?"

I break momentarily from my spiral of self-doubt. "Yeah?"

"Any other ideas?"

I pause. There is literally nothing in the entire rec room that could have been here when it was originally built. Everything has been updated. Meaning that the door to the shelter may only be accessible from the inside. "I guess we could try our luck with the stairwell. I don't think there's any other—"

I stop. I hear something. Kathy hears it too.

Clack. Clack. Clack. Clack.

Faint, but unyielding footsteps.

The kind of *clack*-y footsteps you'd hear from a man wearing dress shoes walking down a tiled hallway. Dress shoes, meaning it couldn't be Jack or Polly. Our SportsGoods sneakers made a small *squeak*, if they made any noise at all.

Kathy mouths something silently. "*Stride?*"

I shrug. It might just be another survivor. Someone well-meaning. Or maybe it *is* Stride and he's not the megalomaniacal tyrant we've made him out to be.

I don't want to find out. The hairs are standing up on my arm. We need to get out of here.

The lounge's only exit leads right into the hallway. Where the footsteps are coming from. My heart is racing. Our best bet is to find the door to the shelter. But *where*?

My gaze falls back onto the photo of the elder Stride. There's a small caption underneath it. *Jacob Stride at the MetroMall opening, 1951.*

There *is* something in this room left over from the mall's opening. *This photo!* I silently remove it from the wall as the footsteps get louder. There is a small knob behind it, like the kind one would use to dim a lamp, but twice as big. I turn it. *Please God, let this be it.*

I hear a small mechanism whirring and the wall across the room gives a small shudder. Then it opens up, revealing the doorway through which we entered the lounge yesterday.

I laugh quietly. "This mall *really* is a goddamn cartoon, isn't it?"

Without a word, Kathy rockets inside the door. I trail behind her when I hear something that freezes my blood solid.

"Is there someone in there?"

It's a smooth male voice. Not one I recognize. From what I can hear, the *clack*-y footsteps are only twenty feet or so away from the entrance to the lounge. And they're beginning to accelerate.

Part of me wants to hang back and find out who this guy is—after all, we don't *really* know if he's a friend or foe—but my gut says to press on. Kathy and I rush through the newly opened doorway.

Back into the abyss.

22

We close the doorway behind us. My heart is pounding against my throat.

"Do you think he heard us?" Kathy whispers.

I put my ear against the door and listen for a few seconds. "I don't think so. But I'm not about to stick around and find out." I proceed down the hallway. "The fallout shelter is down this way."

I should be relieved. After all, this is one section of the mall I've been down before. There's nothing new about this—at least not geographically. From an *existential* standpoint, there's a lot more to fear. I can't help but wonder what barbarity might await us at the end of this tunnel.

Focus, Luke.

"It's just around this corner," I say. "This will lead us to the fake fridge."

"I'm sorry, the *what*?" Kathy asks.

"There are two refrigerators in the shelter. One is real,

and the other one is a fake. It leads to the tunnel we're in right now."

"The fridge is a secret door?" Kathy purses her lips.

"Yes, and there will be time for a lively discourse about how much of a damn funhouse this mall is when we're clear of Stride—or whoever that was." I press on. "Let's go."

We turn the corner and approach the entrance to the shelter. From this side it just looks like a small mint-green door with a silver handle. I grab the handle and open it.

It's locked—because of course it is.

I jiggle the knob harder. "You have *got* to be kidding me. Can we not have *one* task go right the first time today?"

Kathy frowns. "It would appear that ship sailed when the nuke hit us."

I knock on the door. "Jack? Are you in there?"

No answer.

"*Jack.*" I knock again, slightly harder this time.

"Try a little louder."

"I don't want to draw attention to us, in case Patent Leather Man is listening in."

"I don't care if the Zodiac Killer hears us. We don't have time to muck about." Kathy approaches the door and pounds her fist against it. "*Brookie!* Are you in there?"

I hear a muffled commotion behind the door, and my heart skips a beat. The silver handle shakes a bit. I knock louder. "*Jack!* Is that you?"

I hear a stifled male voice from the other side of the door. "*Luke?*"

Jack! It must be him! Who else in the mall would call me by my name? I knock harder. "Yes, it's me! Can you open the door?"

The voice says something, but I can't quite discern the

words being spoken through the fridge door. "Can you speak up? I can't hear you through the door!"

I hear the voice again. It's still unclear, but I distinguish a few words: *tied* and *push*. "Are you tied up? Is that what you're trying to say?"

The voice rings through. "Yes." Then something I can't make out, followed by "*push*" again.

I turn to Kathy. "I think he's tied up. So he can't open the fridge from the inside."

"Is he saying to *push* it open? How can that work if it's locked?"

"I don't know. But if Jack's in there, I'll break the door down if I have to. It's just a fridge door. Those are never *that* solid."

"I thought it was a fake fridge door."

I shrug. "If it's not even legitimate, it *really* can't be that strong. Come on, if we both throw our bodies against it, I bet we can break it down."

Kathy takes off her glasses and wipes them. "Let's do it." She braces her body. "On three?"

"Brilliant." I mimic her stance. "One, two, *three!*"

We throw our bodies in tandem at the door. It opens up easily and we fall into a heap on the floor. *Damn.* That was almost too easy. I can't believe I didn't think of breaking the door down in the first place. *Maybe because you're not Jack.*

No. Not right now, demons.

I realize in this moment that I'm on top of Kathy. "Sorry." I rise and dust myself off.

We're back in the fallout shelter. Everything is as we left it, except there's a new lantern on the table. And there is someone sitting on the bottom bunk, arms behind tied his back and feet bound together.

But it isn't Jack. Or Brooklyn. Or Stride.

It's Lavender Pit Stains Guy.

"*You.*" I realize the uncomfortable fact that LPSG knows my name and I don't know his. "How'd...*you* get here?"

"First things first." LPSG wiggles his arms and legs. Several ropes bind them. "Can you help me out of these?"

"You *know* this guy?" Kathy asks.

"He helped us out of the Electronix gate right at the beginning of everything yesterday morning." I turn to LPSG. "This is Kathy; she's looking for her daughter. And Kathy, this is...uh..."

LPSG snorts flippantly. "Guess I never gave you my name. It's Bruce."

"Bruce, right." I untie the knot behind his hands and around his feet. They're poorly tied, so it takes no time at all. "I was hoping you were okay. You disappeared after we got out of the Electronix."

"Yeah. I was panicked. And apparently for good reason." Bruce stretches his arms above his head. True to form, his pit stains are as striking as ever. "I realized right as you and that scrawny blond kid—Jack, right?—were crawling out that I had absolutely no reason to trust you. So I ran."

"How were you able to see?" I ask.

"Used my cell phone light. Eventually I took shelter in *Doctor Sweetz.* The candy shop. I was there for a few hours before I fell asleep from exhaustion. I had just done a huge workout yesterday morning, so once the adrenaline dropped, I was out. I woke up here, tied up."

"Did you eat any of the candy?" Kathy asks.

I turn to her and frown. "Why does that matter?"

Kathy ignores me. "Did you?"

Bruce nods. "Yeah, I got hungry. I normally try to avoid

simple carbs but figured yesterday was a good day to cheat. Why do you ask?"

Kathy shrugs. "I was wondering if the candy was spiked with something that made you fall asleep."

Bruce stands and stretches his legs out. "It's possible, I guess. I did fall asleep pretty soon after eating some gummy sharks. I just thought I was tired."

Kathy sits next to him on the bed. "Yeah, but you would have woken up if someone tried carrying you away."

Bruce scratches his temple. "Guess I didn't think of it that way."

"That's because you're not a mother," Kathy says.

I'm getting sick of the small talk. We need to find Jack. "How long have you been here?"

Bruce shrugs. "No idea. There's not a clock in here, but it feels like at least a few hours since I woke up. I'm starved, you bring any food?"

"Kathy has some granola bars in her bag."

Kathy grabs one out of her bag and tosses it to Bruce. He places the whole thing in his mouth and swallows after chewing maybe twice. Impressive, to be sure, but I have no time to process this. We have more important items on our agenda.

"Have you seen Jack?"

"Or my daughter, Brookie? She's sixteen years old, wearing a Catholic girls' school uniform."

Bruce shakes his head. "No, sorry."

"Has anyone else been down here?" I ask.

Bruce paces through the shelter. "Right when I was waking up, there was someone. He left the lantern on the table. Late thirties, dark gray suit. Shiny shoes. Couldn't get a good look at his face. I think he saw I was waking up and ran out."

"*Stride*," Kathy says. "It's gotta be him!"

"Could be." I turn to Bruce. "Which way did he go?"

Bruce points through the main door of the shelter—the door that leads to the stairwell. "Through there. I heard him say something on his walkie-talkie. Something about going to the offices?"

"That's our next clue, then." Kathy pulls a brightly colored pamphlet out of her pocket. "The admin offices. They're on the second floor. The new ones Jake Stride Junior built when he turned the old office into the lounge. I had a feeling we might be heading there next."

"Where'd you get that?" I eye her pamphlet.

"It's a map of the mall. They were by the directory. I grabbed a few when we were outside the Candleworks. Men don't notice *anything*, do they?"

"Very funny," I say. "Just one problem. The stairwell is locked. And I don't know if it's safe to go back through the lounge. Stride might still be in there."

"I don't think the stairwell will be a problem." Bruce shifts his eyes toward the table, where the new lantern shines. The light of the lantern reflects off something metallic next to it. "He left a set of keys."

Oh. My God. "You're kidding me!" I jump up and grab them. "He left his *keys* here?"

Bruce shrugs. "I don't know if they'll work in the stairwell, but yeah."

"That's almost *too* convenient." Kathy crosses her arms. "How would he get around if he left his keys here?"

"He probably has multiple sets," I say. "He's the CEO, after all. Plus there's a bunch of custodial stuff right at the entrance to the main tunnel leading to the shelter. He probably swiped an extra pair from there."

"Still, though," Kathy says. "Something doesn't add up. Why would he leave them here with Bruce?"

Bruce sits down at the table. "I *was* tied up. Guess he didn't think I'd get out. He did seem to be in a hurry when I woke up."

"I'm not questioning it." I toss the keyring into the air and catch it. "Kathy, this is our first lucky break since the alarms. We have keys, meaning we may have access to the entire friggin' *mall*, and we need to get out of here before Stride realizes he's left them behind."

Kathy sighs. "You're right. We should take them."

I glance over at Bruce. "You wanna come with us?"

He frowns. "Well, I'm gonna have to, if you have the keys. I tried getting around the mall by myself and ended up tied up in here."

Kathy rises. "Good. We could use your muscles."

"*Hey.*" I try not to look at my soft biceps. "I've done all right so far."

Kathy laughs. "Don't worry, Luke. You're just as pretty as Bruce."

"It's not *that*," I say. "Need I remind you I helped bring that fridge door down?"

"Yes, you're very strong and masculine." Kathy voice is pickled with mock admiration. "Can we go now? I have to save my daughter and you have to save your...Jack."

I try not to think about what my current standing with Jack may or may not be.

I attempt to pivot. "Yeah. Jack and Brooklyn. And anyone else Stride may have abducted."

"You think he's gotten more people?" Kathy asks.

I shrug and gesture at Bruce. "We know he got Bruce. He might be trying to round people up. Get them out of the way. The mall *is* deserted. Polly was the only person Jack and I ran into before we found you guys in the food court."

Kathy shudders. "God, you're right. I figured a lot of them got out before the gates closed, but that still doesn't account for the fact that we've run into so few people in the past twenty-four hours."

"Yeah," I say. "There's definitely something shifty going on. But our best bet of figuring it out is checking out Stride's office."

"Yeah," Bruce says. "Maybe that's where he's keeping your friends."

I pray that Bruce is right. And that Jack is okay.

23

Kathy is about a half-flight behind Bruce and me on the stairwell. "Do we even know what we're going to do when we get to the offices?"

"We'll improvise," I say. "Based on what we find."

Kathy rolls her eyes. "How well has that worked out for you so far?"

I stop and turn around. "That's what we've all been doing this whole damn time, Kathy. And are we not all still alive?"

"Well, *you* are," Bruce says. "Who knows about your friends?"

Bruce is behind Kathy. I repurpose the dirty look I gave Kathy on him. "That's not even remotely helpful, Bruce."

He shrugs. "Just being realistic."

And he's right. For all we know, we'll find Jack and Brooklyn's bodies drawn and quartered in the mall offices—if we find anything at all. God, I *hate* this day. And this mall. And whatever warped demon is the ringleader behind all of it.

"Like Polly said, all we can do is prepare for the worst and hope for the best." I grab the keys out of my pocket as the three of us arrive at the second-floor landing in the stairwell. "One of these should open this door, right?"

Kathy shifts her focus to the keyring. "Is there a master?"

"I don't think so," I fumble through the ring. "They don't appear to be labeled. We're gonna have to do this the old-fashioned way."

I try the first key. No luck there. Doesn't even fit into the lock.

The second key fits into the lock but doesn't turn.

The third key appears to be for a car.

The fourth goes into the lock...and *turns*! Hallelujah!

"Got it!" I say. "I think these keys are about to make our life in this mall a *lot* easier."

"Lord willing." Kathy approaches me from behind. "Do you think they'll open up the offices?"

"Only one way to find out." I open the door.

The second floor of the MetroMall mostly contains smaller family-owned specialty shops. All the big name-brand stores are on the first and third floors. Here on the second floor, there are a few sit-down restaurants, boutiques, and salons. I make a mental note to check out the restaurants later for any extra food.

"Where are the offices located?" I ask Kathy.

Kathy pulls out her map. "We're right by the antiques place right now...here it is! We're gonna want to head to the east wing of the second floor. That's where the admin offices should be."

Kathy leads us down the hallway.

Bruce trails us by a few yards. "Do you two have any weapons?"

Kathy and I both stop and turn around. Kathy is the first to speak. "Why do you ask?"

Bruce pauses. "I mean...just in case we run into someone bad in there. Seems like a reasonable question."

"Fair enough," I say. "Yeah, I have a hunting knife, and Kathy has hers from the sushi place."

Bruce squints his eyes. "No guns?"

I shake my head. "They don't sell guns here. We've found some other weapons, but it's not like any of us brought firearms to the mall."

Bruce laughs. "Betcha wish you had now."

I frown. "If I had the foresight to predict total nuclear calamity and the possible eclipse of all of humanity, yeah, the thought might have crossed my mind. Do you have anything?"

Bruce shakes his head. "I was trying to find one when I got knocked out."

Kathy lowers her map. "I thought you were in the candy shop and you fell asleep."

Bruce runs his fingers through his hair. "Yeah. When the candy knocked me out—if it *was* the candy that knocked me out. I was trying to fashion a large peppermint stick into a shiv when I fell asleep. Obviously when I woke up, it was gone."

Not gonna lie, the idea of this huge, ripped dude desperately trying to lick a peppermint stick into a weapon is oddly comical to me. I can't help but laugh. "*God*, this is a weird day."

"No kidding," Bruce says. "Any chance I could get one of your knives?"

Kathy goes into her pack, grabs one of her sushi knives,

and holds it out. "Here, take mine. You're in the back, and we should be prepared."

Bruce grabs the knife from Kathy and smiles. "Thanks. Are we almost there?"

Kathy nods. "See that double door ahead?

About twenty yards ahead of us, at the end of the walkway, stand two frosted glass doors. Etched into the glass are the words, "*Mall Employees Only Beyond This Point.*"

I pause at the door. "So this is it."

Kathy grabs her own knife. "Yeah. You ready?"

I nod. "Bruce?"

Bruce grips his sushi knife and nods.

We walk in.

The administrative offices are deserted. This is at once a relief—no bad guys—and a disappointment—no Jack or Brooklyn.

I sigh. "*Dammit.* Where could they be?"

Kathy gestures to the far walls of the office. Several closed doors speckle the perimeter. "I think those are the heads' offices. The mall directors, et cetera. They could have hidden Brookie and Jack in there. If they're not here, there may be clues to lead us somewhere else. Let's explore."

"I'll guard the entrance." Bruce grabs a nearby chair and sits down next to the double doors.

I give Bruce a thumbs-up. "Good idea." *And not just because you have the body of a professional wrestler turned actor.*

I take a look at the reception desk. A stapler, a three-hole punch, several sheets of loose printing paper. Nothing out of the ordinary here. A memorandum catches my eye. "*Important Reminder from the CEO,*" it reads. The date on it is the day before yesterday. The last day of normalcy.

Dear MetroMall Administrative Employees,

This is your friendly reminder that, in MetroMall's continued efforts to support its staff, the workday will not begin until 1:00pm tomorrow afternoon. Please use this time to catch up on sleep, spend time with family, or work on personal projects. Happy Employee Relief Day!

Cordially,

Maxwell Stride, CEO

Ironic twist. All of the admins got the morning off the day all hell broke loose in the world. Bet they wish they had come to work after all. At least the mall is safe.

Safer, at least.

Besides the memo, there isn't much to find in the open space of the office. Meaning that Kathy and I will have to search the outer closed-door offices. A knot forms in my stomach.

There are three doors total. The first, on the left, reads *Tanya Shepard, CFO*. The second, on the right: *Sebastián Ortiz, COO*. And in the middle, three words that feel as engraved into my psyche as they are on the brass nameplate:

Maxwell Stride, CEO.

"It's gotta be Stride's office, right?" I ask Kathy. "That's where any clues would be waiting for us."

Kathy nods. "Let's try it."

The CEO office door is made of a smooth, dark reddish-brown wood—different from the other two offices. Walnut, maybe? Or mahogany? *That doesn't matter, Luke, just open the goddamn door.*

I grab the keys out of my pocket. My hand is shaking and they jingle slightly. The first key—the one that was too big for the stairwell door—fits in and turns. I slowly rotate my head toward Kathy and mouth the word, "*Ready?*"

She nods. We open the door.

No expense has been spared in Stride's décor. Potted plants and fine art litter the space. A massive conference table sits in the middle, and a large wooden desk—which I recognize as Jacob Stride's original from the photo in the rec room—stands resolute in the back. And behind the desk, in an office chair—

"*Jack!*" My eyes fill with tears. There's no mistaking the mop of blond hair on his head or the badass pothead skull on his black T-shirt.

Jack looks up. His mouth is covered with duct tape, and he's tied to the chair. But his eyes widen to the size of dinner plates. He grunts through the duct tape. I can only assume he's trying to say my name.

I run over to him and throw my arms around him. "We found you! God, Jack, I was so worried."

Jack continues to grunt behind the duct tape.

I chuckle softly. "Okay, I get it. This may hurt, sorry." I rip the duct tape off of Jack's mouth. A layer of dead skin and some of his stubble comes with it.

Jack doesn't seem to notice. "*Luke!* How the hell did you find me?"

"We followed a trail of breadcrumbs." I dust off Jack's shoulders. "But that doesn't matter right now. Are you okay?"

Kathy enters the office. "Where's Brookie?"

Jack frowns. "F-Fine. I'm fine." He sees Kathy. "I'm afraid I have no idea where they took Brooklyn, though. I'm sorry, Kathy."

"What happened to you?" I ask. "I woke up a few hours after your watch was supposed to end."

Jack swallows. "Yeah, and we were fine. We were maybe an hour in and Brooklyn decided she wanted a Forevergreen. I figured, what the hell, Candleworks isn't *that* far from the food court, and we could all use something to brighten things up a bit. And it's not a bad idea to have another light, one not dependent on batteries."

"So you *left your post*?" Kathy's voice is venomous.

"Yes, and hindsight is *forever* twenty-twenty." Jack's voice is equally as pointed. "Plus she had a small nosebleed, so I figured I'd find some tissue paper at the Candleworks. Two birds one stone, right?"

"So *that's* where the blood came from," I say.

"Oh, yeah," Jack says. "I didn't want to take her with me. A trail of blood isn't exactly great for keeping our location on the DL."

I start to untie the rope around Jack's hands. "So you got to Candleworks?"

"Yeah, never went in, though. I heard some sort of ruckus back by the fountain. I shouted to Brooklyn to see if everything was okay. She didn't respond. So I turned around and..."

"And *what*?" Kathy lip trembles.

"Someone was behind me. A big guy. Bigger than I am. I didn't get to see his face, though, because he grabbed my headlamp and threw it on the floor. He hit me over the head with something and I blacked out. I woke up here. And that's all I know."

"*Stride*," I say. "It has to be him. Same guy who got Bruce."

Jack raises an eyebrow. "Bruce?"

"The muscley guy from Electronix," I say. "The one who helped us with the gate. We ran into him again and he's been helping us out."

Kathy frowns. "But how could Stride be in two places at once? We saw scuff marks from his shoes at the fountain. If you heard a struggle while you were at the Candleworks, it must have been someone else who got you."

"He probably has a henchman, then," Jack says. "Wouldn't be too hard to find some sniveling coward to do his dirty work."

"Doesn't matter." I grab the keys out of my pocket and place them on the desk. "He left his keys at the fallout shelter. We went back there. That's where we found Bruce."

"You went *back* to the shelter?"

"You've missed a lot." I continue working on Jack's ropes. They're a lot tighter than Bruce's were. "Kathy, can you help me with these?"

Kathy doesn't move. "Are they that tight? Bruce's practically fell off."

Jack wiggles his hands around. "I've been trying to free myself for an hour. These aren't moving."

Kathy peers through the door of the office. "Has anyone else come through here while you were awake? If they got you, they got Brookie too."

"I've only been awake an hour." Jack's face falls. "I'm sorry, Kathy. I shouldn't have left her alone."

"No, you *shouldn't* have." Kathy's voice breaks a bit, but she maintains her composure. "But I know my daughter. She's a survivor. She's okay, somewhere in this mall."

"Well, we have one more person on our rescue mission team. *God*, these knots are intricate." I grab the hunting knife out of my pocket and cut the ropes around his arms and legs. "*There*. With you on our team, we'll find her in no time."

"I wouldn't be so sure of that." Bruce's voice comes from behind me.

"*Again* with the negatives." I turn around. "Can't you have a little—"

I stop. Bruce has Kathy in a headlock. The light of my headlamp catches a glint of silver metal. He's holding something against her head.

Oh God.

A *gun.*

24

Bruce holds the gun to Kathy's left temple. "I'm gonna count to three. And you're going to *slowly* put your knife on the floor."

Jack starts to stand, but I instinctively put my hand on his right shoulder to keep him seated. "What the hell? You're a bad guy now?"

"*One.*" Bruce tightens his arm around Kathy's throat.

She whimpers in pain.

"Okay, *okay*. You win. Just don't hurt any of us." I slowly place my knife on the floor.

"Kick it over here."

"Fine." I place my right foot on top of the knife and gently thrust it across the room. "Now will you tell us what's going on?"

Bruce steps on the knife. "The keys, too. Give them to me."

I slowly take the keys off of the top of Stride's desk and underhand them to Bruce. "Anything else? My wallet, perhaps?"

"Easy, funny guy." Bruce keeps Kathy in her headlock and bends down to pick up the knife and keys. Once he has them, he throws Kathy to the floor.

Kathy cries out as her knees hit the tiled floor.

Bruce slowly backs out of the office doorway, his gun still pointed at Kathy. "All of you, behind the desk."

Kathy slowly gets up, sniffling, and shuffles to where we are behind the desk.

"You feel good? Big, strong man throwing around a woman like that?" I realize that mouthing off is likely impractical, but I can't help it. I'm *pissed*. "In case you need a reminder, the two of us *saved* your ass in the bunker."

Bruce laughs. "You idiots. You didn't save anything. I was in the bunker taking stock. I heard you coming from a mile away and threw some rope around my arms."

Dammit. Those ropes did untie super easily. *Why didn't I see this coming?*

Kathy rubs her right knee. "Why on earth would you pretend to be a prisoner? Couldn't you just have shot us when we walked through the door?"

"Oh, it's not my job to kill you." Bruce grins. "Just to...*ensnare* you."

"Ensnare us?" Jack asks. "What the hell are you talking about?"

Bruce brandishes his gun. "I realize it's a big word. I'm trapping you, like animals."

I grit my teeth. "Why are you doing this? Why *us*? Why here?"

"Don't worry. You're not special," Bruce says. "Mr. Stride just believes it will be easier to manage the mall once he can control all the survivors."

"So it *is* Stride," Kathy says. "He's the mastermind behind everything going on?"

"He's part of it." Bruce's smile grows. I can see every grimy tooth in his skull. "I bumped into him pretty soon after I left your sorry asses at the Electronix store. He took one look at my muscles and knew he wanted my strength on his side. So he made me a deal."

"What kind of deal?" Jack quivers slightly.

"I help him with locking up everyone in the mall, and he makes me second in command."

"But *why* imprison the survivors?" Kathy asks. "Why not work together to help each other through this?"

"You're dumber than you look, bitch." Bruce spits on the floor. "Stride knows human beings are inherently selfish. The only person you can wholly trust is yourself. He knew when the mall shut down there would be an immediate run on its resources. If he controls their flow, though, he can ensure long-term survival."

"But there's plenty of food," Jack says. "All the stalls in the food court, plus the meals at SportsGoods. Not to mention the restaurants, the drugstores. We wouldn't run out that quickly. And someone's gonna rescue us eventually."

"You think so?" Bruce asks. "Do you really, *truly*, bottom-of-your-heart think that?"

Jack doesn't respond. The silence is deafening.

I slowly hold a hand up in defiance. "Practical or not, it's the right thing to do."

Bruce aims his gun at me and snickers. "The *right* thing. And what happens if no one comes? Stride has connections to the feds. They called him a few days before and warned him that shit was about to hit the fan. The world was going to end and they couldn't ensure his protection."

"And if someone *does* come to help?" Kathy asks. "What then?"

Bruce smiles. "That's why we're not going to kill you. At least, not *yet*."

Several thousand chills run down my spine. None of us are able to say a word.

Bruce stares the three of us down. "For now, Stride just wants to *control* the people in the mall. Some are locked up in the gated stores. I threw some in bathrooms, some in fitting rooms in the department stores. The three of you are the first to be locked in these offices. Consider yourselves lucky. This office space is one of the more luxurious makeshift prisons we have to offer."

"But *where* is my Brookie?" Kathy's face is bathed in tears, but her composure is resolute. "Did you take her? Is she okay?"

"She's alive. Stride took care of her personally after getting *this* dickhead." He gestures to Jack. "He knocked both of them out with a baseball bat he got at SportsGoods. Guess he learned from your other friend that stabbing was a little"—he clears his throat—"*messy*."

I gasp. "So he *was* the one who stabbed Polly?"

Bruce nods slowly. "He needed the radio in her basket. Last one in the store. And Stride couldn't have *her* reaching out to the outside world. Only he and his most loyal associates should be trusted with that kind of information right now."

"Why didn't he lock her away?" Jack asks.

Bruce rolls his eyes so far I can only see their whites. "Don't you ever *listen*? A man of Maxwell Stride's station hires other people to clean up his messes. But I guess you two jackasses got to the scene and wrapped the girl up before I was able to take care of it."

"But *where* is my Brookie?" Her entire body is shaking.

"Oh, come *on* now." Bruce laughs. "*Why* would I tell you that? Your brat is fine. As long as she watches that pretty little mouth of hers."

Kathy jumps to her feet and slams her hands on the desk. "She is *sixteen*, you bastard."

Bruce draws the gun again and points it directly at Kathy's heart. "Don't do anything stupid. Don't want anything to happen to *Mommy*, do we?"

Kathy backs down, but her hands are clenched into tight fists.

Bruce brings his arm down again. "That's what I thought. Now, I believe you mentioned there are two more bozos in the food court waiting for me. *Ciao*." He closes the office door.

The lock clicks a few seconds later.

I slowly slump down to the floor and place my head in my hands. "Jesus *Christ*. I should have seen this coming."

"Give yourself a break," Jack says. "How on earth could you have predicted *any* of this?"

"The loose ropes, the keys conveniently left behind, Bruce asking about our weapons. The red flags were *right* there, laid out like a goddamn picnic, and I trusted him without a second thought."

Kathy places a hand on my shoulder. "I trusted him, too, Luke. It's not your fault. We're all in the same boat. We had no other choice. Your assumption that people are innately decent is a *good* thing."

"Still, though, the writing was on the wall, and it was crystal clear. Now we're right back where we started."

Jack turns to me. "Not true. You found me."

He's smiling. The same way he smiled when we were flirting at the SportsGoods. Has he come around? *Not the time, Luke.*

"We did." I return the smile. "Small mercies. But we're still locked away. With no knowledge of what's coming next."

Jack cocks his head to one side. "Not *exactly*. We know he's headed to the food court. And he'll likely trick Polly and Don the same way he tricked you. Lure them into a corner and trap them."

I groan. "Somehow, that doesn't make me feel any better."

"I'm not trying to make you feel better," Jack says. "I mean —not that I don't *want* you to feel better. I'm just saying that Bruce will be gone for at least half an hour. Probably longer. And the meathead forgot to tie us up."

I look around the office. "He still locked us in, though."

"Yeah, and I'm guessing that a mall administrative office isn't exactly a military fortress." Jack stands. "One wooden door stands between us and freedom. I think we can handle that."

"What, you wanna break the door down?" I glance at the door. "It looks pretty solid."

"Yeah, so does every object in this office." Jack grabs a large black globe from Stride's desk. He strains slightly under its weight. "Take this thing, for instance. It's made of solid marble. I've been in here a while, had a chance to take stock. With the three of us combined, I bet we could take that door down."

I have to stop myself from swooning. Jack is *so* hot right now.

Kathy walks over and examines the door. "Do you really think we could bring it down?"

"Yeah." Jack gestures to some of the small sculptures

ornamenting the space. "You each take one of those statuettes. We can pound the door with them until it's weak enough for us to kick open."

I grab a bronze bust from a nearby bookshelf. I recognize the subject almost immediately. It's a nearly life-size effigy of the head and shoulders of the elder Jacob Stride, bolo tie and all. Oddly poetic that Papa Stride should help us out of the quandary into which his grandson placed us.

Kathy handles some sort of contemporary deconstructed figure of a lion—or at least that's what I think it is—made of steel. Also a symbolically appropriate choice.

Jack, carrying the globe, approaches the office door.

I grab his arm. "Wait. Won't this make a ton of noise? What if Bruce hears us? Or what if Stride walks into the admin space?"

"That's a risk we're gonna have to take," Jack says. "We don't have any other options."

"We could just wait it out and hope for the best."

Jack shakes his head. "Bruce made it pretty clear that Stride intends for us to die in here. Maybe not today or tomorrow, but that's our ultimate fate. If that's the best we can hope for, I'm not sold."

"He's right," Kathy says. "And us being here won't do Brookie any good."

The three of us line up at the door with our chosen objects in hand.

Jack grabs a permanent marker off the desk and draws an X on its center left segment. "We're going to want to aim close to the doorknob, but not right on it. That's the weakest point of the door."

"How on earth do you know that?" I ask.

Jack smiles. "Not my first rodeo."

"How many doors *have* you knocked down?"

"Story for another time. Let's take turns. Me first, and then Luke, and then Kathy."

I silently pray that there are no malicious persons nearby.

Jack raises the globe—I catch a quick glance of his beautifully chiseled arms—and brings it down on the X. The clash of marble on wood resounds through Stride's office.

My heart stops for a moment—if anyone heard that, we'll be seeing them soon. But there is no response to the noise.

"Guess it's my turn." I tentatively lift Jacob Stride's head over mine and pummel his bust, shoulders first, at the X. My resulting clamor is not nearly as impressive as Jack's—nor is my lifting form—but it leaves a small indentation in the door.

Kathy brings her lion down right after me. We repeat the cycle four more times. The gouge in the door slowly grows.

Jack takes a look at our progress. "Okay, that might do it. Stand back."

"Wait," I say. "Can I do it?"

Jack lowers his globe and cracks a small smile. "Go for it, Chesterfield."

I step a few feet away from the door, then run at it and kick the X with my right foot. The door buckles in on itself. I give it a few more kicks and it's down.

Huh. Maybe *I'm* hot too.

Jack admires the mahogany remains. "Luke! Nice job!"

I turn to him. "It was your idea to bust the door down."

Kathy marches out the doorway. "Call it a team effort. Now what?"

"We know that Bruce is down in the food court," I say. "But he took our weapons, so we don't stand a chance against him."

"Don't be so sure." Kathy grabs her bag from behind the desk. "He didn't take my second knife."

Jack laughs. "Wow, he is *really* bad at detaining people. And we *do* have some heavy, blunt objects. We're not *completely* defenseless."

I eye the marble sphere in Jack's hand. "Do you really want to carry that globe all the way through the mall?"

Jack shrugs. "It weighs less than it looks."

I eye Jack's bicep. *Yeah, right.*

"Also, we have no way of getting back down to the first floor without the keys," I say.

"What about through the lounge?" Jack asks.

"Not a great option. Stride almost caught us when we came through the lounge to the bunker. He's probably in and out a lot."

"Then we'll figure something else out." Jack glances up at a clock in Stride's office. "It's been about ten minutes since Bruce left, so we need to at least get out of here."

"We need to find a place to hide, then." Kathy slowly spins around, examining the offices. "Maybe we can settle into another one of the offices? We can regroup and plan from there. And we still need to find Brookie."

"Here isn't a great idea. Bruce could come back." I pause for a moment, then it hits me. "*But* there are a bunch of restaurants on the second floor. We can hole up in a kitchen. We could even grab something to eat, maybe see if we can find some more cutlery to defend ourselves."

Jack smiles. "Good idea, Chesterfield. Plenty of places to hide in a restaurant, too. Under tables, in a pantry. Just in case someone nasty comes in."

"Brilliant," I say. "Where do you think we should go, then?"

Jack picks Kathy's map up off of the desk and unfolds it. "*Chez Océane* is nearby. You like French food?"

"*But of course,*" I reply in a horrible French accent.

Jack chuckles. "Then we're decided. *Allons-y!*"

We walk out of Stride's office and pause at the double glass doors of the admin area. We crack the doors open and peek through. No Bruce, no Stride.

Chez Océane is about a fifteen-minute walk from the administrative offices. At first, I was concerned that it was too close to Stride's office and that Bruce may find us here, but my anxieties are instantly alleviated when I see the size of the MetroMall bloc of fancy restaurants. A complete search of the area would take at least an hour. And Bruce and Stride won't know we've escaped for a while. We're safe, for now.

The exterior of the restaurant is bedecked in a series of jewel-encrusted fish. More tacky than classy, in my opinion, but then again no one consulted me in the design process. We walk past the hostess podium to the interior dining area. There are fifteen or so tables, each one covered in a luxurious red tablecloth with an iron candelabra centerpiece. Several broken dishes litter the floor, but every candelabra has managed to steadfastly remain on its respective table.

We walk to the back of the restaurant, through a door marked *La Cuisine*, and into the kitchen. We search every cupboard and drawer, but there is nothing sharp in sight.

"*Dammit.*" Jack closes the final drawer. "Stride or one of his lackeys must have cleared the kitchen of any potential weapons. I bet he's done the same to all the restaurants on the second floor."

I sit on the counter. "Why not the first floor? There was still plenty of stuff in the food court stalls."

"Most of the restaurants don't open until evening." Jack

paces the kitchen. "They would have been the first place he could clear out without anyone noticing. He was probably trying to clear the food court when he abducted me and Brooklyn."

I walk into a pantry. "At least there's food. Now that things have calmed down a smidge, I'm starting to get a little hungry."

"Yeah, check the freezer," Jack says. "Maybe there's something in there that's already cooked up. Some cured meats, perhaps."

The freezer is to the side of the kitchen, opposite the pantry. A solid silver door with a large handle stands guard. I pull a few times, but it's stuck. "Freezer door isn't budging."

"Just pull a little harder," Kathy says. "I used to work in a restaurant kitchen. Freezer doors can be a little testy sometimes."

I yank the door handle a few more times, and finally the door gives way. It swings open and the sight I behold causes me to let out a yelp.

I'm greeted not by a collection of meats, but by a woman. Very thin, long black hair and wearing a white chef's jacket and black pants. She looks me straight in the eye and smiles weakly.

"*Dieu, merci.* You have saved me."

She collapses into my arms.

25

A petite and possibly French woman lies unconscious in my arms after having fallen out of a freezer. I am understandably flummoxed.

I crane my neck toward the pantry. "Uh...guys?"

Jack is shifting through the kitchen drawers. "What?"

"There was a woman in the freezer. And she fainted. And now I am holding her."

"I'm sorry...*what*?" Jack stops what he's doing and runs over.

I pivot slightly, taking care not to move Unconscious Petite French Chef Woman in case she's injured, but enough to reveal her to Jack. "I opened the freezer. And she was apparently inside."

Jack brushes her hair off her face and takes a look. "Yikes. And she's alive?"

"Yeah, she fainted, but she said something to me before she fell unconscious."

"How long do you think she was in there?" Kathy asks.

I shrug. "No idea. Can't have been too long, or else there's no way she'd be alive."

"The freezer wouldn't be on since the power went out. Still, though, it would have been pretty cold. Let me feel her heartbeat." Jack presses two fingers under her wrist. "Her heart's beating, but it's weak. Probably hypothermia. We need to warm her up. Help me get her away from the freezer."

Jack lifts Unconscious Petite French Chef Woman's legs, and we carry her toward the pantry.

I slowly lower her to the floor. "Kathy. Can you grab some of the tablecloths from the dining room? We can use them as blankets."

"Good idea." Kathy runs out of the kitchen and comes back a few seconds later with two tablecloths in tow.

We wrap UPFCW up. A few minutes pass and she slowly comes to. She looks around in fretful bewilderment at her burritolike swaddling.

Jack leans down next to her and speaks softly. "Hey. I'm Jack, and this is Luke and Kathy. Everything's okay. You're safe. We're just warming you up."

UPFCW takes a moment to garner the energy to speak. "Thank you." Her words are slurred, but I'm not sure if it's because of her condition or her accent. "I thought I was a— how do you say?—*goner*."

I crouch down. "Not on our watch."

She coughs lightly. "Véronique. My name."

"Pleased to meet you, Véronique," I say. "I know you need to rest, but can you tell us how you ended up in the freezer?"

Véronique closes her eyes. "It was but a few hours ago. I had been hiding in the kitchen. I worked here before. Head chef. Best *sole meunière* in the city. I was the only one in the restaurant. It was early when *l'explosion* occurred."

"Why were you in so early?" Jack asks.

"Once a week to take inventory. I guess it was my lucky day. Or unlucky. I suppose it depends on your thinking."

I frown. "And you were hiding out here the whole time?"

"*Oui*. I had no idea if anyone else in the *centre* was alive. But I had the entire kitchen to myself. I thought nothing of it. I went to the pantry and waited for rescue to arrive."

"And then someone *did* show up," Kathy says.

Vèronique nods. "A man, very big. *Beaucoup de* muscles."

I slowly exhale. "Bruce."

"Is that his name?" Véronique opens her eyes. "I did not learn it. He had sneaked up behind me and grabbed me. Threw me in the freezer. Lucky it was not too cold. But cold enough to worry."

"My God," Kathy says. "What a monster."

"*Oui, un monstre horrible*. As I say, I thought I was to die. If not from the cold, then lack of air. I have no idea why a man such as that would attack me in this way."

"He's working for Maxwell Stride, the mall's CEO," Jack says. "They're trying to lock up all the survivors in the mall so they can keep all the food and resources to themselves."

"*Monsieur Stride?*" Véronique sits up slightly. "This cannot be possible. He is a frequent patron of my restaurant. I saw him just last week. He said hello on his way to the offices."

"Well, that was then." Kathy stands up and paces the kitchen. "Rich, entitled men do horrifying things when they're afraid."

"*C'est terrible*. I regret having ever served him a single bowl of *bouillabaisse*."

Jack surveys the counter. "Looks like Bruce also cleared the kitchen of all your cutlery. Did you have anything in the freezer with you that we could use as a weapon?"

Véronique squints her eyes. "You are preparing for a battle?"

"We just want to be prepared for anything," I say. "We know Bruce has a gun. Stride probably does too."

"I see." Véronique raises her hand slowly and motions to the freezer. "In the icebox, there is a cleaver. It was inside when I was attacked."

"Perfect." Kathy walks into the freezer—the door is still open—and walks out brandishing a large meat cleaver.

I glance around the kitchen. "If Bruce has already been here, it's unlikely he'll return, at least for now. Véronique, I know you need your rest. But is there anything in the freezer, maybe something protein heavy, that we can prepare without heat?"

Véronique nods. "We have ingredients for *charcuterie*. We are mostly serving seafood at *Chez Océane*, but it is very popular for appetizer. Everything will be on the second shelf on the right."

"Wonderful," I say. "Now relax. You've gotta get your body heat back up to normal."

"*Merci encore*, Luke," Vèronique shuts her eyes again. "*Mon sauveur*."

I know just enough French to be flattered. "All I did was open the door. Take a nap. We'll have some food ready for you when you wake up."

From Vèronique's charcuterie shelf, we find duck *pâté*, pork liver *mousse*, and something marked *Jambon de Bayonne*, which appears to be the French version of prosciutto. We find a silver serving platter in the pantry and pile as many meats as we can on top. Kathy grabs another tablecloth from the dining room and we arrange a nice little picnic. Jack even takes a moment to tastefully arrange the platter's contents.

For a fleeting moment, things feel normal.

Well, as normal as things *can* feel next to a hypothermic French woman wrapped in two velvet tablecloths.

I want to punch myself in the face when I realize that this is *technically* my second date with Jack. And this food is a *lot* fancier than the rehydrated camping food at the SportsGoods.

Then I remember that Jack and I have some major unpacking to do. It's not like we can talk about whatever it is we're going through with Kathy and Véronique—conscious or otherwise—around.

Then I wonder: *Will Jack and I ever get privacy?* Based on the vibes he's been giving out since we rescued him, I *think* he wants to talk to me. Maybe about last night? About his sudden change of heart? If I'm willing to share the *saucisson sec* that I found on the shelf next to the *jambon*? All equally legitimate concerns.

Also, gentle reminder, the literal world is ending. So maybe now isn't the time.

Jack and I can talk later. For now, we need keep the group together. People tend to disappear when left alone in this mall. Like Brooklyn. And likely Polly and Don at this point. I know Polly would give Bruce a hell of a fight, especially with her crossbow. I'm sure the two of them are okay, even if Bruce managed to intern them in the end.

That said, one thing is for sure: the worst is ahead of us.

26

———

A few hours pass. Véronique is still asleep, but we're monitoring her vitals and she's improving. As far as her body temperature goes, we have no idea if she's warming up or not. Jack did find a meat thermometer in one of the kitchen drawers, but the implications of using a thermometer designed for culinary use on a human being hit a little too close to home in our post-apocalyptic hellscape.

Jack, Kathy, and I have been sitting on the pantry side of the kitchen discussing our next move. But we've run out of ideas on how to get back to the first floor.

"Do we even want to get back down to the first floor?" Kathy surveys the MetroMall map. "My guess is they're locking most of the people up here."

"If by most, you mean at least four." Jack snags the map and lays it on the floor. "There are several places in the mall that Stride could turn into makeshift prisons. Bruce said they're using bathrooms, any space available. For all we know they've gated the food stalls and locked Don and Polly right where they left them."

A moment of silence passes.

I raise my hand. "Is there any more ham?"

Jack and Kathy stare blankly.

"What? It was good."

"Your unwavering commitment to your aesthetic is staggering," Jack says. "Check the freezer. There was quite a bit of food in there."

I walk across the kitchen. Véronique is stirring. I'm craving *jambon*, but I'll check on her real quick.

I kneel down to her level. "How's it going? You feeling better?"

Véronique smiles faintly. "Yes. Much better. And warmer. The three of you?"

"We're doing fine. We're trying to plan our next move."

"Next move?" Véronique sits up. "Why not just stay here?"

"Bruce and Stride want to lock everyone up in the mall besides themselves. And they're eventually going to realize that we escaped the admin offices. They'll be checking around to see if anyone else has escaped, too."

Véronique's eyes widen. "*Non.* They cannot put me back in the freezer. It was death."

"I'm sure it was. But we're gonna figure something out. You're welcome to join us."

"I will. I cannot be a sitting duck. An especially hideous fate for a chef, as it is I who is to cook the ducks, you see?"

I chuckle. "Sitting duck *a l'orange*, as it were."

"I realize the joke does not quite work, as my specialty is seafood. But it is the best I can do under the circumstances."

"Well done." I offer Véronique my hand. "Want to come join us by the pantry?"

Véronique gets on her feet. "It would be my pleasure."

I run into the freezer and grab one more slice of ham.

Then the two of us join Jack and Kathy on the opposite side of the kitchen.

"How are you feeling?" Kathy asks.

"Better, thank you. No more ice grip on my throat."

"The ideal state of one's throat," Jack says. "Véronique, I don't suppose you have any ideas how to get down to the first floor? Our friends are in the food court, and we want to check up on them."

Véronique frowns. "You have not tried the stairs?"

I shake my head. "The stairwell is locked. And we don't have a key."

"Not the stairwell." Véronique browses the map and points. "The escalators. In the *Beds n' Better* store. It is how I get to work every day."

"Oh my *God*." Jack slaps his palm to his forehead. "How could I be so dumb? Here I am thinking of ways to parachute downstairs and the easiest solution is right in front of me."

"How so?" I ask.

Jack places his finger on a large section on the map's right-hand side. "*Beds n' Better* is a furniture and home goods store. One of the biggest stores in the mall, and the only one that has two floors. One on the first story of the mall, and one on the second."

I gaze at the map. "And there's an escalator?"

"Well, with the power down, the technical term would be *staircase*."

"Funny. So we've had access to the second floor this whole time?"

Jack nods. "Guess I got tunnel vision, thinking about the stairwell. It didn't really matter at the time since we were trying to get to the third floor. No store in the mall has three levels."

"We shouldn't waste any time, then," I say. "We should go down to the food court now. Polly's still down there. We can regroup and search for Brooklyn together."

Jack bites his lip. "Polly has likely already been locked up somewhere. But she's smart and she's tough. Plus she has her badass crossbow hidden away. She's fine."

"Still, though." I pace the kitchen. "Shouldn't we check up on them?"

"If she's locked up, there's nothing we can do," Kathy says curtly. "I say we keep looking for Brookie. Just because you found *your* person doesn't mean our search-and-rescue is over." She silently beelines into the restaurant's dining area.

I don't even have time to ponder the significance of Jack's being called *my* person, nor to comment on the undeniable flair of Kathy's dramatic exit. "Kathy's right."

"We *do* have access to the first floor," Jack says. "We can search the area where Brooklyn was taken. Which just happens to be the fountain near the food court. We can check up on the others and search for clues about Brooklyn."

"All we found were scuff marks on the ground and a few drops of blood," I say. "Those have both been explained. We have nothing more to go off of."

Jack shrugs. "Maybe that's all *you* found, but eight eyes are better than four."

"Valid," I say. "Plus we could see if the scuff marks lead anywhere."

Jack places his hand over his heart in mock admiration. "Ladies and gents, take note. Luke had a good idea!"

"Hey!" I gently shove Jack's shoulder. "I managed to save *your* ass pretty well." I gently shove his shoulder.

"You got yourself locked up on the way, but credit where credit is due." Jack bites his lip. "Though, to be fair, you're only one for two on saving people. Fifty percent isn't exactly a great record."

I gasp. "*Jack*. That's a horrible joke."

"Which is why I didn't make it until Kathy left the room." Jack crosses toward the kitchen's exit. "Come on, let's go get her. Véronique, you good to go?"

Véronique stands up and raises two fists in the air. "*Oui*. Let us go and kick ass."

"Love the spirit," Jack says.

We enter the dining area. Kathy has fashioned a sack from one of the tablecloths. "I figured we should stock up on whatever we can find here. Don't worry, I already packed more of that pretentious prosciutto you like, Luke."

I glimpse at Kathy's tablecloth bag. "What else did you get?"

Kathy grabs one of the candelabras off of a table. "Stride may have cleared the kitchen of knives, but he didn't take everything. These are solid iron, and they're quite thorny. And there's a few shards of china on the floor that could work as blades." She finishes putting her pack together and hands it to Jack. "Who wants to carry this?"

I motion toward Jack. "I think most recently rescued should be pack mule."

Jack clasps his hands together. "Wouldn't that technically be Véronique?"

"Sorry, guess I should have clarified. Most recently rescued with a *normal* body temperature is the pack mule."

Kathy foists the sack into Jack's arms. "This *really* isn't the time to be joking. God only knows what that maniac is doing to my daughter."

Jack and I freeze and exchange uncomfortable looks.

"Right, sorry." Jack slings the makeshift rucksack over his left shoulder. "Just trying to lighten the mood."

"I get that. But Brookie needs me. You two can play house once we've rescued her." Kathy brandishes her cleaver in one hand and her sushi knife in the other. "That bastard has no idea what's coming for him."

Véronique peeks her head from the kitchen and shuffles to the front of the store. "Should I have something?"

"Grab another candelabra," Kathy says. "They won't do much against a gun, but it's better than nothing."

"*Fantastique.*" Véronique grabs a candelabra from a table near the front entrance. "I was always believing that these were too *rococo* for the atmosphere anyway."

"A much-needed update," I say. "Shall we, then?"

The restaurant sector of MetroMall is comprised of seven unique restaurants, each one offering its own distinct worldly cuisine. After the restaurants is a pharmacy—I'll keep them in mind if we need medical supplies—and a gift basket shop.

Finally, we behold the glorious monument to capitalism that is the second-floor entrance to *Beds n' Better*. The great maw beckons us inside with promises of soft affordable bedding and fluffy overpriced towels.

I take in the industrial splendor. "We should just spend the night here. This all looks much better than that sleeping bag."

Jack turns to me. "You didn't like the sleeping bag?"

I blink. "I didn't *mind* the sleeping bag." *Not the time, Luke. There will be time to discuss last night later.* "Sharing it, I mean. It was...*fine.*"

To be fair, the only time I've used that sleeping bag, I was enveloped in a vortex of despair and self-doubt, so I can't give a truly honest review of its functionality. I try to read Jack's expression, but he has a great poker face when it comes to matters of the heart.

Jack graciously chooses not to acknowledge the gargantuan elephant in our room. "Keep an eye out for anything we might use as a weapon. Or for protection."

I hold up the bust of Jacob Stride from the offices. "No worries there, I've got Daddy Jake on my side."

Jack guffaws. "*Daddy Jake*. Incredible."

"I thought you'd appreciate that one."

"I am at once fascinated and deeply unsettled."

Véronique walks up between the two of us. "You two are funny. You are clearly very good friends."

Very good friends who spent a half-hour making out last night.

"Yeah, Luke's a great guy." Jack places a hand behind my right shoulder. "I'm lucky to have met him."

Alarms start ringing in my brain. Jack is either confirming that he wants us to be friends and nothing more, or he's trying to flirt his way back into romance. He's toeing the line with the grace of an Olympic gymnast.

Kathy points toward the center of the store. "The escalators!"

Jack breaks eye contact with me. "There they are."

We take the escalators down to the first floor. All is clear. Not a single maniac wielding a pistol, which I have to admit is a pleasant surprise.

"We're not too far from the food court now, right?" I ask.

"Not far at all," Jack replies. "We're on the other side of the mall, but the food court is at the center. No matter what, we'll never be more than a stone's throw away."

"Brilliant design on the elder Stride's part."

"Indeed."

Véronique hops off the escalator. "And we are to meet with your other friends?"

Kathy nods. "Yes. To check on them and look for any clues."

We pass through the great behemoth that is the *Beds n' Better* first-floor entrance—even more magnificent than its second-floor counterpart—and carefully saunter toward the food court. A familiar chill passes through my spine. A stone the size of my bowling ball in my gut tells me something sinister has happened here.

The top spout of the fountain comes into focus first. Then I see the food court stalls. All of them are wide open except the Cluck Hut. The metal gate is down. A perfect ersatz prison for Bruce.

I run to the entrance. "Polly! Don! Are you in there?"

I shine my headlamp inside. A figure lies across the floor. It's not until my headlamp catches a glint of several metallic strips—*duct tape*—that I realize it's Polly. She's sprawled across the floor, facing away from me. And she's not responding.

"*Polly!* Are you okay?"

Jack runs over. "Oh, God. What's the matter?"

"She's not responding." I look back inside the Cluck Hut. "*Polly! Wake up!*"

Finally, Polly's silhouette shifts. She turns around and shows her face. "Luke?"

"Yeah. It's me. And we found Jack. Kathy's here too. We're back."

Jack shakes the Cluck Hut gate. "Are you all right? You took a while to respond. We were worried."

"Fine." Polly rubs her shoulder. "In a relative sense, at

least. Some meathead attacked us a while back. Locked me in here. I guess I fainted."

"His name is Bruce, and he's working for Stride," Kathy says. "Did he hurt you?"

"He didn't lay a finger on me." Polly squeezes her eyes shut and her body lurches. "But Don...he...that man *killed* him."

My heart stops. "He's *dead*? That can't be right. What happened?"

Polly winces. "I screwed up. I was looking through the fridges in all the stalls, taking inventory of the food. I was honestly just bored, needed something to do. I was in here, in the Cluck Hut, when I heard the gate come down all of a sudden. I turned around—I honestly thought it was a draft or something—and I see that guy, *Bruce*, I guess. He brought the gate down and put a lock on it before I even realized what was happening."

"And where was Don?" I ask.

"Don was over at the Burger Palace. I shouted once I realized I was locked inside, and he came out to see what was going on. Bruce drew his gun and aimed at him, telling him to back down. And he did."

Jack is trembling. "Then what?"

"Bruce backed him up to the Rockin' Roll. He was trying to trap him in there. And I guess Don saw the extra knives on the counter and decided to try and fight back. So he grabbed a few and lunged at Bruce, and—"

Polly face contorts as she attempts to contain a sob. She swallows before continuing. "Bruce had holstered his gun at that point, but he was able to fend off Don's attack. It was clear that Don had no idea what he was doing. Bruce blocked him and returned with an uppercut to Don's chin. Don fell to his knees, dropping the knives. Bruce grabbed one and stabbed him, right through his chest, before he could even get back up."

A lump forms in my throat. I struggle to contain myself. "*Jesus.*"

The one thing getting me through this was the knowledge that Bruce was just locking people up, not *killing* them. No matter what happened with us, we would still be alive at the end of the day.

That appears to no longer be the case.

Jack finally breaks the silence after a moment. "Where's the body?"

Polly tries to speak but can't. She motions toward the fountain. I flash my headlamp over there for a minute and see a macabre trail of burgundy leading from the sushi stall to the fountain. I immediately look away, but I can't unsee it. It takes every atom of energy in my body to not keel over.

The bodies in the Electronix didn't bother me nearly as much as this does. Those people died because some*thing* fell on them. This trail of blood was directly caused by another human. It's so gruesomely twisted, not unlike the multitude of knots forming in my stomach.

Véronique approaches the stall. "I am so very sorry. To lose a friend in such a wicked manner. It is simply unthinkable."

Kathy wipes a single tear from her eye. "I'm so sorry you had to witness that, Polly." She turns and faces the group. "Don may be gone, but we can still save Brookie."

"Kathy's right." I turn to Polly. "I realize this is a stretch, but did Bruce happen to mention where he had detained Brooklyn?"

Polly bites her lip. "We didn't really talk much. And I

certainly didn't want to engage with him after what happened with Don."

Kathy frowns. "Nothing?"

"He pulled out a walkie-talkie after," Polly says. "And I couldn't quite make out what he said on it. But he *might* have said—and let me stress the ambiguity in that *might*—something about the *brat in the bookstore.*"

Jack furrows his brow. "The bookstore? How can you lock someone in a bookstore?"

"No idea," Polly says. "That's the last thing I remember hearing before I fainted."

"He said he was using bathrooms and the like," I say. "Maybe he locked her in a bathroom in a bookstore?"

Jack shakes his head. "The only bookstore in this mall is GobbledyBooks. First floor. It's a small shop, no gate. No bathroom."

"How would you know that?" I ask.

"The technicians at Electronix get asked all the time where the nearest bathrooms are. It's literally one of the first things we learn about when we're doing new-hire training." Jack grabs the map out of his pocket and unfolds it. "The only bathrooms on the first floor are *here*, outside of the shops. And there's one in the Trixie's and one in *Beds*. That's it."

I bend down and look at the very small square on the maps denoting the bookstore. "Well, maybe there's a back office or something."

"It doesn't hurt to check, but don't get your hopes up," Jack says. "We can't leave Polly alone, though. Bad things happen when we leave people behind."

Véronique raises her hand. "I can stay."

"All by yourself?" I ask.

"Not by myself. With Polly." She stands on her toes and

peers inside the Cluck Hut. "Hello. I am Véronique, head chef at *Chez Océane.*"

"Charmed," Polly says dryly.

"I have many years' experience of picking locks," Véronique says. "An old hobby taught to me by my brothers."

I frown. "What the hell did your brothers do?"

"They were…not chefs." Véronique pulls a pin out of her left jacket pocket. "The skill has come in use to me before. I am often forgetting my keys to *Chez Océane*'s gate, so I am often jiggling myself inside."

Jack examines the lock. "Can you *jiggle* yourself through this one?"

"With a little time, yes. This gate is different from mine, but the lock is similar. If you go ahead to save the bookstore girl, I will stay here and do my best to release Polly. Then, if there is time, I will be happy to prepare a meal for the family."

"And you'll be fine?" I ask.

"Bruce the Muscle has already been through here, *non*? So it is my understanding that he will not be coming back to the food court anytime soon. And he believes us all still to be locked up. Time is on our side for now. But you should go."

Kathy grabs the map. "Véronique is right. We need to get to Goblin Books."

"*GobbledyBooks*," Jack corrects.

Kathy shoots him a dirty look.

Jack steps back a few feet. "But your version works too."

Véronique is already fiddling with the lock.

"And you're sure you'll be okay?" I ask.

"Not at all. But none of us can be sure of anything right now, can we? And when we are unsure, what is important is made clear."

A beautiful, if slightly muddled, sentiment.

I face Jack and Kathy. "She's right. And what's important now is saving Brooklyn."

Jack nods. "*Aye*. All for one and one for all. Right, Lucas?"

I appreciate the callback to yesterday, but I'm unsure if this is another hint from Jack or if I'm just romanticizing again. Besides, there are more important things to focus on—rescuing Brooklyn.

"We'll be back soon." Kathy grabs her tablecloth sack. "Set a table for six, Véronique. We're gonna save my daughter."

27

We walk past GobbledyBooks twice without realizing it. It's that small.

Jack peers inside the tiny shop. "Again, I have no clue how anyone could be locked up in here. It's so dinky."

Unlike the rest of the stores in the mall, GobbledyBooks has no huge sign in front broadcasting its wares. The long name is written in cursive on a small plastic board on the front window of the store. Piles of haphazardly stacked dusty books on either side of the sign are the only forthright indication of the store's product.

We walk inside and find that the store is much bigger than it looks from the outside. The ceilings are nearly twice as high as they were in the MetroMall walkway outside. Rows of bookshelves tower over us. Several books are strewn across the floor and a few shelves have collapsed, but the majority of the store seems to be so densely packed in that The Boom had comparatively little effect on its condition.

One thing we don't see, however, is Brooklyn.

I stroll down an aisle of shelves. "She's not here. I think this is a dead end."

Kathy grits her teeth. "No. We turn this place upside down. No stone unturned."

Jack crosses his arms. "Kathy, I realize you're upset, but there's no reasonable location in this store where someone could be locked up."

Kathy freezes. The venomous electricity scorching from her eyes stops Jack and me in our tracks. "You wanna talk *reasonable*? Tell me, Luke, is it less reasonable than, I don't know, finding a French woman in a *freezer*? Or how about finding your boyfriend in a locked office? Or how about the entire godforsaken time we've been in this desolate mall?"

"Jack isn't my—"

"Newsflash, brainiacs: every *goddamn* second I've spent here has been the absolute opposite of *reasonable*, and I'm not about to be told by two kids what I am or am not to do in order to save the most important person in my life. So would you kindly shut the *fuck* up?"

The weight of Kathy's words nearly knocks me off my feet. I take a quick beat to declutter my brain before responding. "You're right. I'm so sorry. I can't even begin to imagine what this must be like for you, Kathy. Knowing your child is in danger has to be the worst possible pain for a parent. Jack and I are with you."

Kathy inhales deeply. "I'm sorry." She pauses. "I mean, I'm *not* sorry about what I said, because it's one hundred percent accurate, but I suppose I could have delivered it with a bit more...*poise*." Her face contorts.

I grab a tissue from a nearby table and hand it to her. "No apology necessary. You're absolutely right. We were *way* out of line."

Kathy blows her nose. "Little bit, yeah. Let's continue our search. If what Polly said is true, Bruce has locked *someone* up in here. Whether or not it's Brookie, we can do some good."

Jack nods. "Good point. Luke, you have our best light. You lead."

I turn the brightness on my headlamp up a few notches. I walk down a row of bookshelves, turn a corner, and head down another row. I continue snaking through, looking for any possible clues, but nothing pops out.

We end up in an empty alcove that appears to be a reading area. Several cavities in the carpet mark where furniture once stood.

Jack walks into the nook and scratches his head. "That's weird. Where did the reading couches go?"

Kathy cups her hands around her mouth and shouts. "*Brookie!* Are you in here?"

No response.

"*Brookie!*"

Then we hear it. A very faint, but very much genuine, response. "Mom?"

Kathy's face lights up. "*Brookie!* That's her!" She anxiously scans the area. "Yes, we're here, sweetheart! Where are you?"

"Look up."

The three of us raise our gaze.

Jack is the first to speak. "Sweet Jesus, I forgot about the Tree House."

GobbledyBooks is apparently famous for its elevated children's reading loft, colloquially known as the "Tree House," even though there is nothing arboreal in sight. It spans the size of a one-car garage and is connected to the rest of the store by a small white staircase in the children's area at the rear of the store. The entire thing is surrounded by a white vinyl fence.

Through the slats of the fence, portions of Brooklyn's face peek through.

Tears rolls down Kathy's face. "I *knew* it. We're coming, honey! How do we get up to the loft?"

Brooklyn tries to say something but begins to cough. After a few seconds she has caught her breath. "There's a staircase. But that guy in the purple shirt blocked it off."

"His name is Bruce," I say.

"And his shirt is more of a lavender color," Jack adds.

"Like it *matters*." Brooklyn coughs again. "Just get me out of here, Mommy. It's dusty!"

Kathy places a hand over her heart. "Oh, God, her asthma. We're coming, Brookie! Just give me a minute to figure out how to get you out."

We run to the children's section. Lifesize cardboard cutouts of beloved children's story characters guard the entrance. The staircase is intact—thank God—but several pieces of furniture block our way up.

"I've gotta hand it to Stride," Jack says. "Using the GobbledyBooks Tree House as a detention unit is inspired. Menacingly dark, to be sure, but inspired."

"Guess he ran out of bathrooms by the time he got to the two of you." I approach the staircase. "What's the damage? Can we drag it away?"

Kathy is already standing at the base of the entrance surveying the blockage. "Looks like a few couches and chairs. And a big table on its side."

Jack comes up from behind me. "Those must be from the reading area. Stride and Bruce must have knocked Brooklyn out and moved all the furniture onto the staircase to block her in."

I cross my arms. "They clearly weren't planning on keeping her here forever, then. This was a last-minute choice after they left you in Stride's office."

"They had other offices, though. Why not fill those up first?"

"And have you communicated with the other prisoners?" I grab a small chair from the staircase and drag it to the side. "It makes sense they'd want everyone in our group separated. Once we got together, we *were* able to escape pretty easily."

"True."

"Boys"—Kathy has made it halfway up the Tree House entrance—"if you can find a moment to stop staring at each other, I could use a hand with the couches."

My mouth sputters for a moment. "We're not—that is to say, we aren't—"

Jack snorts. "*Coming.*"

We make pretty quick work of the furniture. It's easy with three people. We clear a full-sized couch, one loveseat, and two armchairs. At the very end is a large conference-style table, blocking the door to the Tree House at the top of the staircase. It's heavy, but we're able to remove it. Kathy opens the door.

"Mommy!" Brooklyn runs across the loft and embraces Kathy.

"Oh, sugar bear." Kathy runs her fingers through Brooklyn's hair. "I was so worried you were hurt."

Brooklyn begins to cry. "I'm sorry I was so nasty earlier. I really do love you, Mommy."

Kathy smiles. "And I love you too, sweetheart."

Brooklyn abruptly breaks the embrace and coughs several times into her elbow.

"The dust." Kathy instinctively reaches into her bag. "Do you have your inhaler, sweetheart?"

Brooklyn shakes her head. "I left it at home."

On a dime, Kathy switches back into stern-mom mode. "*Brooklyn May*, what am I always telling you?"

"It's a little late for a lecture, Mom. I'm fine, it's just—" She coughs again.

"Not another word." Kathy grabs Brooklyn's arm. "I'm taking you upstairs. There's a *Right Drug* up on the second floor. We can break into the pharmacy and find you some albuterol."

Brooklyn stops coughing for a moment and looks up at her mother. "Break in? Isn't that illegal?"

"Sure is, babycake." Kathy smiles. "But less illegal than abducting and confining a teenage girl. I'll take my chances."

Jack draws in on the reunited duo. "You need us to come with you?"

"No," Kathy says. "I'm all Brookie needs. As long as we're together, we'll be fine. You two go back to the food court and help Véronique get Polly out. Come on, sugarplum."

Arm in arm, Kathy and Brooklyn walk out of the GobbledyBooks in the direction of *Beds n' Better*.

For the first time since we shared a sleeping bag, Jack and I are alone together.

Oh, God.

I think I'm gonna be sick.

28

I look at Jack.

Jack looks at me.

The two of us are alone in the Tree House.

We have total privacy. There are countless things I want to say, but my tongue and brain don't seem to be able to collaborate to form any of the statements I am thinking.

"We are alone."

Bravo, Luke.

Jack smiles. "There's that English degree again."

A glimmer of fleeting courage rushes through me. I decide to pounce on it. Screw it, right? "So...kind of funny how Kathy called us boyfriends."

Jack's smile fades slightly. "Yeah. I guess one could say we're...uh...elevated somewhere *beyond* friendship."

I furrow my eyebrows. "Are we? Because I've been trying to figure out what's going on between us since last night. We were about to go to bed. I figured we were about to partake in...um...well, *something*. At least a goodnight kiss. Then, out of nowhere, you put all these walls up."

Jack's face falls. "You're right. I did. And I'm so sorry if that made you feel weird or anything."

"Not weird." I sit at the top of the Tree House staircase. "But...I mean...I didn't *love* it. It made me wonder if you had lost interest."

"Oh, God, Luke." Jack closes in on me. "That is the furthest possible thing from the truth. You've gotta know that, right?"

I shrug emptily. "I figured you were into me when we were at the fountain. But then I assumed you had regrets afterward. And things just haven't felt the same since."

"Well, to be fair, I *was* kidnapped."

I raise my hand. "Don't try and make this a bit. I was hurt, Jack. And I've been trying to figure out exactly what your thoughts are regarding us since then. It's been one mixed message after another."

Jack places his hands on my shoulders and looks me directly in the eye. "Luke, I like you. I *really* like you. More than I've ever liked another person—at least I think that's the case."

"Then why did you cut me off so abruptly last night?"

Jack sighs. "It was when we met Don and Kathy. They're right about the same age as my parents. And Don was a dead ringer for my dad. And all this pain from last year—pain I thought I had finished processing—came flooding back."

"Why didn't you *talk* to me about it? I would have been happy to."

Jack bites his lip. "I already unloaded on you in Ball World. I'm not about to open a can of even *more* pent-up trauma on a guy I just met."

"So you decided to block me out instead?"

Jack breaks eye contact. "I guess so. I didn't want to deal

with it. It was easier to just shove my feelings down. I've been on my own for a while now, even before my parents left my life. I wanted to deal with this independently, too. And I didn't think I could process with my own internalized issues about my sexuality while also fooling around with you."

"*Fooling around?* Is that all it was to you?"

"Oh, God, no." Jack meets my gaze. "I wish there were a better way to articulate it. But it was *never* you, Luke. Don't think for one goddamn second that it was you."

"So you're saying *it's not you, it's me*? You realize, Jack, that that's the oldest excuse in the book?"

Jack inhales slowly. "But it really *is* the case here. Or at least it *was.* I figured you'd hang around until I had finally figured everything out and then we could pick up where we left off."

I clap my hands on either side of my head. "How the *hell* was I supposed to figure that out? I'm not a mind reader."

Jack smiles very slightly. "Guess I missed that question on the boyfriend interview."

I sigh. "You realize you make everything a joke when things get too serious for your comfort?"

Jack laughs. "Yeah, not the first time that's been mentioned to me."

"Well, it's a real pain in my ass. You *and* your sense of humor."

"Don't pretend you don't love it."

I exhale. "I do. But you need to be a little more honest with me. Because I like you too, Jack. Like, a *lot*. And I really am willing to help you untangle the damage your parents inflicted on you, but you need to let me in for that to happen."

Jack brushes a single tear off his cheek. "Really? After everything I've put you through?"

I close in on Jack. "How's this for an answer?"

I bring my lips right next to his and close my eyes.

We kiss.

The first time I have *ever* initiated a kiss in my life, and it feels damn good.

Jack's lips are even warmer and softer than they were last night.

Jack slowly lies down on the floor of the Tree House. I am on top of him. Our lips don't break once. I slowly place a hand under his shirt and feel his chest. *So* tight. *Ugh.*

Jack takes the hint and shimmies out of his shirt. His hands are tugging at the bottom of my shirt as well. Our chests come together. Utter bliss. I don't even care that mine is significantly less toned than his. None of that matters.

I navigate downward with my right hand. Past Jack's chest, down the line of fine blond chest hair leading to his bellybutton, down to the cuff of his jeans. Dare I move lower? Jack certainly seems into the idea. I can tell by his kissing, as well as by the small tent forming between his legs.

I am about to cross the barrier, when—

"Boys? You still here?"

Jack breaks his lips from mine. "Who is that?"

The voice calls out again. "Jack? Luke?"

I recognize it. "It's Kathy."

Damn. Could her timing *be* worse?

Jack stands and quickly throws his shirt back on. "We're up here."

Thank God Kathy can't see us.

"Still? What on earth are you doing up there?"

I exchange a glance with Jack. I stifle a giggle. "We were

just checking out the bookstore. Seeing if Stride left any clues up here."

"Isn't the Tree House empty?" Kathy asks. "Anyway, we already searched the rest of the store. Come on, Véronique was able to free Polly and she's prepared dinner."

Jack smiles. "That was nice."

"It was," I say. "More later?"

Jack laughs. "If you're good." He calls down from the Tree House. "We're coming down. Give us a second."

He grabs my hand and reels me in for one final kiss. *God,* I want to hold Jack to me for eternity. But all I get is two extra seconds before he gives me a quick hug, stands, and leads me down the staircase back to the main section of GobbledyBooks.

Once I see Kathy's face, I can tell immediately that she knows exactly what we were doing in the Tree House, and that it was definitively *not* searching for clues. My cheeks warm. I look at Jack. His ears are bright pink.

But Kathy doesn't say anything. Possibly because Brooklyn is next to her, or possibly because it's none of her business. Probably a combination of the two.

"Come on, you two. We're starting to put a plan together."

Kathy and Brooklyn lead Jack and me back to the food court. Jack grabs my hand as we leave GobbledyBooks and interlaces his fingers with mine. I squeeze his hand back.

I smile.

Mine.

29

Véronique has prepared the finest possible meal with the shoddiest possible ingredients.

"Chicken tenders *au vin* and hamburger *bourguignon*. On the side we have a simple country salad with a honey-mustard vinaigrette and French-fried potatoes *au gratin*."

My jaw drops. "Véronique, this looks incredible. You did all of this with our little Pro Bro?"

Véronique shrugs. "It was not very difficult. I have excellent training. And I watch many garbage shows on the television where people are cooking strange things. This was easy by comparison."

"I, for one, am very glad you guys found Véronique." Polly raises a glass of red wine.

Jack's mouth is agape. "Where did you find *wine*?"

Véronique clasps her hands together. "We needed a bottle for the chicken and the beef. The gift basket shop by the pharmacy. Many of them have wine inside. It is by no means fine, but good for cooking. And drinking, if you are Polly."

"You see my shirt?" Polly pulls on the edges of her novelty wine-mom garment. "*Ask questions later*, babe."

Véronique eyeballs the Pro Bro. "Perhaps later we can go back to *Chez Océane* with this mini stove and make something real."

Polly finishes her glass of wine. "Absolutely. Once we figure out our next move. Jack and Luke, you weren't here, but Brooklyn has some new information about Stride."

"Yes, you were too busy *searching for clues*." Kathy elbows me.

I ignore Kathy's absolutely accurate insinuations. "What is it?"

Brooklyn sets her plate down. "They're in the movie theater. Stride and his CFO, Tanya Shepard. They cleared out a theater and have been using it as their hideout."

"Bruce told you this?" Jack asks.

Brooklyn nods. "Yeah. He's got a loose mouth. Thinks he's real clever."

I grab the map off of the Cluck Hut counter. "Where in the movie theater is he? I know the area pretty well. My mom would often take me to see a movie after an afternoon of shopping."

Brooklyn scours the map and places her finger on it. "Theater Thirteen."

"Theater Thirteen?" I ponder a moment. "Theater Thirteen is *never* open. It's been closed for years. When I was in middle school, kids would talk about how it was cursed."

Brooklyn shrugs. "Stride himself may have fabricated that myth to keep it closed for his own use. I'm guessing he and Shepard spruced it up to their liking. Maybe they turned it into a sex dungeon."

Kathy gasps. "*Brookie.*"

"Oh come *on*, Mom. You *know* they've gotta be banging."

Kathy stares at her daughter, but she doesn't argue.

"*Anyway*." I return to the map. "Should we plan on ambushing them, or what?"

Polly takes a bite of hamburger *bourguignon* and swallows. "I think so. Bruce has a gun, so I think we can assume Stride and Shepard have guns, too. We only have our knives and my crossbow."

Jack raises an eyebrow. "You still have your crossbow? Bruce didn't take it?"

"It was already in the Cluck Hut with me when Bruce locked me in. And I sure as hell wasn't going to tell him I had a weapon."

"But couldn't you have shot at Bruce while he was fighting Don?"

"I thought about it, but I couldn't get a clean shot through the slats of the gate. And I didn't want to give away that I had a weapon, otherwise Jockface would have taken it from me. The fight with Don all happened so quickly. I was in shock."

Polly's face drops.

Jack places an arm on her shoulder. "It's okay. No one's blaming you."

Polly looks at Jack and smiles. She grabs the map. "If we are presuming that they're armed, then we are literally taking knives to a gunfight. So I propose we attack at night. We can catch them while they're sleeping. At the very least, they'll be off-guard."

Kathy nods. "The element of surprise is our best hope. They all think we're locked up, so if we attack at the right moment, we may be able to overwhelm them."

Jack holds up a hand. "How do we walk in, though? Even if we luck out and they *are* in the theater when we get there, it'll be a big space. And we'll be blind until we shine our lights in. And there's no way of knowing if they'll be sleeping or keeping watch."

It hits me. "The projection booth! The entrances to the projection booths are separate from the theaters. That way people who are drunk and stoned at the movies can't come traipsing in and ruin the movies for everyone."

"Well, then how do we get in?" Jack asks. "Assuming we're not drunk or stoned?"

"Bold assumption." Polly pours herself a second glass of wine.

I close my eyes and picture the space. "It's a separate entrance. An *Employees Only* entrance. It was never locked when I used to go there with my mom, though."

Jack crosses his arms. "How do you know this?"

"I *may* have wandered off once or twice during the previews and explored."

"What a rebel."

"Save me from myself."

Polly rolls her eyes at Jack and me. "Superfluous flirtation aside, it's a good idea. We can sneak into the projection booth for a little pre-ambush reconnaissance. Get the lay of Stride's lair. See if there's any place where he's left himself exposed."

"Then we can formulate a plan of attack," Kathy says.

"With a little good fortune, we can take them down," Polly says. "Once they're out of the way, we can free anyone else they locked up in the mall."

"So when do we do all this?" I ask. "The spying and subsequent strike?"

Brooklyn gets on her feet. "It has to be tonight. It's our only chance. They'll probably check on all their prisoners in the morning. Give out rations, the like. Once they find out we're no longer locked up, we lose our advantage."

Polly nods. "I say we lay low until midnight or so, then investigate. If we're in the projection booth by then, we can see when they go to sleep. Then we figure out what to do."

My nerves surge into my fingers. "Just to be clear, is there a possibility of using...*lethal* force?"

Polly's face darkens. "They used it on Don. We have to at least be prepared to use it in return."

Deep in the inner recesses of my stomach, several butterflies emerge from their chrysalides and spread their wings.

I don't like this. "Can we at least figure out some sort of non-violent method first? If we have to act in defense, that's one thing, but can there be a first-draft plan where we just tie them up or something?"

Polly sighs. "If we can get their weapons away from them, they lose their power. Or at least the playing field will be evened out. So, *if* we get their weapons and *if* they don't attack us anyway, then sure."

This predictably does absolutely nothing to mollify my butterflies. But we'll do what we have to do.

I nod. "Okay."

Kathy crouches down to where I'm sitting. "Think of it this way, Luke. I would do *anything* to protect Brooklyn. And I think you feel the same way about Jack. As long as we're all on the same page there, we can attack as a team."

I nod. "You're right. But what if it doesn't work out?"

"Then they kill us," Polly says.

My butterflies begin to perform an advanced gymnastics routine.

"Best case, they lock us back up and *then* we die. Either way, that's our destiny if we stay here. Our only hope of shifting the balance in this mall is taking them down before they take us down. By whatever means necessary."

Kathy nods gravely. "I think Polly is right. This is our only shot. Are you in?"

I look at Jack.

Jack looks back at me.

I wish we could just run away and make out in the Tree House. Or by the fountain. Hell, I'd even take Ball World. Just away from the mess of MetroMall, away from the evil of the world, away from our nuked city, where we can live freely and not have to potentially take another person's life—no matter how cruel and deranged that person is—in order to survive.

But that's not the hand we've been dealt. That's not the hand any of us have been dealt.

I look around me. Polly, Kathy, Brooklyn, Véronique.

I owe my life to Polly, several times over. Kathy is incredibly kind but still willing to call Jack and me both out on our BS. Brooklyn acted as a spy, even in captivity, and passed priceless intel onto us. Véronique and her badassery got Polly out of the stall using only a hairpin *and* made a gourmet meal out of fast food and basket wine.

I owe it to them to join them in their crusade.

I turn my gaze to Jack. My mind dwells on our moment in the Tree House. Our first encounter at the fountain. The hours we spent in the Electronix, huddled together.

Then I think about the four incredible women in our group. They've each been through their own personal hell. Their resilience inspires me beyond measure.

Then I think back on my mother and brother. Maybe they're still alive. It's possible that they found shelter. We may still reunite when this is all over.

Finally, I think of Dad. The time he took me to a batting

cage for the first time. The way he hugged me after I missed five balls in a row. I hear his voice. "You've *got* this, Luke. Just focus."

I see the fire in Jack's eyes. Flames kindle within my own body. "Yes. We're in."

30

Night falls.

It's getting close to midnight.

We've gathered everything we could possibly use as a weapon. Polly has her crossbow, Kathy has the meat cleaver, Brooklyn has an assortment of sushi knives, and Véronique has the *Chez Océane* candelabra. Jack has the marble globe and I have the bust of Jacob Stride. The two of us also have our hunting knives in our pockets.

We are well-armed.

Jack and I are packing our backpacks up at the Cluck Hut.

"Hey, Luke."

"Yeah?"

"Just in case this doesn't go well, I want to say—"

I hold my hand up. "No. Don't say that. It'll be fine."

Jack sighs. "We don't *know* that. I just...want you to know how much the past two days have meant to me."

I look up from my backpack. "It's meant a lot to me, too, Jack."

Jack throws his arms around me. "I've never met anyone quite like you, Luke."

I scoff. "Are you kidding? You're the special one. You're brilliant, and you succeed at everything you do."

"Oh, God, *please* stop." Jack breaks the hug but keeps his hands on my shoulders. "But thanks. Let's just agree that we're both great?"

I smile. "Fine."

Jack brings me in for a quick kiss. "Guess I'll see you on the flipside, Chesterfield."

We break apart right as Polly approaches the Cluck Hut counter.

"You two ready?" she asks. "We're gonna be heading out soon."

"Yeah, we're good," I say. "You?"

"Yeah. Kathy and Brooklyn are finishing up their packs now."

Kathy, Brooklyn, and Véronique close in.

I gulp. "I guess this is it, then?"

Jack gives my hand a squeeze and leans into my ear. "Nah, there'll be plenty of *it* waiting for us when we get back."

"*Jack.*"

Polly claps her hands over our shoulders. "What *am* I gonna do with the two of you?"

Jack chuckles. "You love us, and you know it."

"Despite the two of you being the biggest pain in my ass, I guess I do."

The six of us are now gathered. No one speaks. We just stand still and allow the gravity of the moment to wash over us.

Kathy breaks the silence. "To the theater then?"

"*Allons-y*," Véronique says.

We begin our final trek to the MetroMall Cineplex.

"The movie theater takes up a full third of the space on the first floor and contains fifteen separate cinemas and two concessions," Jack explains. "There is also a small Japan-themed arcade in the foyer and a fully stocked tiki-style bar between theaters eight and nine. Only place in the mall where alcohol is served."

"I make a motion that we stop there on our way out, then," Polly says.

"Let's focus on our main initiative first," Jack says. "Then we can celebrate."

Polly staggers slightly.

I lean over and whisper in Jack's ear. "Is she okay?"

Jack glances at Polly's gait. "She's a little buzzed. Kathy told me that she grabbed Polly some pain meds for her shoulder in the pharmacy, so between those and the wine she had with dinner, she's probably feeling pretty good right now."

"Should we have maybe waited for her to sober up?"

"No time. And she's fine. I wouldn't necessarily want her driving a car, but—"

"But firing a crossbow is okay?"

"She's *fine*."

"Okay, if you think so."

The Cineplex entrance dwarfs *Beds n' Better*'s in comparison. The six of us behold an immense red wall, thirty feet tall, with eight monstrous silver letters spelling the word *CINE-PLEX* above three glass revolving doors. Red rope separated by bronze stanchions marks the entrance area's perimeter.

"The employee entrance is to the side." I cross underneath the *X* of *CINEPLEX*. A small door, the same color as the wall, stands stalwartly on the right side of the entrance.

"Is it open?" Jack asks.

I jostle the handle. "Yes. They keep it open. Normally there is someone standing just inside of the red rope taking tickets, so they need easy access to the employee entrance."

"And you managed to sneak past a ticket-taker when you used to come here with your mom?" Kathy asks.

I shrug. "They were distracted by the tickets. Plus I was a little kid. No one gave me a second thought. They eventually caught me and brought me back to my mom. I told them I was looking for the bathroom. The mall security bought it. My mom didn't."

"Guess she knew you too well." Jack elbows my ribs.

"You have *no* idea," I say. "I got a stern talking-to on the ride home. We didn't see a movie for a while after that."

"So this whole ordeal is really just poetic closure for your childhood?" Jack asks.

I crack the employee entrance door. "I suppose so."

"Definitely worth it, then."

The six of us walk inside. It's dark. No emergency lights in here. Polly and I have the only remaining functional head-lamps, so we lead.

Polly looks over her shoulder to the rest of the group. "Be careful, everyone. As far as we know, Stride and Shepard are in the theater, but they could be hiding anywhere. Keep your weapons at hand."

Luckily, though, no one interrupts our journey to the projection booths.

"It is Theater Thirteen that we are looking for?" Véronique asks.

Polly nods. "It's probably toward the end of the hall."

"*Pardonnez-moi,* but it is right here." Véronique points to a door right next to her. A small gold plate on the door reads the words *Theater 13 Projector*.

Brooklyn claps softly. "Nice one, Véronique! I thought this was just an office."

Véronique shrugs. "Sometimes short people notice things. I am happy to help."

We gather around the door. A small yellow wedge keeps it slightly ajar.

I try the handle. "It's locked. But as long as we don't close the door while we're in there, we should be fine."

We pile inside the booth, keeping the door opened a crack. The room is small, and a large gray box with a piece of silver tubing rising out of it fills up much of the space.

I gesture to the gray box. "That's the projector."

"Where's the reel of film?" Jack asks.

"Back in the eighties," I say. "All movies are broadcast digitally now."

"Well, *la-dee-dah*."

"*Hush*." Polly stands by the window that looks into the theater. "Stride and Shepard. They're in the theater."

"Yeah," Brooklyn says. "You can continue your flirt-fest later."

I don't respond. Jack looks at me and grins before discreetly patting my ass. It takes everything in my power not to make a noise.

But now is not the time. The six of us huddle up to get a view.

The theater is well lit. Stride has clearly diverted some of the emergency power into his space. There is a bed—I recognize the model from our jaunt through *Beds n' Better*—two couches, and a minifridge. A shelf of canned foodstuffs similar to the ones I saw in the fallout shelter stands next to the fridge, next to a small poker table surrounded by wooden chairs. In the leftmost wooden chair sits a man. In one hand he has a smartphone, and in the other he has a handgun. He's tall, thin, and wearing a charcoal suit with those goddamn patent leather shoes.

Maxwell Stride. Our villain.

Sitting on the bed, wearing stiletto heels and a black power suit—overly padded shoulders and all—is a woman. Long flame-red curly hair cascades down her shoulders. Her lipstick perfectly matches the shade of her hair. She's wielding what looks like a large knife and appears to be sharpening it with a metal file.

This must be Tanya Shepard, Stride's second-in-command.

These two well-groomed monsters are responsible for all the distress we've been through today, and they're clearly not finished.

A small black object sits next to Stride on the poker table. A small AM/FM wireless radio—the one he stabbed Polly for. It's switched off now, but I imagine Stride has been tuning in every half hour or so to see if any broadcasts mention the nuclear strike. Just in case he has to free all his prisoners and make everything look like a big misunderstanding for the courts.

The door to the theater opens. Bruce enters. The window is thin and the theater is a resonant space. We are able to hear him pretty well.

"The last of the prisoners have been locked up, sir." He places the MetroMall keys on the table next to the radio. He keeps his gun in his hands.

Stride lifts his eyes from his phone. "No casualties?"

"Only one, sir. A man in the food court who attacked me from behind."

My heart takes a dive into my stomach. *Don.*

Shepard peers over her knife and narrows her gaze. "How was he dispatched?"

"With a knife. I didn't use any bullets, as you requested."

Stride grins. "Good boy. We have to save those."

Bruce pulls out a sheet of paper. "I took a record of where I imprisoned everybody, for food rations in the morning, sir."

Stride places his phone down on the table. "Food rations?"

"Yes, sir. I figure we feed them once in the morning and once in the evening. But if you had another plan in place, I of course will defer to yours."

Stride cackles. "Those lowlifes aren't getting any of *my* food."

Bruce raises his eyebrow. "Then what food are they getting? There's plenty in the restaurants—"

"Imbecile." Shepard rises from the bed. "The plan was *never* to feed them."

Bruce blinks for a few seconds. "What do you mean? You wanted to lock them up so they wouldn't run rampant. I only assumed—"

Stride slams his hand down on the table. "*What?* Those filthy little ingrates sucking on the teat of my grandfather's fortune? I owe them *nothing.* Our only hope of survival is keeping all of the resources in my mall for ourselves."

"But, sir, they'll starve."

Stride's smile widens. Even from the projection booth, the whiteness of his teeth is almost blinding. "That's the plan."

"You mean to tell me that I've been locking people up in their own *coffins?*" Bruce's body tightens.

Stride circles Bruce. "Just thank your lucky stars you're not one of them." He tightens his grip on the gun. "You saw an opportunity with me and you took it. You'd make a great businessman."

"Sir—"

Stride stops walking and stares Bruce down. "Bruce, I know my mall. I know everything about this space. And when my contact at the Pentagon let me know that we were days away from all hell breaking loose, I crunched the numbers. Three people could live here for years, especially once we rewire the emergency generators to our refrigeration units. The dozens of people still left in this mall—the ones I didn't hurry out the doors—would suck us dry in a manner of weeks."

"But—"

"I'd watch what you say, Bruce." Shepard brandishes her large knife. "Providence has blessed you. Max here originally offered the third spot to our COO. He didn't take it, so you got it."

"COO?" Bruce asks.

"Sebastián Ortiz." Stride scowls. "Complete moron. Had an attack of the goody-goodies at the last minute. Decided to fly to his extended family in Venezuela instead. He thought South America had a better chance of making it through the strike."

Bruce squints his eyes. "Why didn't you flee?"

"Look around you, Bruce." Stride extends his arms to either side of his body. "I have the greatest nuclear shelter in the world. Our shields are impenetrable. The one good thing my grandfather left me was the insurance that I'd survive any sort of nuclear disaster. Good gamble on his part. His contemporaries—even at the height of the Cold War—thought he was nuts."

Bruce is silent for a moment.

"But...sir, can't we feed the prisoners for a little bit? We can always cut down if the food supply dwindles."

Shepard laughs. "Every day we give *them* food, we're sacrificing a month's worth of food for us. I don't like the return on that investment."

"But don't we have some kind of *moral* obligation?"

Stride and Shepard make eye contact for a moment and then throw their heads back in a rich guffaw.

"*Moral obligation?*" Stride mocks. "In case the events of the past forty-eight hours haven't clued you in, there is no such thing as *morality*. The models of goodness and wickedness were invented by the religions millennia ago to keep people from killing each other. To keep society from crumbling. There is absolutely no room for your *ethics* in our new world." Stride crosses his legs. "Let them starve. You locked them away. It's not like we'll have to *see* it happen."

Bruce sits at the table for a minute. His posture deflates momentarily, but then he straightens his spine, stands, and draws his gun, aiming directly at Stride. "No. We are *all* in this together. The prisoners deserve enough food and water to live. I agreed to lock them up to prevent a run on our resources, but I can't get behind this."

Shepard is about to lunge toward Bruce, but Stride holds a hand up, stopping her in her tracks.

A wicked grin divides his lips. "You foolish boy. I'm your best chance of survival. You really want to kill me?"

"I don't *want* to kill anybody." Bruce falters slightly, but keeps his gun pointed at Stride. "That's the whole point. It was one thing when I took out the old man in defense, but no more. It's not too late. We can undo this."

Stride's smile magnifies to jack-o-lantern proportions. "Then shoot me, coward."

"I'll do it." Bruce's voice is cracking. "Don't test me."

Stride places his gun on the poker table and spreads his arms apart. "Clean shot, Bruce. Go for it."

Bruce closes his eyes and pulls the trigger on his gun.

A gentle *snap* sound ricochets across the theater.

I almost gasp. Even a firearms novice like myself knows what we just heard was not the sound a gun makes.

Bruce appears to have arrived at a similar conclusion. His eyes widen as he looks down at his weapon.

Shepard giggles. "You really thought we'd give you a real gun?"

Bruce doesn't move.

"Fool," Stride says. "I picked that up at the toy store right after I met you."

Bruce drops the toy gun and steps back. "No..."

Stride picks his gun off of the poker table with his left hand. "My gun, on the other hand, is fully functional." He draws and shoots Bruce straight in the chest.

Bruce's body crumples to the floor.

Stride stands over Bruce and spits on his spasming body. "Sweet dreams, Bruce."

He aims his gun at Bruce's forehead.

The six of us in the booth cannot stand it anymore. We all look away—Véronique actually runs out of the booth—but we hear the second shot from Stride's gun.

Bruce is dead.

Stride's voice echoes through the projection booth. "Tanya, be a lamb and help me with the body."

Shepard doesn't respond.

I look back up—I have to. We need to know what's going on. Brooklyn stands up and joins me.

Shepard has wrapped Bruce's body in a bedsheet.

"This was perfectly good Egyptian cotton," Tanya mutters.

Stride hoists Bruce's swaddled body onto a dolly. "I'll throw this in the snack bar freezer. Can't have Bruce putrefying in here."

Shepard blows him a kiss. "Come back soon, darling."

"I'll count the minutes." Stride reels Shepard in for a passionate kiss, then grabs a flashlight and exits the theater.

Shepard retires to the bed. She slowly strips off her power suit, revealing bright red, lacy lingerie.

"I *knew* they were boning," Brooklyn whispers in my ear. "Gross."

Brooklyn shifts her gaze back to the group. "We should attack now."

My heart stops. "What?"

"Yeah." Brooklyn pulls her knife out. "Y'all, it's now or never. Stride is out of the room and Shepard couldn't be more vulnerable than she is right now. I say we take her out."

Kathy shakes her head. "Sweetheart, we don't know when Stride will return. Best to wait until they're both back so we can make one clean strike."

"I'm with Kathy." Polly reaches her hand out to Brooklyn. "Sorry, Brooklyn."

Brooklyn slaps it away. "*No.* You don't know these people as well as I do. Stride visited me while I was locked up in the Tree House. The way he spoke to me"—she crosses her arms and looks down—"you have no idea the evil this man is capable of. Our best bet is to take them separately. They're too strong together. Shepard doesn't even have a gun."

I peek through the projection window. "We don't know that, Brooklyn. She could have one hidden away. I think we should wait, too."

"Fine. Wait if you want." Brooklyn snaps the light off of my head. "I'm going." She runs out the door of the projection booth.

"*Brookie!*" Kathy grabs her cleaver and sprints into the hallway.

Jack gasps. "Kathy! The door!"

But Kathy accidentally knocks the wedge out from under the door. Véronique is somewhere outside, and Jack, Polly, and I are on the other side of the booth. Before any of us can reach the door, we hear the small *click* as it closes.

We're locked in.

31

J ack, Polly, and I are trapped.

And it's not as if we can pound on the door. We might inadvertently alert Stride and Shepard to our presence.

Jack slowly slinks to the floor. "Okay, this *looks* bad. But Véronique is out there. She ran out when they shot Bruce."

"She may have just run away, though." I sit back down on the floor and bury my face in my hands. "There's no way of knowing if she's just outside or on the other side of the mall."

Polly drops on all fours and peers under the door jamb. "How could she even open the door? She doesn't have a key. Even if she is just right outside, there's no way she could get us out."

Jack inhales slowly and clutches his hands together. "Maybe she'll find a set of keys in the employee area some-where. We're not toast yet. Have a little hope."

Polly stands on her knees and dusts herself off. "You think Kathy got to Brooklyn in time?"

"Only one way to find out." I move over to the projection window.

Shepard is still lounging on the bed in her underwear.

Jack walks up next to me. "She may just pull this off. It'll take Stride a while to dump Bruce's body. They've got a solid fifteen minutes, at least."

"Yeah, but it's only two of them, and they're not exactly trained fighters."

Polly joins us. "Neither is Shepard, though. I mean, she's a heartless banshee, but I can't imagine she's got any extensive training in combat."

I spy a small movement in the corner of the theater. "The door's opening. Look!"

The door's shadow lengthens. The hinge lets out a faint squeak.

Shepard positions herself sensually on the bed. "Back already, my pet?"

A quick flash of blue and red darts across the theater—it's Brooklyn. She stops, looks around, and slowly walks into the theater, like a leopard stalking its prey.

"Maxie?" Shepard sits up in the bed. "Is that you?"

Brooklyn wastes no time. She swiftly shifts into a quick onslaught, running at Shepard with her knife aimed right at her exposed belly.

But Shepard reacts in time, rolling off of the bed. Brooklyn ends up stabbing her knife through the mattress topper. She pulls it out, taking a few feathers with it.

"And *who* are you, pumpkin?" Shepard runs for her knife.

Brooklyn sneers. "One of your prisoners. Guess you didn't do a great job there."

Shepard presents her knife with a flourish. "Maxwell was

in charge of delegating the lockups. Your grievance is not with me."

"Cut the bull." Brooklyn raises her sushi knife. "We know everything. How you planned to starve us to death and keep the mall to yourself. You coldblooded shrew."

"*Well* then." Shepard dusts her lingerie off. "With that in mind, you must know what's coming next." She charges at Brooklyn.

I gasp. Shepard's weapon isn't a knife at all. It's a katana. A single-blade, curved sword, the same kind samurais used. I've seen it before. It used to hang in the Cineplex arcade, behind the ticket counter.

It's going to cut through Brooklyn's sushi knife like butter.

Brooklyn seems unaware of this because she advances on Shepard anyway.

Shepard parries her strike, and the two go at it.

My head is reeling, but I can't peel my eyes away. "Brooklyn's holding her own. She's not bad."

"I think Kathy mentioned that she fenced when she was younger," Polly says. "She could pull this off."

"But Shepard has that huge sword," Jack says. "There's no way. Unless Kathy comes in to help her."

"Where *is* she, anyway?" Polly asks. "She was right behind Brooklyn, wasn't she?"

"Yeah, but she doesn't have a headlamp," I say. "It's probably taking her longer to get to the theater without it."

Shepard nicks Brooklyn slightly in the chest. She cries out in pain. It's not life-threatening, but it's no papercut, either. A small circle of blood forms on Brooklyn's left side, soaking through the blouse of her uniform. But she's okay. The swordfight with Shepard continues.

Brooklyn keeps fighting and manages to get a hit in on

Shepard's right leg, causing her to trip slightly.

Shepard regains her footing and returns the favor, delivering a much stronger strike onto Brooklyn's leg. Brooklyn falls over, dropping her knife.

I gasp softly. "Oh, *no*."

Katana in hand, Shepard slowly treads toward Brooklyn. She kicks the sushi knife out of the way.

Brooklyn doesn't move.

"So sorry about this." Shepard raises her sword. "Nothing personal, I assure you."

Shepard aims for a deadly blow, right through Brooklyn's heart.

Brooklyn closes her eyes.

A small sob escapes Polly. "Lord, have mercy."

The next two seconds transpire in slow motion—at least, that's how it feels. As Shepard begins to bring the sword down on Brooklyn, a figure rushes across the room at what seems to be supersonic speed, landing right between the two women right at the moment of crucial contact.

Time returns to normal. The synapses in my brain are finally able to put the picture together. Kathy stands between Shepard and Brooklyn. It is her body, not her daughter's, into which the katana has plunged.

Christ, it's bad.

Shepard struck her right in the soft part of her belly. A small sliver of metal peeks through the other side of her abdomen. She slowly collapses to the floor.

"*Mommy!*" Brooklyn crawls over to her mother as she lies bleeding out.

"No matter, then." Shepard removes her sword from Kathy's stomach. Bright red liquid drips off its blade. "Second time's the charm, I suppose."

Shepard raises her sword, but she never brings it down. Instead, an ornate candelabra crashes onto her head and she collapses to the floor. Behind her stands the tiny but triumphant figure of Véronique.

My jaw drops to the floor. "*What?*"

"Where the *hell* did Véronique come from?" Jack gasps.

"She must have been hiding," I say. "Trying to get Shepard's back turned before delivering a fatal blow."

"That little spitfire," Polly says. "I knew adding her to our rotation was a good move."

Blood pools where Shepard's head slapped the concrete floor of the theater. Véronique slowly walks to her wrist and feels for a pulse. She looks straight up into the projection booth and gives us a thumbs-up.

In her own words, Tanya Shepard has been dispatched.

Our focus returns to Kathy. Véronique rushes over, where Brooklyn is crying over her mother's body.

"Mommy." Tears stream down her face. "I'm so sorry, Mommy."

Kathy raises her hand and touches her daughter's face. She's trying to say something, but I can't make out what it is from the projection booth. Even from the booth, though, I can see the same fire in Kathy's eyes that I saw when she was searching for her daughter. Two tiny flames, slowly shrinking as Brooklyn weeps.

"I love you too, Mommy. So much."

Kathy forms a weak smile, and she stares ardently at her daughter until she can no longer keep her eyes open. A moment after her eyes close, her hand drops and her face falls to the side.

She's gone.

32

I can't believe it. I've never seen a person die like this before. Just watch their consciousness slowly fade to oblivion.

Kathy could have made it. She *should* have made it.

Jesus Christ, it could have been any one of us.

I can't even begin to fathom what this is like for Brooklyn. When I lost my dad, I at least knew he was on his way out. He was sick for so long; it was almost a relief when he passed on. But to lose a parent so suddenly—so *violently*—is beyond my comprehension.

Never in my life have I felt so helpless. Being stuck in the projection booth while all this unfolds is the icing atop the horrible shit cake forced down our collective throats.

I reassign my gaze from Kathy's body to Jack and Polly in the booth. Silent tears spill down their faces.

I bring my hand up to my own cheek. Without even realizing it, I've been crying too. No one has spoken a word since Kathy's eyes closed for the final time.

But we don't have time to process. Not yet. Stride could come back at any time.

Véronique also seems aware of this. She removes her hands from Brooklyn's shoulders and crosses to the table, where Bruce left his keys. She picks them up and waves them back up at us in the projection booth.

I motion through the window that we're locked inside. Véronique nods, and a few minutes later she's at the door. I hear the lock shift and the door swings open.

Polly runs to the door and embraces Véronique. "Thank God. Véronique, you're incredible."

"I suppose then that we are even." Véronique jingles the keys. "You unlock me, I unlock you. Very fair trade."

"Guess you're right," I say. "Thanks, Véronique."

"It is my utmost pleasure."

"So what's our next move?" Jack asks. "Stride could be coming back any moment."

"He will be a moment," Véronique responds. "I saw him when I was walking to the theater. He took the body of Bruce to the snack bar, near the entrance of the theater, but he had not stowed it away yet. He was just beginning to enjoy a cigar when I left."

Jack crosses his arms. "How big was the cigar? My dad used to smoke them all the time. The big ones take a while."

Véronique closes her eyes for a moment. "It was very big. I assume he will be indisposed for at least twenty more minutes."

"Assuming he finishes the whole thing." Polly runs her hands through her hair. "Any chance he heard the noise in the theater?"

"I don't think he would," I say. "The movie theaters are soundproofed, so the noise from one movie doesn't bleed into the theater next to it. Since the snack bar is so far away, I don't think there's a chance."

Jack grabs the map of the mall. "Then our best plan for right now would be to take him down at the snack bar. We can go through the main entrance. His accomplice is taken care of. With the six of us—"

"Five."

Jack takes a deep breath. "Right, *five* of us, I think we've got a good chance, especially if we ambush him from behind."

"What's the snack bar like, Luke?" Polly asks me.

I shrug. "It's not bad. Normal movie snacks. Popcorn, soda, candy."

Polly sighs. "No, genius. Is there a good angle for attack?"

I blink. "Right. That makes more sense." I scan the theater section of the map. "It's kind of open-ended. I think the freezer is in the back, meaning he's behind the popcorn machines and the hot dog rollers. We've technically got him backed into a corner, but that doesn't mean a whole lot when he has a gun and we just have our blunt objects."

"And my crossbow," Polly says.

"That too." I strain to picture the Cineplex entrance in my head. "Even so, our best shot would be to lure him into the open space in front of the snack bar. Near the arcade. Then we at least have a few angles on him."

Jack nods. "Seems smart. Is there a way to lure him out of the snack bar without alerting him to our location?"

"Honestly, I can't remember exactly what the entrance looks like. It's been a few years since I saw a film here. We may have to improvise once we're down there and hope for the best. It's not like we have a whole lot of time."

"What about the theater?" Polly looks out the window. "We need to clear the bodies out in case he returns."

Véronique raises her hand. "I will assist with that. You three can go ahead and take Stride. I will move the bodies and take care of Brooklyn."

I eye Véronique's petite physique. "Can you move the bodies all by yourself?"

"*Oui*," Véronique responds. Her face darkens.

I can't help but wonder if this is another skill Véronique has learned from her brothers, but we'll save that conversation for later. I observe the crimson puddles strewing Theater 13.

"What about all the blood? Surely he'll notice that."

"There is already blood on the floor from Bruce," Véronique says. "But I will find a way to clean it up. If *Monsieur Stride* returns, he will instead think that his lover has wandered off somewhere. And that is *only* if he is making it back to the theater in the first place."

"Right," I say. "Hopefully it doesn't come to that. But you two had better be ready in case he does."

"We will be." Véronique waves her candelabra above her head. "It is apparent that I am skilled with the *candélabre*."

"Plus you can steal Shepard's katana."

Véronique crinkles her forehead.

"The sword she used," I explain. "I'm assuming she won't fight you for it."

"Oh, I see. Very good idea." Véronique saunters into the hallway. "Then it is settled. Brooklyn and I will plan for the backup attack in the theater in the case Stride escapes you."

Jack nods. "Let's move, then. No time to waste."

The four of us sneak back to the front of the theater. I take stock of Polly's posture again. Her walk is a little less balanced than it was when we were first walking to the theater, but that could just be nerves.

I'm overthinking this. Jack's right. She's *fine*.

We make it to the entrance, and Véronique breaks off and heads back to Theater 13. The remaining three of us loom over the concession.

The Cineplex has two snack bars, and the one at the entrance is quite large, with ten separate cash registers, five large popcorn machines, and a huge display of overpriced candy. There's a large self-serve soda fountain to the left of the first cash register, and large television screens above, where movie times and meal combo deals would normally be listed. Right now, of course, the screens are turned off—several are cracked from The Boom, and a few shards of glass litter the ground. A small light glistens behind the first popcorn machine.

Polly points to the glow. "That's gotta be Stride."

"I think you're right," I say. "How do we get him out? A bird call or something?"

Jack exhales slowly. "Yeah, because there are so many exotic birds in this mall."

I turn to him and frown. "Well, then what do you suggest? It's not as if we can just shout."

"We need to do something that alerts him but doesn't make him think that there are people here," Jack says. "Can we make some sort of non-threatening sound?"

I survey the area. I point at a small display of plastic jewelry on the ticket counter of the arcade. "That little stand of necklaces. It's cardboard. Someone can push it over. Stride will think it's a draft or something. But the metal of the jewelry hitting the floor should make enough of a sound to get him to come check it out."

"Love it," Jack says. "I'll push it over. You and Polly can position yourselves on the right side of the snack bar entrance. If he comes out, Polly can shoot. Luke, you can be backup."

"Great." Polly readies her weapon. "Let's position ourselves."

Jack tiptoes to the arcade. "Count to twenty. That's when I'll knock over the jewelry display."

I hold up a hand. "Twenty Mississippi?"

Jack sighs. "Sure. Twenty *Mississippi*. Starting now."

We position ourselves and slowly start the count, maintaining an eye on the light in the corner of the concession the entire time. Jack's Mississippis are a bit faster than mine, because I'm only on eighteen when I hear a small *thud* in the arcade. Close enough.

The light shifts slightly. "Tanya, is that you?"

Stride's voice is even colder, more menacing, without a window muffling it. Even the innocuous words he has spoken send icy shudders through my entire body. The small trace of light augments, and the shadowy outline of Stride's upper body appears next to the leftmost popcorn machine. There's a glint of red from the tip of his cigar as he places it on the counter, still lit. He pauses.

"I think I can do it." Polly raises her crossbow. "I can hit him from here."

Her body is swaying slightly. "Are you sure?" I ask. "We should wait until he gets a little closer, don't you think?"

"I don't think he's getting any closer, Luke. And if he does, he'll see us."

"Polly, wait—"

But Polly doesn't listen. She aims the crossbow. Right as

she fires, though, a tremor shoots through her body and she lets out an involuntary squeak.

A *hiccup*.

The most poorly timed hiccup in medical history.

God *dammit*. I *knew* it.

The arrow flies several yards over Stride's head and lodges itself in the ceiling. Stride reacts instantly and draws his pistol, firing.

Luckily, he misses, too. He doesn't know our position yet. He bellows out in fury.

"Who the *hell* was that? Show yourself!"

Polly and I stare at each other silently. We don't have a plan for this.

But apparently Jack does. He runs at Stride and lobs the big-ass globe in his direction. It ricochets off of the popcorn machine and bangs into Stride's left shoulder. He yells out in pain and grabs his shoulder but quickly switches the gun to his right hand.

Stride's eyes lock onto Jack. "*You*. How the hell did you get out of my office?"

Jack flashes his famous smile. "Guess you should have locked me up yourself, *sir*. Turns out Bruce is really bad at his job."

"Good thing I relieved the bastard of his duty, then." Stride raises the gun, now in his right hand. He shoots, but the bullet misses.

Stride must be left-handed. *Good move, Jack.*

I look down at the bust of Jacob Stride in my hands. It's about a third of the weight of the globe. There's not much I can do with it. I quickly scan the area. There's *nothing* I can use as a weapon.

Meanwhile, Polly is advancing on Stride with her crossbow. She shoots a second arrow, which also misses, hitting the soda machine. It begins to leak out a pale-yellow liquid. Lemonade.

My dad's voice shoots through my head. *You're creative, Luke. And creative people find creative solutions.*

Maybe I *do* have a weapon.

I crawl in front of the snack bar as a third bullet whizzes out of Stride's gun. The blast from the firearm nearly bursts my eardrum, but I'm able to make it to the soda machine. I grab two of the largest cups available. One hundred and twenty-eight ounces. I take a moment to silently contemplate the insinuations that cups this size assert on the state of the country as a whole before filling them up with lemonade.

Beverages in hand, I crawl back in front of the bar. I wait for Stride to fire a fourth bullet. Immediately after I hear it— this one thankfully also misses—I pop up and throw the contents of both of my cups straight into Stride's face.

I hit my target square on. The acidity of the lemonade burns Stride's eyes and he cries out in agony. He instinctively brings his hands up to his eyes and rubs them. He is temporarily blinded.

"Nice one, Luke!" Jack runs out of his hiding space and pumps his fist in the air.

But we're not done yet. Stride still has his gun. Until he is disarmed, we can't overtake him. I look around the snack bar, trying to find something else I can use. I could go back to the soda fountain, but that's too far. Then inspiration strikes again when I see the popcorn machine in front of Stride. More specifically, the rectangular vessel of fake butter imme-diately to the right of it.

"Polly! Aim for the left side of the popcorn machine. The butter container!"

Polly switches her gaze to the popcorn machine and smiles. "Gotcha." She closes in and aims her crossbow. She shoots and hits her target with aplomb. No hiccups this time.

A flood of bright-yellow hydrogenated soybean oil bursts out, greasing the floor of the immediate area. And Stride, still rubbing his eyes, steps right into it and slips. He lands flat on his ass and drops the gun.

All three of us are close enough to dive for the gun. Unfortunately, we don't choreograph our movement ahead of time and we all go for it at the same time. We dogpile on top of Stride, groping in every direction, hoping to find the weapon. The only light we have is from Polly's headlamp and Stride's flashlight, and all four of us are struggling to find the gun.

Stride, however, knows the area better. He elbows Jack right in between his eyes. Jack falls on his back, unconscious.

This distracts me from the immediate task at hand. "*Jack! Are you okay?*"

Jack doesn't respond.

Stride takes advantage of my distraction and snaps the headlamp off of Polly's head, breaking the band in half. He kicks Polly square in the chest and locates his gun. He grabs it off of the floor. It's soaked in oil, but it looks like it's still fully functional.

Polly and I lock eyes.

Game over.

We slowly raise our hands over our heads.

"You little *weasels*." Stride points the gun at the two of us. "Thinking you could outsmart me. This is *my* mall. You never stood a chance."

"We managed to take out your girlfriend, asshole." Polly spits defiantly in Stride's direction.

Stride laughs. "Saved me the trouble. As if I'd share my wealth with that sycophantic whore. I *was* looking forward to getting my rocks off with her before taking her out, but I'll somehow move on."

"If you lock us back up, we'll just escape again," I say. "Or someone else will. You won't get away with this, Stride."

"Very good point." Stride aims his gun right at my forehead. "That's why I'm not going to give you the chance."

A single tear rolls down Polly's cheek. "You *wouldn't*."

"Oh, sweetheart, I assure you I *would*. First you, then the rest of my prisoners. Your little coconspirator is right. Best to just slaughter the lot now. Leave nothing to chance."

I think back on the scared little girl sitting in her father's lap in the Electronix. "There are *children* in this mall. How could you be so evil?"

"Evil is relative, boy." Stride touches the gun's barrel to my forehead.

The metal is at once the coldest and hottest thing I've ever felt. It's as if my brain is melting inside of my skull. Chills envelop my entire body.

Oh God, he's won.

"You won't get away with this," Polly says. "You may kill us, but justice *will* prevail."

"I'll take my chances." Stride cocks the gun. "Any last words?"

I *really* want to say something clever, but my mind is blank. It's over. I close my eyes and think about my first kiss with Jack. I want that to be the final image etched into my mind when my soul departs this planet.

"No?" Stride asks. "No matter, then. Say hi to Tanya for me."

Polly screams. I squeeze my eyelids together. It will all be over soon.

A distant voice hits my ear. Gruff, low, masculine. *Dad? Is that you?*

"Not so fast, Stride."

The cold metal of the gun's barrel departs my forehead. I fall back to earth. I'm still alive. I open my eyes and see that Stride has moved his gun away from me and Polly and pointed it toward the entrance of the Cineplex.

Stride's bloodshot eyes squint slightly, but he cracks a small smile.

"Sebastián Ortiz, you son of a bitch."

33

I shoot a glance in Polly's direction. She mouths a single word.

"*Ortiz?*"

I shrug. I mean, I know who he is. We heard Stride talking about him with Bruce, and I saw his office door, directly to the right of Stride's. But I have no idea if he's on our side or not. The only thing I know in this moment is that he's a sharp dresser. Ortiz is wearing a black suit, with a bright red dress shirt on underneath. On his left lapel is a rose boutonniere matching his shirt. He's older than Stride, and his hair is thinning. Most importantly, he has a revolver in his right hand that is aimed directly at Stride.

Stride steadies his gun. "I thought you took off to Caracas. You didn't want a part in our plan."

Ortiz smiles. "I almost did. Purchased tickets and everything. In the end, I sent my mother down there. I hope to God she's safe. But I was standing at the entrance to the airport and couldn't get something out of my head."

"And what was that?"

Ortiz raises an eyebrow. "*You.* At first I was thinking, hey, he can't be *that* bad a guy. After all, you offered me a spot on your ark when the floodgates were beginning to open. But then I thought back on a conversation I had with your father years back."

Stride rolls his eyes. "Oh, what did *Papa* have to say?"

"Your father had his flaws, Maxwell. I'm the first to admit that. But he knew how to run this mall. When the labor scandal hit the press, he acted swiftly to make things right."

Stride curls his lip. "He just did that to protect his own image. As if he gave a damn about any of those entitled janitors."

"That may be so, but at least he adapted when it was required of him. A proclivity that he knew you lacked."

"What do you mean?" Stride steps forward. "I inherited the mall when he died. He wanted me in charge."

"You and I both know that's not true," Ortiz says. "He wanted *me* as CEO when he died. He knew you were unstable, that something wasn't quite right in your head. And you were so young when he had that stroke. Barely out of school."

"You lie!" Stride shouts. "I am the *rightful* heir to the Stride legacy!"

Ortiz takes a few steps toward Stride. "His will was never found, and there were whispers that you took him off of life support when he could have pulled through. It doesn't take a rocket scientist to put two and two together."

"Those allegations were never proven," Stride says. "Besides, the board of directors gave me my title. I earned it."

"You never learned the difference between fear and respect, did you? The board was *frightened* of you. You're an unhinged despot, but they figured there was only so much power the CEO of a shopping mall could realistically wield."

"Joke's on them, then, isn't it?" Stride cackles. "They're all six feet under at this point."

"Likely yes," Ortiz says. "They didn't know your capacity for ruthlessness. Not like I do. So I put my mother on the plane and turned around. I knew you'd be doing something horrible. I arrived at the mall yesterday morning and waited for your plan to come to fruition."

"Why didn't you confront me earlier, then, you coward?" Stride takes a step forward. "You could have saved the lives of some of the unwashed souls you love so much."

"When the bomb hit, a piece of debris knocked me unconscious." Ortiz rubs a small welt on his head. "I only came to an hour or so ago. I've been searching for you since. And judging from what I see, my timing couldn't be better."

"*Impossible*. My henchman locked everybody up in the first twenty-four hours. How'd he miss you?"

Ortiz shrugs. "It's a big mall. I was in a fitting room in Trixie's. Maybe he saw me and thought I was dead. Or maybe you're bad at delegating. Another one of your father's concerns."

Stride shoots his gun up in the air. Particles of drywall rain down from the ceiling. "*Shut up!* I am a few heartbeats away from a lifetime of safety in this mall, and I'm not about to let your mawkish words stop me." He closes in on Ortiz.

Ortiz draws his gun and cocks it. "Not one step closer, or I'll shoot, Maxwell."

Stride laughs. "You don't have the nerve, Seb. You watched me grow up. You're really telling me you're gonna blow me to kingdom come?"

Ortiz holds the gun steady. "I will if it means saving the poor souls you've locked up here."

Stride rolls his eyes again. "And what about the souls outside of the mall? How come their lives have less value?"

Ortiz's face softens slightly. "I'm only one man."

"Don't worry. You'll join them soon enough." The muscles in Stride's legs tense. He's about to charge at his former subordinate.

"It's not too late," Ortiz says. "You can undo this."

"The hell I can!" Stride begins to shake. "You may have pledged allegiance to my father, but my only duty is to myself. I've *killed*, Seb. And you know what? I relished every goddamn *second* of it. Because it's survival of the fittest out there, and I'm at the top of the food chain. It's *good* to be king."

"Are you really king if you murder all your subjects?" Ortiz places his finger on the trigger. "I'm afraid you're too far gone, Maxwell. May your father's spirit forgive me."

He pulls the trigger, but the bullet misses. Stride's entire body convulses instinctively.

I have a split second to react before Stride regains control of himself. I jump up from behind him as he's about to shoot and wrap my arms around his neck.

Stride wheezes and shoots the gun in all directions.

Luckily no one is hit. Polly grabs his cigar, still lit, from the counter and thrusts it into Stride's left leg.

I feel Stride's larynx spasm, but my grip on his neck keeps sound from escaping. Polly takes the cigar out and hits Stride in his other leg. The second burn, combined with the lack of air in his lungs, brings him to his knees. Once he's down, Polly tackles him from the front in an attempt to get the gun out of his hands.

Then a gunshot. Polly shrieks in pain.

Her leg is bleeding. She's been hit. Her grip on the front of his body loosens and Stride returns his focus to me.

He shakes his entire body and reaches the gun back and shoots, but he's not able to get a clean shot. The glass in the popcorn machine behind us shatters as bullets fly through and around it.

With no options left, I open my mouth and bite down on Stride's right ear. His entire body jerks in agony and his weapon falls out of his hand.

Polly pounces on the gun. She draws, aims, and shoots Stride twice, once in each leg. She must have hit an artery, because blood pours out.

Stride stumbles for a moment and his face turns green. His eyes roll to the back of his head and he tumbles to the floor. Out like a light.

"Now we're even, jackass." Polly carefully places the pistol on the floor. "Luke, find something to tie him up."

I sprint over to the front of the snack bar. There are several stanchions connected with polyester belts normally used to delineate the lines for the cashiers. I snap a piece of the belt off and use it to wrap Stride up around the middle of his body. I grab a second length and wrap it around his legs. He's tied up like the prize steer at a rodeo. Maxwell Stride isn't going anywhere.

I look up from my handiwork. "Polly, are you okay?"

She's in the corner, nursing her shot leg. The bullet grazed her left calf. I grab one more piece of line-control belt and wrap it around her leg tightly. "This should help with the bleeding."

"Thanks, Luke."

I smile at her. "We did it."

Ortiz runs over to the snack bar. "I'll say you did! Sebastián Ortiz, COO. And you are?"

I look up at Ortiz. "Luke. This is Polly, and the guy napping in the corner is Jack."

Ortiz beams at our little trio of misfits. "I had no idea there was anyone else behind the counter."

I shrug. "Stride was about to murder our asses, so we're glad you showed up."

"Same to you." Ortiz draws his gun and points it at Stride's head. "Now let's finish what we started."

I stand and block Stride with my body. "No. He's detained. Shooting him now would be wrong."

Ortiz raises an eyebrow. "Are you aware of the havoc this man has wreaked? He's too dangerous to be kept alive."

"Maybe he is. But if we kill him, we're no better than he is. I vote we lock him up somewhere secure and bring him three meals a day while resources allow."

Polly ambles over. "Luke's right. There's been enough death today."

"*Oui, plus de mort.*"

Right on cue, Brooklyn and Véronique walk out from the shadows. Véronique is carrying the candelabra, and Brooklyn has graduated to her late mother's meat cleaver.

"Hello? Friends? We heard of many gunshots. Is everything okay?"

I wave the two of them over. "Yeah, everything's okay. We knocked Stride out. Polly shot him in the legs."

Brooklyn sees Ortiz and raises the cleaver. "And who's this?"

"He's cool. This is Sebastián Ortiz. He was COO of the mall. He saved our lives at the eleventh hour. Stride was about to take us out, execution style."

Véronique places her hand over her mouth. "*Mon Dieu*." She kneels down next to Jack. "And funny Jack? How is he?"

Jack has a nasty bruise in between his eyes, but his breathing and heartrate are steady and normal. "He's going to be fine." I gently pat his cheeks in an attempt to wake him up.

Jack's eyes flutter for a moment and then squint as they adjust to the light from the headlamps.

"Luke?"

I smile as a tear runs down my face. "Yeah, Jack. It's me."

Jack brings his hand up to the bruise between his eyes and winces slightly. "Did we get the bad guy?"

I laugh lightly. "Yeah, we did. Thanks in part to you. You've missed a lot."

A small smirk forms across Jack's face. "Polly misses a lot, too." He points at her crossbow.

"Keep talking like that and I'll knock you out again, Jacklov."

Jack sits up. "And everyone's okay?"

Tears well up in Brooklyn's eyes. "Everyone except my mom."

Véronique wraps her arms around her. "She died protecting the one she loved the most. Every mother worth her salt is willing to do that."

"I'm so sorry, Brooklyn," Jack says. "I lost my sister a few years back. It's the most horrible pain."

"And I lost my dad two years ago," I add. "We're here for you."

"We all are," Polly says.

Brooklyn wipes her eyes. "Thanks, guys. I just wish I hadn't been such a bitch to her."

"She knew you didn't mean it." Véronique brushes Brooklyn's hair from her eyes. "She loved you. And you loved her. And love is all we have in this world."

Love is all we have in this world. A slightly cloying thought, but it tracks.

I look back down into Jack's eyes. Those gorgeous shamrock-colored eyes. And he stares right back at me. I lean down and kiss him.

Polly groans and Véronique squeals. I pay them no attention. I don't care if they see. We've won, and the man who's gotten me to the finish line deserves a smooch.

Our lips part and I smile at Jack. I behold his gorgeous, striking face. His messy blond hair. His glasses slightly fogged up from our kiss. The bruise forming between his eyes somehow only adds to his allure.

"I love you, Jack."

Jack's jaw drops. For once he's the one who's dumbfounded. For a fleeting moment I worry that I've tipped my hand too much. We *have* only known each other for twenty-four hours.

"I love you, too, Luke."

"Aww!" Polly voice is half-mocking and half-authentic. "You *guys*!"

"Shut up, Polly." I lean down and give Jack a second quick kiss. "Wanna be boyfriends?"

Jack smiles. "I thought you'd never ask."

34

Two months have passed since the Battle of the Cineplex. And things are going well.

Thanks to Bruce's record-keeping, we were able to locate and free all of the mall prisoners. A few familiar faces—like Navy Suit Stepdad and his stepdaughter—but mostly new folks. There are thirty-six survivors total in the mall, including the five of us, Ortiz, and Stride. As Don had theorized, most people left the mall before the shields came down.

We were also able to cremate the bodies of Kathy, Don, Bruce, Shepard, and a dozen or so other people who perished in The Boom. We held a candlelight vigil—courtesy of Candleworks—before incinerating the bodies in a large pizza oven on the second floor.

I know it sounds dark and dystopian, but it actually proved to be quite poignant.

We keep Stride in Tanya Shepard's office. Of course, we removed everything from there except for a chair, a mattress, and a few magazines from the Right Drug. As we promised, we bring him three meals a day from the food court.

The five of us run the food court. Véronique is our master chef, but Polly is working directly under her and prepares the majority of the vegetable-based dishes. The two of them have collected more propane stoves from the SportsGoods and have a pretty good system. Three times a day, the mall's inhabitants line up and receive their rations. We've set up a bunch of battery-powered lights throughout the food court so people aren't tripping over each other. A significant portion of the lighting comes from the Christmas section of *Beds n' Better*, so it's very festive.

The refrigerators ended up lasting longer than Jack originally predicted, which was a pleasant surprise. We've unplugged most of them and have consolidated our perishables into a few main refrigerators we keep behind the Cluck Hut, to ensure we're using as little power as possible. We're beginning to explore possibilities of keeping food cold once they finally do go out. Temperatures should be dropping soon. Véronique is thinking the mall's basement may be getting cool enough to serve as a makeshift freezer.

At mealtimes, Jack and I usually help pass out the rations, while Brooklyn makes sure no one cuts in line or tries to get unauthorized seconds. Ortiz's job is to stay in his office on the second floor, keeping an eye on Stride. When she's not Véronique's *sous chef*, Polly is in charge of guarding the mall's main entrance, the only one with direct access to and from the outside world.

It's not a perfect system. The people in the mall are a little restless, but our one rule—besides the aforementioned unauthorized seconds—is that no one ventures outside. We have no idea how devastating the destruction may be, and there's the threat of radiation.

So far, no one has tried to break that rule. We enjoy a relatively peaceful existence.

On top of that, the nasty little voice of self-loathing in my head has abated substantially since the Cineplex. At first I thought it was because I finally got with Jack, but I'm coming to realize that it's actually because I've proven to both the world and myself how good I am at taking charge of my own life. It's a good feeling.

It took the world ending for me to get there, but I try not to dwell on that too much.

I wake up on the morning of Jack's and my two-month anniversary. We still live in the Cluck Hut, but we brought down a Queen-sized mattress and a downy duvet from *Beds n' Better*, which has proven to be far superior to the double sleeping bag.

Jack's already out of bed and dressed. He's sitting at the Cluck Hut counter, fiddling with the radio we stole back from Stride. I get out of bed and grab a robe hanging off a hook on the wall.

I walk over next to him and kiss him on the cheek. "Morning, handsome."

"Hey."

I lean on the counter. "Hear anything interesting? You've gotten nothing but static every day since you brought that thing back from the theater."

Jack slowly turns a knob on the front of the radio. "Yeah, I thought I caught something earlier this morning. I was just playing around with the frequency. But I haven't been able to pin it down yet."

"Let me know if you hear something. I'm gonna get things ready for breakfast."

I walk over to our dresser—another treasure from *Beds*—and open the top drawer. On the left are Jack's flamboyantly designed briefs, and on the right is my more conservative collection of boxers. I grab a pair from my side and slide them on. I grab my jeans off of the floor and throw on a tank top—the striped one I was wearing on the very first day. We found it the day after we locked Stride up and dried it out. It's my only remaining piece of clothing from before The Boom. Everything else is stuff I scavenged from Trixie's.

I walk over to Burger Palace, where Véronique is riffling through the cabinets, preparing the ingredients for breakfast. Polly is just arriving, too. She's using a cane.

I give her a gentle pat on the shoulder. "I see you're no longer using the crutches."

"I'm really moving up in the world." She pokes me in the shoulder with her free hand. "Jacklov still playing with his favorite toy?"

My cheeks warm. "I'm not his *toy*. We enjoy each other's company."

Polly laughs. "No, dumbass. The radio."

"Oh, right." I shift my gaze toward the Cluck Hut. "I guess he's been messing with it all morning. He says he thinks he heard something a while ago."

"Good timing." Véronique peeks her head over the counter. "We are beginning to run a little low on supplies. Nothing drastic yet, but we should start considering other options for food."

I sit down. "We'll figure something out. You still think we could store food in the basement?"

Véronique nods. "I intend to go down later today and check it out."

Polly turns to me. "Are you going to Brooklyn's thing later?"

"Brooklyn's thing?"

"She put together some sort of art installation by the fountain. In honor of her mother and of all those who died."

"That's today?" I ask. "Guess I'll have to check my calendar. Make sure I don't have any important engagements."

"You can push your morning make-out session with Jack back an hour," Polly says. "She's making her presentation right after breakfast, so you're on line duty. Jack can help pass out the meals by himself today."

I check the clock in the Burger Palace. People will be lining up any minute. I cup my hands around my mouth and call across the food court. "Jack! Breakfast time!"

Jack waves and walks over, bringing the radio with him. His hair is messier than usual. I tousle it flirtatiously.

Today's breakfast is pancakes with a side of bacon. Véronique found a massive box of pancake mix in the kitchen of one of the diners on the second floor, and this is the third morning in a row that she's used it.

Adam—the personage formerly known as Navy Suit Stepdad—sighs. "You're kidding me. Pancakes again?"

"*Technically*, yesterday was waffles."

Adam rolls his eyes. "You know damn well that's the same exact thing."

Adam's stepdaughter, Annabelle, tugs on his shirt. "But Daddy, waffles have dimples."

"Yeah, *Daddy*." I smile. "Véronique found a big box of mix and she's been using it a lot since it's nonperishable."

"It's *fine*. Any chance of extra bacon?"

"You know the rule. Only after everyone has had a turn. Then we'll see. Véronique knows how much food we have, so it's her call."

"Fair enough," Adam says. "Let's go, Annabee."

They grab their food and Jack helps serve the next person in line. About twenty minutes later, everyone has their breakfast.

After Véronique, Polly, Jack, and I finish our pancakes—and get Adam his second helping of bacon—we walk over to the fountain. Brooklyn is standing in front of some sort of monument, about as tall as she is, covered in a bedsheet.

Ten or so of the other mall inhabitants gather round as well.

Brooklyn takes a few notecards out of her pocket. "Thank you, everyone, for coming today. As you know, the first two days of our little community were absolutely horrific. A lot of us lost friends and family. My mother was one of those who was killed, as was our friend Don, as were several other people killed in the initial explosion."

We bow our heads in solemnity.

"I've been working on this tribute for the last several weeks." Brooklyn gestures to a woman in the crowd with dirty blond hair wearing a paint-caked apron. "With some help from Regina from the craft store, I was able to put together an homage to those we lost in those turbulent forty-eight hours."

She pulls the bedsheet off of her project. It's an obelisk, made of clay and painted bright white, about seven feet tall. Into the monument's four sides, Brooklyn has carved out, in gorgeous calligraphy and surrounded by a tasteful amount of glitter, the names of all the fallen. On the side facing us, I make out two of the biggest names.

Donald Smith and *Kathleen Braxton.*

All of us are teary-eyed, but Polly is the first to let out an audible sob. "Brooklyn, it's beautiful."

My own eyes moisten. "It really is. Congrats."

Regina, the arts and craft lady, applauds enthusiastically. The rest of the small crowd joins in.

"Thank you all so much." Brooklyn's voice wavers slightly, but she presses on. "Every day without my mom has been rough, but putting this together really helped me in my grieving process. Please feel free to leave any trinkets in tribute to those we lost."

"I've got one." Jack walks forward, takes Don's watch out of his pocket, and solemnly lays it at the base of the obelisk.

Véronique raises a hand. "If you would all like to join, I have prepared cupcakes in honor of Brooklyn's showcase. We will be serving them in front of Taco City. They are, if I may say, *fabuleux.*"

"Cream cheese frosting?" Brooklyn asks.

"*Mais, oui.* Only the best for you, Brookie."

Brooklyn hugs Véronique.

We walk over to the Taco City and grab a cupcake. Except Jack. He's gone back to the Cluck Hut with his radio.

I take a bite out of the cupcake. "Oh my God, these are divine. Véronique, you've done it again."

"It is a simple recipe, but thank you, Luke."

Brooklyn tosses her cupcake wrapper in a nearby receptacle and then peers across the food court. "Where did Jack go?"

"He's playing with his radio," I say. "I'm sure he'll be over in a minute."

Polly finishes her cupcake and throws her arm over Brooklyn's shoulders. "I hope you know how proud of you we are. Not just for your art project, but for all the growing you've done in the last two months."

Brooklyn smiles shyly. "Thanks, Polly."

Polly gives Brooklyn's shoulder a squeeze. "Now that this project is done, what's next?"

"Not sure. The monument was for everyone, of course, but I honestly felt a little selfish while I was putting it together. It was really for me, something to help me process losing Mom. Now I'd like to do something for the other people in the mall. Maybe put some sort of social club together, something to keep morale up."

"How about a sports team?" Polly asks. "Pick-up football and the like? I'd love to join."

I laugh. "Need I remind you that you're still recovering from getting shot in the leg?"

"Gotta get back in the game sometime, Chesterfield." Polly slaps my back. "I'm sure you'll be spending all your time canoodling with your boyf."

I smile and reach into my pocket. "Actually, I picked this up for him." I take out a small jewelry box and pop it open. Inside are two tungsten wedding bands.

Polly gasps. "*Luke!*"

I smile sheepishly. "I was passing by the jewelry store the other day and saw these. Figured I'd better snag them before someone else did. They may come in handy sometime soon."

Véronique examines the rings. "They are gorgeous. He is a very lucky boy."

Brooklyn hugs me. "You both are."

"Thanks." I smile. "I found out a week ago that Ortiz is ordained, too. Not that it really matters in here, but if we do decide to go in that direction, he told me he'd be happy to do the honors."

"*Incroyable,*" Véronique says. "And you do not think it is too soon?"

I laugh. "When you spend every day wondering if a second nuke is gonna take you out, it speeds the dating process up a tad."

"Guess you're right there." Polly grabs another cupcake and raises it in the air. "To perspective!"

We all grab a cupcake and raise them, laughing. We've settled into our new normal, and I've gotta admit, it's kind of nice.

Jack runs across the food court to us, interrupting our adorable cupcake toast. I quickly pocket the jewelry box.

Jack is breathing heavily. "Guys! I found it. Listen!"

He holds the radio up and turns the volume all the way up. It's mostly static. But, very faintly, I can make out the short message being broadcast.

"*Acting Governor Wilson is calling all survivors, no matter their location, to come to Jackson City Hall this coming Thursday at noon for supplies and further instructions regarding Project Rebuild. Acting Governor Wilson is calling all survivors—*"

Jack turns the radio off. "It's on a loop. I'm guessing they've been playing it all morning. Our signal is weak, since the mall's walls are so thick. Most people outside won't have as hard a time tuning in."

I mentally count the days. "Thursday. Isn't today Wednesday?"

Jack nods. "You got it, Chesterfield."

Polly frowns. "City Hall is far, though. And unless you find a car in the parking lot that isn't destroyed *and* figure out how to hotwire it, you'd have to walk."

"I figured it out." Jack pulls a piece of paper out of his

pocket. "I have a map of the city from the pharmacy. It's about forty miles from the mall. It's walkable."

"Forty miles?" I quickly do the math in my head. "That's a whole day of walking."

Jack slowly nods. "Guess you'd better start packing."

I scratch the back of my head. "Should we all go? We can't bring the entire mall with us. We should maybe just send a representative on our behalf. Then they can bring a helicopter or something over and rescue the rest."

"Luke is right." Polly sits on the Taco City counter. "And some of us need to stay behind to keep things moving. The mini-civilization we've created would collapse without us."

"Then who should go?" Brooklyn asks.

Polly laughs. "We all know it's gonna be the boys. I'm still recovering from my injury, Véronique is the only cook we have, and Brooklyn is starting a football team."

"We never landed on football."

Polly rolls her eyes. "Fine, a squash league, then. That'll be thrilling. Anyway, Ortiz can't go because he's in charge of keeping an eye on Stride. That leaves the two of you. And I'm sure we could all take a break from the two lovebirds."

"Hey!" Jack says. "I think we've kept it discreet."

Polly laughs. "Discreet as two peacocks on full display."

Jack scoffs.

"Hush up, I'm joking. We all ship the two of you hard, don't worry."

"All personal attacks aside, Polly is right." I turn to Jack. "It should be the two of us who go. Plus, if our families survived, this may be our best chance of locating them."

Jack smiles. "Fixing to introduce me to your mom?"

"Maybe." I smile playfully. "Let's pack a bag. Polly, can you prep the mall entrance?"

She nods. "I figured out how the shield works a while back. It'll be interesting to watch it rise up over the doors, though."

"Great." Jack glances at the clock. "It's nine-thirty now. Let's regroup at lunchtime."

A few hours later, Jack and I have packed our bags. We each have the two backpacks from the first day. Jack's beige one from Trixie's and my green one from SportsGoods. In it, we've packed a few meals, a change of clothes, and an assortment of camping supplies. Jack has rolled up our double sleeping bag, which is strapped to the bottom of his pack.

Jack looks over at my backpack—overflowing with supplies—and grins. "You packing for the end of the world? It's just a day. We don't need that much."

"You seem to forget that the world literally ended." I stuff the backpack and manage to zip it. "Plus you're assuming that nothing goes wrong while we're out there. Luck favors the prepared."

"Luck favored me, that's for sure." Jack grabs me by the waist and gently kisses me on the neck.

I shudder but recover after a moment. "You used that line on me last week."

"Yeah, and it's *still* adorable."

"Fair. *Anyway*, better to be primed for the worst, just in case."

"As long as you're willing to carry it all." Jack gestures outside of the Cluck Hut. "C'mon, Polly and the others are waiting for us."

We walk over to the mall entrance, right by the fountain where our romance first budded.

Polly is standing next to a large lever next to a sign labeled *For Emergency Exit Only*. "When I pull this, the front shield should come up. But I can't promise it will be up long. The two of you are going to have to scurry under it."

"How will you know when we're back?" I ask.

"I'll check every day before lunchtime, starting tomorrow. If you bring a rescue party, gather them then."

"And if they bring a helicopter?" Jack asks.

"Have them land it on the roof of the mall. I'm sure someone will hear it and report it to us. Otherwise, worst case, I'll check at noon."

"Okay." I look around the food court. "And you're sure you've got everything here under control?"

Polly smiles. "I'm offended you'd even have to ask that."

Jack laughs. "Pretty sure Polly has everything under control. Lucas is just gonna miss you."

"Can't argue with you there." I give Polly a hug. "Thanks for being a badass, Polly."

"It comes naturally. Thanks for learning to be one."

I smile. Véronique is next.

I embrace her. "*Merci pour tout. Tu es un chef merveilleuse et une meilleure amie.*"

Véronique beams. "When did you learn French?"

I hang my head and laugh lightly. "I didn't. I found a French dictionary in the bookstore and learned how to say that and only that."

She brushes a tear from her eye. "We will have lessons when you return."

"Deal."

Finally, I turn to Brooklyn. "You've been through so much. And you've turned it into something so beautiful. I'm proud of you."

Brooklyn smiles. "Thanks, Luke. I'm proud of you, too."

Polly rolls her eyes. "All these sentimental goodbyes. I

know the thought of being away from me for even a minute is painful, but you'll see us soon."

"That's the plan," Jack says. "Right, Luke?"

"Definitely." I turn to Jack. "You ready?"

Jack nods. "Yeah. You?"

I nod. "Polly, the lever!"

Polly nods. "It'll only be up for a minute or so. Be quick."

She pulls the lever as I take one last look at my Mall Family. These people have been my world the last two months. The thought of leaving them breaks my heart. But we'll be together again soon, God willing.

The wall in front of the entrance lifts up about ten feet.

"Now!" Polly says. "We'll catch you later."

I look into Jack's eyes and see the familiar verdant fire I've fallen in love with.

Jack decides to ruin the moment and makes the same grand goofy gesture that I made two months ago when we first met. "After you."

"You are the literal worst." I grab his hand and squeeze it. "We'll go together."

The two of us walk, hand-in-hand, into the unknown world outside.

ACKNOWLEDGMENTS

First and foremost, I must thank my incredible mom for taking the time out of her *New York Times* bestselling schedule to help me bring this novel to life. Additional thanks to her for giving me life as well.

Thanks to my fantastic cover artist, Kim Killion, for dealing with every meticulous request I made in our process and turning out a gorgeous product.

And thanks to you, dear reader, for joining me on this journey. I hope you enjoyed yourself as much as I did.

ABOUT THE AUTHOR

Eric J. McConnell is a professional opera singer who started exploring writing when certain 2020 events made his day job illegal for a year. *Mall* is his first novel. He holds degrees in music from the University of Miami and Northwestern University, and is an Eagle Scout, a blackbelt in Tae Kwon Do, and a zealous collector of rubber ducks. He is the son of #1 *New York Times* bestselling author Helen Hardt.

Find him at http://www.ericjmcconnell.com.

www.ingramcontent.com/pod-product-compliance
Lightning Source LLC
Chambersburg PA
CBHW060912190726
48286CB00002B/464